Praise for

MW00560276

5-Star Review from Heidi Scheer, Mrs. Universe TCP

"This story of three generations of women struggling to balance their frustrations and their love for each other during a pandemic is SO relatable! Being able to connect with these women on so many levels made this book reflective of many journeys we've all experienced. It's refreshing to read about honest thoughts, feelings, and emotions that we can all relate to. Highly recommend!"

5-Star Reviews from Readers' Favorite Book Reviews & Awards

"*UnMasked* by Julie Cadman offers a focus on relationships and how secrets have the power to destroy relationships. "I don't usually enjoy novels written in the first-person narrative because most of the time it feels a little forced. However, this is not so in *UnMasked*. Julie Cadman breathes life into each of her characters and makes sure the narrative style feels like a conversation with a friend. The story uses the COVID-19 pandemic as a background but also as a driver for the story. It changes how our protagonists look at things and try to work their differences out. The lockdown is almost treated as a blessing for the Blake family. The secret is not so much a secret but a catalyst for how it will all play out for these women from three different generations."
—Rabia Tanveer

"The characters learn small things about themselves and become closer than they were at the beginning as they strengthen their bond. Each character's story will be relatable to different age groups. Written in the first-person narrative, the style of this literary novel is optimistic and thoughtful. I recommend it to those who love to read about life events and enjoy a family focused approach. The ideologies presented may differ from that of the readers but it will help by providing a different perspective to consider."
—Manik Chaturmutha

"What I loved about *UnMasked* by Julie Cadman is the use of multiple narrators. This allowed me to experience each narrator individually and from their narration, I could resonate with each of the character's feelings, thoughts, and emotions. I understood why they acted the way they did and what made them think the way they did. This helped me connect with each character and made the experience enjoyable. I also liked how well the characters were developed, with each playing their role perfectly to make the storyline entertaining and realistic. I recommend it to readers who love family dramas; it will keep you enthralled and leave you wanting more."

—Grace Ruhara

5-Star Review from Readers' Choice Book Awards

UnMasked is an honest and heartfelt novel by author Julie Cadman. This is a fictional novel, written in the first-person perspective, which alternates between the voices of the three women. The novel deals with some of the key challenges faced by ordinary people during the pandemic, including fear of catching the virus, vaccine hesitancy, loneliness, isolation and mental health issues, working from home, home-schooling, travel restrictions, and many more. It also describes some of the benefits of lockdown, such as lie-ins, cooking together, and family time. I particularly enjoyed reading about the different experiences and perspectives of three strong female characters, each in a different boat in the same storm. This is an engaging and insightful book, that will resonate with women and girls of all ages.

5-Star Review from Readers' View Book Awards

"Unmasked" by Julie Cadman is a compelling family saga about secrets, survival, and discovering what's important. This is the story of three generations of females whose lives could be altered in irreversible ways. This drama will absolutely suck you in and won't let you go until the last page.

Cadman brings us a rich tapestry of story by way of multi-dimensional and believable characters so real, you feel like you could know them in real life. Her style of writing is easy, but packed with emotion, heart, and weight–every sentence counts. It's easy to get lost in a story like this because it's so relatable in today's world.

One of the things I admire about this book, and there are many, is the frank and open way the author handles the issues that come up. It's like giving us a peek into the private lives of a family behind closed doors. Maybe you see yourself in this story, and maybe you don't, but it will leave a powerful impact. These women are strong, each experiencing life in her own way. Young women and girls will be moved in some way. The author is skilled at showing how occurrences in people's lives shape them into who they will become.

Even though the subject matter is sometimes serious, touching on complex issues, there is an overall feeling of positivity about the book that will leave you feeling happy that you've read it. There are life lessons here that you can latch onto, thanks to the ability and sensitivity of the author. In some ways, it could be taken as a form of self-help, but just know that it could trigger some readers. I also think the multiple POVs work wonderfully well in this book.

Kudos to this author for having her pulse on the multi-generational experience during the pandemic, and her insightful way of addressing generational pain. Her book reflects real life, in that not all issues are handily resolved. If there is one pandemic-centric family drama to read this year, make it "Unmasked" by Julie Cadman.

—Tammy Ruggles

UnMasked

UnMasked

Julie Cadman

Suanne —
Stay "UnMasked!"

Julie Cadman

To my husband, Dana,
and our three kids, Luke, Jessica, and Katie.
Thank you for your constant encouragement and support.
I love being on this incredible adventure with you!
God knew exactly what He was doing
when He put our family together.
I love you all so much!

Chapter One
Patti

January 8, 2020—According to my husband Joe, I'm a young, sexy-looking grandma. Actually, my grandkids don't call me grandma—they call me Granda. That's *grand* with an *A*. My granddaughter Kylie started calling me Granda when she was little. I still think it's pretty cool.

I MAY BE SEVENTY-THREE, but I look and act much younger. I honestly don't know where the years have gone. Sometimes I feel like I'm still Kylie's age. Those years between sixteen and now, they went by in a *blink*. My husband Joe and I were babies when we married and became the new Mr. and Mrs. Clarke. He was twenty and I was nineteen years old. Our first few years were a little rough. We had a hard time getting pregnant and didn't have our first child, our Jenni, until I was twenty-five. Against the odds, we've stayed married for fifty-four years and raised our kids in our hometown of Grand Blanc, Michigan.

Joe and I are blessed to have three children. Lori, like my Jenni and Clint, is gorgeous, successful, and looks much younger than her years. Lori will be forty this year, Clint will be forty-four, and Jenni forty-eight. When I look in the mirror, I just can't believe I have children this age!

I'm often mistaken for the mother of my grandchildren. And I was last carded on my fifty-second birthday. Take that, Muriel Rogers!

Muriel is kind of my best friend—or frenemy. We've known each other for over forty years, and we compete in almost everything. One reason we've stayed friends is because she and her husband, like me and Joe, are still together. Many of our friends have divorced through the years, with a lot of the men trading in for younger models.

On my fifty-second birthday, Joe and I went to lunch, so I celebrated with a hot chocolate with Baileys Irish Cream, and the waiter asked to see my driver's license. My son loves to tease me, and he said, "Ma, they carded you because they card *everyone* who orders liquor."

I choose not to believe him. And so does my Joe.

I have a beautiful picture from that day of me in my light pink sweater. My auburn hair is styled a bit above shoulder length, kind of between my chin and my shoulders. I'm wearing my contacts, so my blue eyes are sparkling and my makeup is applied perfectly. In the picture, I look absolutely fabulous as I show off my license.

And, yes, I made a copy for my Joe to carry in his wallet. Too bad the Facebook didn't exist twenty-one years ago! But no worries, my granddaughter Kylie showed me how to use the Facebook, and I put the picture on my status. I got over one hundred likes and over fifty comments.

We started the winter season with a delightful Christmas with two of our kids and their families. The holiday was perfect, with just a light dusting of snow—giving us the first white Christmas in years. Correction: almost perfect, since Lori and Wallace weren't with us. But they plan on visiting us in Florida.

Lori and Wallace have purposefully decided not to have children. Every time I think of them, old and alone, with no one to keep them company or help take care of them, I fight back tears. I don't understand why my Lori doesn't want kids. Family is so incredibly important. It must be that husband of hers. I've tried to talk with her, and she refuses to discuss the subject. She says, "Mom, Wallace and I made the decision together. You need to let this go."

Whenever I see a baby, I instantly think of the beautiful child my Lori would have. I know when she's ready, she will talk to me. If it's a fertility problem, her dad and I are willing to help with whatever they need. Money for IVF or for adoption. She just needs to ask us for help.

I truly hate putting my ornaments and decorations away in January. Joe is the original Scrooge or the Grinch that Stole Christmas. He gets cranky and hates anything associated with decorating. He refuses to use my system and doesn't take the time to carefully wrap our ornaments. Each ornament and decoration must go back into a specific container that I've labeled.

Before I retired, I was an executive secretary for over twenty-five years for the president of Stone International, a commercial development company. I know a thing or two about being organized and having everything in its place.

It's January ninth, I've put all the decorations away, and I just finished packing. We're now ready to head to our condo in Florida.

Notice, I said "I"—that is not an oversight. My Joe is wonderful. He's just not very good at packing. I make lists of everything we take to Florida, and I have a master list on my computer of what is in each container. There have been times when we've forgotten something, and I've had to call one of our kids back in Michigan. They love to make fun of my organizational skills, but they don't tease me when I can tell them exactly where to find something. My kids call me the "list diva."

When we leave for Florida, we take our time and drive to St. Augustine in three days. Gone are the days when we powered through and took turns driving to get there in eighteen hours or less. We're older now, and as I tell Joe, "Slow down—let's enjoy the journey. We don't have to be in a hurry." And surprise—he agrees!

Once we arrive in St. Augustine, it's time to chill for a short time and then let everyone know we're here. Joe teases me that I act like a teenager, because as soon as we're in town, I head to the balcony. I always leave the University of Michigan flag rolled up next to the balcony door, ready for our arrival. I'm exactly five feet one inch tall, so sometimes, if the wind is blowing, I need Joe's help. After freshening up, hoisting the flag is the first thing I do.

About two years ago, we arrived at our Florida home to a blustery day. On that particular day, I started to hang the flag up when the stand tipped over and fell toward the balcony. I thought it was going to drop over the edge, so I leaped forward and grabbed it. The flag line caught in my feet, and I found myself in the precarious position of being astride the top of the railing with my arms flat out. Picture the *Titanic* scene where the girl is acting like she is flying. That was me.

I was afraid to move, terrified I would fall three stories down. All I could do was scream for Joe. He came running, and after he extricated me, he sat down hard on the deck chair. I followed suit, collapsing in the chair next to him.

Joe sat there and laughed! I swear, he laughed for about five minutes as I glared at him, before I began to see it was kind of funny. So, we sat there like two old geese, cackling away. We would stop, look at each other, only to begin laughing again.

That is what I like about my Joe. He has a strong laugh and sense of humor as well as being strong and capable. He is able to easily lift my one hundred and ten pounds. Actually, I just tipped the scale at a hundred fifteen pounds. I will be back to normal now that I can go walking with my friends on the beach. I'm home, and I'm so happy.

When our flag goes up, the phone starts ringing, and I'm in my element. It's time now to start planning cookouts, card games, and sign up for activities. I've already planned our first two dinner parties in great detail. Typically, I let my friends have the first couple; this way, I know how I need to up my game for the season.

Muriel Rogers is an excellent party planner. She is always trying to outdo me, but she doesn't stand a chance. There's an art to putting together memorable parties. People still talk about my Murder Mystery Party we had ten years ago. It was a super big hit. We had our friends in the complex playing the actors. My Jenni and her Ben wrote the murder mystery. The story was tantalizing and helped to bring even the quietest, most shy participants into the fun of guessing "whodunit."

And don't get me started on the food. We put a special menu together that showcased some of our favorites. There was succulent roast beef, green beans almondine with a butter sauce, homemade hot rolls, mashed potatoes, roasted potatoes with several dipping sauces, and a hot spinach salad with bacon and special dressing. Dessert was my special "Death by Chocolate" cake. For giggles and grins, we made a special poster board that had "deathly" names for each of the foods and had everyone select their individual courses. It was super fun. Some people had Death by Chocolate first, while others asked for Murderous Irish Beast—the roast beef. Others started with the Guilty Party—a special cheese ball dip we had created just for the party.

That's not all we do. Joe and I are both active in our Homeowner's Association (HOA), and I lead the members' activities. My favorite activity is our monthly progressive dinner held the last Saturday of the month, January through March. My favorite night is Italian night. We make pans of lasagna, spaghetti, and fettuccini Alfredo. We also put together an array of dips for everything, ranging from garlic bread to tomato sauce, to vegetables and fruits, and then tables and tables of desserts.

We divide our attendees into smaller groups with individual and sometimes multiple couples hosting different courses. By the time we're finished with the main course, it's time for dessert. We then bring everyone together in our courtyard by the pool, where they can mingle under the moonlight and stars. We set up smokeless candles—lights that look like candles. Everyone then has the chance to walk around and see and visit with their neighbors.

It's been an incredible mixer for our condo members. And since it was my idea, I know everyone and have become close friends with many of our neighbors. You would be amazed at how many people kiss my butt, trying to get moved into specific groups.

We also have weekly gourmet dinner clubs, yoga, pickleball, tennis, bi-monthly trips to St. Augustine and the surrounding cities, plus golf course outings, a book club, and two swimming pools. One pool is indoors and one outside, and depending on interest, there are morning water aerobics and a senior night swim.

There is so much to see and do here in St. Augustine. And the best part is not only do we wake up to the gentle sound of the ocean, but we also have that small town feel. On rainy days, everyone else goes to the outlet malls to shop, and our beautiful beach is empty. In my opinion, St. Augustine is one of the best kept secrets around.

To me, this place is perfect. I'm able to visit with fun and interesting people, and I get to walk the beach. Just a short distance from our back door, we come face to face with nature. We cut up strawberries and bananas and leave them for the tortoises to find. After nearly twelve years, we have some spoiled, well-fed tortoises.

The average age in our complex is fifty-four years old, so Joe and I are kind of the old-timers, though you wouldn't know to look at us. We keep up just fine with people much younger than us, and we often have family and friends visiting. When my husband and I aren't wintering in St. Augustine, we rent our condo.

Truly, I wish we'd found this place sooner. Joe and I both worked hard our entire lives, and about twelve years ago, we decided to take the plunge and buy a condo. So now, our typical day begins with sharing the newspapers—yes, I said newspapers. We read *The Wall Street Journal* and *The New York Times* and sometimes the *Detroit Free Press*. Our kids have taught us how to get our news online. We sit on our wraparound porch, drink our coffee, have fruit and eggs or a protein shake, and watch the ocean. We can look out at the sunrise and see the beach slowly begin to fill up.

Our home back in Grand Blanc is much larger than our condo. We raised our three kids in our two-story colonial Tudor. The interior of the house is painted white with some blue and gray pictures and pillow accents. Our kitchen is white, with marble counters and stainless-steel appliances. It's a little big for us with five bedrooms, four bathrooms, a library, living room, formal dining room, and our kitchen.

One of my favorite rooms in Michigan is our sun room. It's different from the rest of the house. The walls are painted a creamy butter, and there are tall windows that run the length of the room, with a set of French doors that open onto our patio and pool. It's a lovely, relaxing place. When I'm in Florida, I miss my Grand Blanc sun room. Yet, when I'm in Grand Blanc, I find myself missing my St. Augustine balcony, my special coffeemaker, and sitting outside watching the ocean.

I never thought I'd say this, but I like having a small place. It's easier to clean and doesn't get as cluttered. The gray of our wood laminate floors offers a contrast to the vibrant teal and aqua accents throughout our condo. It's similar to the colors in our Grand Blanc home, just a bit more of a beach vibe. Our decorations are whimsical. Lots of paintings that we picked up at local art fairs. I even got a little wild last year and had one of the walls painted a bright turquoise. You hate it or you love it. I *love* it!

I really enjoy taking pictures of the early morning sunrise and sending them to our kids to encourage them to visit. I always include several pictures of my handsome Joe, showing his silver white hair, dark tan, and slim, six-foot-two build. My Joe doesn't like to pose for pictures, so I've learned to snap really fast. If I ask for more, I'm guaranteed to get the famous Joe scowl, with his green eyes sparking thunderbolts. I always send a couple angry pics as well, which makes everyone laugh. Our kids tend to call more quickly after receiving one of Joe's scowling pictures. They always ask, "Mom, what did you do?" Seriously, all three will ask me the *same* question.

It's been at least four years since Jenni and her family visited us in Florida. I mean, seriously, we bought a three bedroom for a reason. Clint comes about every other year, sometimes more, and Lori visits at least three times during the winter. Jenni and Ben make enough money; it shouldn't be a problem for them to get away to the sunshine at least once a winter. Granted, it's been hard with Mark, I get it, but I'm her mother and I need to see my grandbabies. Jenni is keeping them away from me by not coming to Florida. What catastrophe has to happen to convince my daughter to spend more time with me?

Chapter Two
Jen

January 8, 2020—This year, I will lose twenty-five pounds, organize my office—*once* and *for all*—and get my *life* in *balance*!!! I've walked ten thousand steps the last three days and I made it safely through the holidays without killing any family members. We're planning on visiting my parents in April. Kids are super excited to be traveling to Florida for spring break. I want to be down fifteen pounds by then, but I'm going to be realistic... six pounds sounds about right... My mantra is ten thousand steps a day—I've got this!

HAVE YOU EVER BEEN SO tired that you feel like there's a hazy paste over your eyes, preventing you from seeing clearly? All you want to do is go to bed and sleep through the night, or forever, whichever comes first. Because, seriously, you can't remember the last time you slept for seven whole hours.

The minute you lie down, you're instantly awake, your eyes won't close, and your mind is spinning. Thoughts are racing through your head. You even tried putting a pen and notebook next to your bed, hoping to capture your ideas and calm your mind. But you still can't sleep. One thought brings forth more thoughts and, before you know it, a couple hours have passed. Your mind is in a continuous loop that won't shut off.

Melatonin and other sleep aids don't work. Sure, they work for a couple of nights, but you're too afraid of getting addicted to sleep medication, so you stay away from medications your doctor offers you. After an hour or so, you get back up and return to your in-home office. Your mind is racing with thoughts and projects and things on your to-do list, things you need to finish.

That's how I feel. That's how I've felt for years.

My name is Jennifer or Jen or Jenni Blake, depending on how long you've known me. I live in Medway, Michigan, a suburb of Metro Detroit. I'm the chief organizer of our family of five, six if you count our miniature Goldendoodle Rex—or The Rexter, as we call him. He's our family protector, all thirty-two pounds of rust-colored muscle.

My eye is seriously twitching as I write a long list of items. My to-do list includes helping my husband Ben and three teenagers. In descending order, they are Kylie, our fifteen-year-old sophomore in high school, Jill, our fourteen-year-old in ninth grade, and Mark, our thirteen-year-old in eighth grade. Added to this constantly evolving to-do list are my kids' sports and driver's training, my paying job and projects, as well as figuring out our schedules to see family and friends.

And, if the truth is known, I'm kind of over being the last person in the family to get my stuff done. There aren't enough hours in the day to get everything completed. The smiles on my kids' faces, their extra big hugs, and their "I love you" at the end of the day are part of what keeps me going. I'm caught between total exhaustion and needing to do just a couple more things. Mom guilt is real, and I feel like I'm not doing enough for my family.

And I miss my husband. I have the best husband, and I miss having more time with just us, just Ben and me. I'm always at the bottom of my to-do list. For example, because I keep putting off my own dental cleaning, I paid the price. I ended up with two cavities, and one of the teeth was so far gone I needed a crown.

As of late, the individual requests from each family member have me in an overwhelmed state. My family has absolutely no idea how much I do, and I keep telling myself that I will get a large board and write out everything I'm doing for them. I need to keep better track of my time, and I think the family needs to be aware of how much is on my plate. I will just finish helping one kid then, within five minutes, my office door will open and in walks the second kid, only to be followed by the third a few seconds later. And, if that weren't enough, my parents Patti and Joe have been calling with subtle demands. Christmas this year was especially challenging. In addition to everything else on my plate, my mom requested that I make my "famous" six-layer coconut cake with raspberry filling and coconut frosting, plus a gluten-free/dairy-free dessert for our son Mark, as well as two additional sides for our family gathering.

Christmas has been my favorite holiday since I was a little girl. My earliest memory is going out for a midday dinner and then church. My parents started taking us out for dinner on Christmas Eve when we were tiny. Mom says that, otherwise, it was too hard for us kids to wait for Santa. On the way back from dinner, we'd sing carols at the top of our lungs, competing to see who could sing the loudest. Once we arrived home, we'd write Santa a letter, drink some hot cocoa, and snarf down a few luscious cookies. Then we'd rush to bed, eager for morning.

If I see a thumbprint cookie rolled in coconut or nuts with either red jelly or green apple jelly, I'm transported back in time. And I can't wait to enjoy and cherish the memories.

My mom decks the house out and makes a huge meal with all the trimmings. Because my parents leave for three months after the holidays, the family tradition is to celebrate with my parents before they leave for Florida. Like most years, we listened to my mom's latest story about her recent conversation with my sister Lori—short for Lorinda.

Lori lives in California and phones my mom nearly every day. My mom *lives* to tell us about these conversations. The worst is when she talks to Lori in front of us and then gets off the phone to recount the conversation. It's like someone coming to your home to introduce you to their new baby and, instead of holding the baby, you spend the whole visit looking at *pictures* of the baby.

That's what it feels like to be with my mom and hear, again and again, how *busy* my sister is, and how hard it is for her to get away for the holidays. My brother Clint and I usually just roll our eyes, but when it gets to the point that Mom pulls out her cell phone and you see that the screenshot includes a picture of just her and Lori and Dad... well, that's when it gets a little over the top.

One benefit to my sister missing the holiday is we don't have to deal with Lori and Mom competing over who spent the most on gifts. It's hard to take when Lori receives incredibly extravagant presents and I receive things like a dish towel that states, "It's more precious to give than to receive." Yeah, right, tell that to my mom when she doesn't like what she's received. Or if, heaven forbid, you buy the wrong size. Mom is quite petite and will give you a specific list of exactly what she wants for Christmas, the size, color, name of store, etc. One year I bought her a size medium blouse, and she proceeded to sneer at the gift and rip it in half.

Our family is comprised of the good, the bad, and the little bit crazy. Being with the extended family over Christmas can definitely be a challenge. Spending time with my brother and his family, watching as Clint teases Mom, and seeing how much fun the cousins have together somehow makes it worth it.

But, as dysfunctional as it can be, at least it's a relationship. Despite our success in recovering our son Mark from many of his diagnoses, our single-minded focus has resulted in lost friendships and me taking care of everyone *but* me. I can remember when I was in my mid-twenties and a colleague told me that she weighed 150 pounds. I remember thinking, *Wow, I won't ever weigh that much, even when I'm pregnant...* Famous last words.

I wish someone would invent a magic pill that allowed you to eat anything you want and be in shape and look and feel fabulous. Instead, I go on crazy diets, lose twenty or so pounds, and start feeling good. But within a few months of going off my diet, I've gained all the weight back, and sometimes more than what I started with. I've managed to keep a BMI that is overweight and, at five feet six inches, I'm getting too close to the next category (the word that rhymes with deceased—no special message there!).

It's not fair. Why is food so good? And why did I hurt my knee so I had to stop doing the only exercise that put me in my happy place? Running used to be my thang—by myself or with friends. I *loved* the sound of my heels pounding along wooded trails and along the crest of the sand just before it hit the water on my favorite beach. It was the sound of stress leaving my body. My whirling mind would become still, the staccato of my feet pounding their own special rhythm. I could also eat virtually anything I wanted with no worries about gaining weight, and I had no problem sleeping.

I'll never forget my last run. I was on a business trip on the East Coast during a snowstorm. Since the weather was sketchy, I decided to stay inside and run up and down the hallway to get in my cardio.

I finished and was sprinting to my room. My foot caught on a piece of loose carpet and I went flying. I hit the floor with a thud that reverberated through my entire body. My knee instantly swelled up, and I could no longer walk or run without extreme pain.

I remember long weeks of physical therapy as the swelling reduced and my knee got stronger. Then it happened. The happy day I was finally allowed to run again.

I cautiously stepped onto the treadmill, slowly began walking, and then increased my speed to a gentle jog. I hadn't smiled or felt this joy since my injury. Suddenly, there was a sound like my back cracking, only the sound came from my injured knee. I fell to the ground. The pain was easily a twenty on a scale of one through ten, and I felt nauseous. I was convinced I'd broken my femur—I couldn't straighten my leg for three days without screaming.

After the ultrasound confirmed a torn meniscus, my doctor suggested I switch sports. The middle of his forehead was heavy with frown lines as he said, "Jen, I know that you love to run. But you're in danger of another injury, and your body can't take it. It's my recommendation that you consider walking, biking, or swimming."

I listened to my doctor and I stopped running. He'd scared me. I wanted to be walking and not limping or in a wheelchair when I entered my fifties. I still remember the mental and physical pain after my knee surgery. I tried biking and walking, but neither felt as good. Running made me feel free, and, that feeling was now gone.

Even though I'm forty-eight, I look like I'm in my late thirties—in decent shape, but nothing close to the body I've had all my life. I'm five feet six inches tall, with green eyes and dark brown, shoulder-length hair. I seriously only have three gray hairs. I like to believe it's one for each of my children. (My husband is very happy that he hasn't caused a fourth.)

I'm feeling very blessed as I look at our son, Mark, and realize how far he has come. For the most part, life has been good. Our kids have matured, and all three are doing well in school, enjoying their sports and friends. Surprisingly, the kids get along well.

I've been back in the workforce for almost exactly one year when suddenly the world comes to a standstill. Although we aren't aware, life as we know it will end. March 2020 marks the beginning of the pandemic. In our home state of Michigan, COVID-19 results in some of the strictest lockdowns in the country.

Chapter Three
Kylie

January 10, 2020—Lately, I've been feeling like I'm stuck between my mom and my Granda. I love them both. I wish they got along better. It seems like everything I do has one of them fiercely supporting me, while the other says, "Hmmm... are you sure you want to do that?"

Plus, I think I need a new place to hide my journal. It wasn't where it's supposed to be. Jill, I know you're reading my journal! STOP IT!!! *Right now*—or I'm telling Mom and Dad, and you'll be in BIG trouble.

AT ALMOST SIXTEEN, I'M THE oldest. The thing that stinks about being the oldest is that I'm always the one who has to go first.

Basically, my parents are learning how to parent on *me*! And then I have to teach Jill and Mark how to do things, like how to navigate school and how to play sports. I *really* wish I had a big brother who played sports. Instead, I'm always the first. I was the first to play soccer, then basketball, and now lacrosse.

At a young age, I learned the definition of the word perseveration. To perseverate means to get stuck on a topic and never let it go. My brother, Mark, is on the autism spectrum, and he has been stuck on one or two subjects for as long as I can remember. He will repeatedly ask questions like:

"How tall am I?"

"How tall was I when I was in sixth grade?"

"How tall do you think I'll be?"

He's also fascinated by feet and pointedly asks strangers, "What size shoe do you wear?" Jill and I get secondhand embarrassment every time he does it. He doesn't care, and Mom and Dad are patient—too patient, if you ask me. He needs to learn to stop asking strangers bizarre questions.

At Christmas, my grandparents gave Mark a book about pirates. Now, we're hearing 24/7 about all the lost, buried treasure in St. Augustine. This is life in the Blake House.

My mom and Granda are so different. Granda's car and home are always clutter-free. Her house's furniture and carpet are all various shades of white. Everything is neat and clean and has a specific place. We grew up with Mom being afraid one of us kids would break Granda's precious art objects. One of my earliest memories is Granda telling my parents, "I'm not putting things away. Children need to learn how to *behave* appropriately." And Mom would roll her eyes *every* time.

I'm not a neat freak like my Granda Patti and my sister. Mom says, "The organization gene skipped a generation and went directly from Granda, passed me and Kylie, to Jill."

I'd be surprised if Grandpa Joe has ever seen Granda without makeup. My Granda is a tiny, "perfectly put together" woman, as my mom says. She watches everything she puts in her mouth. She weighs much less now than she's weighed her entire life and is super proud of her figure. I play a lot of sports, and Granda Patti has this way of looking down her nose whenever she sees me with a candy bar or soda. She'll say, "You're going to eat that?" Or, "Do you know how much sugar is in your pop?"

Yes, Granda… and I run three miles every day. I think I can drink a soda with real sugar in it!

Mom is pretty athletic. She loves to go walking and attend yoga classes with her friends. She dresses pretty casually in t-shirts and yoga pants and is not even close to being "perfectly put together"—except for her business meetings or family get-togethers. She doesn't exactly appreciate it when we tell her, "*Wow*, you look nice. Where are you going?"

And seriously, pretty much the only time Mom wears makeup is at a family get-together or if she's got a business meeting. Dad is pretty soppy, and he always gives Mom a big hug and says, "Your mom is naturally beautiful. She doesn't need to wear makeup."

Our house is cluttered, especially Mom's office. She has four paintings of the ocean and sailboats, a big desk, and a credenza that is filled to the top with papers and books and stuff. I swear, there's no way she knows where *anything* is in her office. She even has piles of paper on her floor.

We all know to leave her alone when her door is shut, or she'll go crazy on you. I'm the only one who doesn't walk into her office during the day. Jill and Mark are constantly in there. But the *one* time I have a question, she explodes at me. It's not my fault my brother and sister are in her office all day!

I'm an interesting mix of my mom and Granda. I'm petite, but I have my mom's wavy, dark brown hair and crazy sense of humor. Granda used to have the same hair color as us, but now it's reddish-brown. I've got Granda's blue eyes, and Mom has Grandpa Joe's green eyes. Granda always has to be right, even when she's wrong, and Mom wants to make things fair. My friends think it's funny because I get on my soap box about things being fair.

Granda can be extremely biting and rude to my mom. It's the one thing that really bugs me about her. She's nice to me, but it takes her a nanosecond to get into it with my mom.

Politically, I'm somewhere in the middle. I'm definitely a feminist—you can't be Jen Blake's daughter and not be a strong, empowered woman. But somehow through the years, my mom has kind of gravitated toward the middle. She dresses up when she has to, but for the most part, she's super comfortable in yoga pants and t-shirts—outfits my Granda wouldn't be caught dead in. Mom is pretty laid back about house cleaning, but she does get on my case about keeping my room clean. Thankfully, she's not an organization freak like Granda, and we don't live in a house completely decorated in white.

When I announced I was running for homecoming court, I got complete acceptance from Granda Patti. "Kylie, your Grandpa and I are so proud of you. You are just like me at your age."

I remember thinking, *Well, not quite. I'm not a cheerleader, and I don't have guys falling at my feet.* Granda just flutters her eyelashes and both young and old guys will pick up heavy things and flex their muscles. She laughs when I tease her and says, "Kylie, your old Granda still has it!"

When I told my mom I was running for homecoming court, she hugged me, then looked me squarely in the eye. Next came the question I'd been dreading. "So… what made you decide to run?"

I'd rehearsed my answer. I knew Granda would be super excited. Mom was the one that I was worried about. When Mom was nominated for homecoming court, she told her friends, "Don't vote for me."

Can you believe it? Can two people be any more different? Granda Patti, an ex-homecoming queen who loves to give me makeup and clothing tips, and my mom, a staunch feminist who openly campaigned against homecoming. I knew I had to explain exactly what I was feeling—why me, why now, and why homecoming court.

"Mom, I've been thinking a lot about what I want to be. Everyone sees me as this major tomboy. I love sports. I'm super competitive, but I'm tired of being in the friend zone with my guy friends. I want them to see me as more than a little sister." I'd rehearsed my answer, and I thought it sounded pretty good.

Mom raised her eyebrows, and then zeroed in on what I was trying to keep to myself. "Hmm… does Paul have a little something to do with your decision?" she asked.

My face flushed, then I quickly pushed forward. "Mom, if I'm elected to homecoming court, then Paul *has* to notice me. I'm really tired of him treating me like one of the guys." I paused as I gathered my thoughts. I had hoped my mom wouldn't realize the real reason I wanted to be on homecoming court. I swear my mom has a third eye. I'm seriously not anything like my girly friends, and I have a lot of good guy friends. I just want Paul to *see me* as more than his little friend.

Mom surprised me with her next sentence. "Honey, I'm so proud of you. You've decided you want this, and now you're going for it. I think you'll make a great sophomore attendant."

The next week was definitely interesting. Everyone in the tenth grade voted, and I was one of the five finalists. Then we voted again; this time, everyone was given two votes, as there would be two sophomore attendants. Student Council was tabulating the votes, and as I walked the halls, I was constantly getting stopped by people saying, "Hey, Kylie! I voted for you."

It felt good. I really wanted to win, but if I didn't win, at least I'd put myself out there.

They announced the court at assembly a week before our homecoming game. I was super nervous. First, they started with the freshman, then it was the sophomores' turn.

Suddenly, my best friend Paige was screaming and jumping up and down next to me. I couldn't believe it. They called my name. Woohoo! I was elected to homecoming court. I couldn't wait to tell Granda and Mom! And the best news—Paul gave me a high five and stared at me the whole time I was on stage. Step One complete—Paul was definitely noticing me. I couldn't wait for him to see me all dressed up.

Once I was elected to the court, my mom, Jill, and I went into overdrive. I needed a long dress for homecoming. We went to three dress shops, and I was so tired by the end, I would've literally picked anything—but, no, we had to keep going until my mom and sister found the "perfect" dress. I sat down and begged for a cheeseburger—after all, it was almost two o'clock and I hadn't eaten since breakfast.

Mom wasn't in the best mood as she snapped, "Kylie, we have to find your dress today. We'll probably have to alter it, and we're running out of time!"

We were debating between two blue dresses when my mom told the saleslady, "I like the royal blue dress, but it's a bit flashy. Do you have something more classic?"

I lost it. I flopped on the floor and sat with my legs crossed, like back in kindergarten. I was tired, and it felt like I hadn't eaten in a year.

"Kylie—I told you, we are *not* stopping to eat until we find your dress. Have a granola bar," my mom said as she looked through another rack of dresses.

"But Mom, I'm hungry. I want real food." Surely, she would take pity on me. But no, we started a huge discussion. Before I knew it, we were in a full-blown fight... I just wanted to be done. "We've been to three stores. Can we please go to lunch?"

"Kylie, I'm sure you can find something here you can eat!" At this point, exasperated, my mom reached into her purse and began to toss food at me. My mom had brought my favorite snacks. First, it was a bag of corn chips, then peanut butter crackers, a candy bar, and finally some cheese sticks. She'd been so caught up in the "dress" that she hadn't really listened to me and realized how hungry I was.

I dove into the food. I was already feeling better.

Just then, the saleslady brought out a plain blue dress. The shop was having a sale, and we'd found a dress for two hundred dollars, a dress that was marked half off. I didn't get why it was so expensive. And it was about three feet too long for me. We would have to cut a bunch of the fabric off. The shop owner assured us the dress would fit perfectly with some minor alterations. She suggested we have the seamstress use some of the extra material to make a wrap to match. The dress was simple, so my mom found a sparkly diamond and pearl belt to add a little bit of bling.

Homecoming court wasn't the huge deal everyone makes it out to be, but it was fun. I talk to everyone, which is probably why I was voted onto the court. I guess my parents constantly telling me to treat people like I'd like to be treated sunk in. I don't walk around like I breathe different air. Even though I kind of do, being so close to the ground and all. I can hear my mom now: "Kylie, stop it. That is a disparaging remark. You shouldn't cut yourself down."

Of course, I would respond, "I'm already so short, there's nothing left to cut." Yup, that's how I roll. Keep the jokes coming, and duck and weave before anyone knows what I'm doing.

One day, I asked my parents why I was so short. Dad joked, "Have you seen Grandma Debra?"

I instantly laughed. My dad is six feet tall and his mom is four feet eleven inches. Point taken.

Grandma Debra is one of the most selfless people you will ever meet. We're her only grandchildren, and Dad says, "My mom was made to be a grandma." She used to take us every summer for a week. We called it Camp Grandma, as she and her sister Ellen would keep us busy with all kinds of activities. We would go blueberry picking, swimming, to the movies, for walks in the woods, camping in her backyard, and fishing at the nearby pond. Grandma Debra would plan fun crafts to mirror our interests. We were always so proud to show Mom and Dad our creations.

She's also a wonderful baker and makes the best cookies in the world. I think everyone should have a Grandma Debra. She has been really helpful to my parents through the years. Now that I'm older, I realize how important it is for them to get downtime. It was especially important during the early years when my brother Mark was acting out.

Mark used to get really mad if anything happened outside of his plan. He had to sit in a certain place during family movie night, would eat all the cereal or chips in the house, plus had a limited number of foods he would eat. He would have meltdowns where he screamed, yelled, cried, and threw things.

For years, we had holes in the walls, and we all learned to be careful we weren't upsetting him, especially if he was at the top of the staircase. A couple times, he got angry and threw himself down a flight of stairs. Fortunately, he wasn't hurt too badly. He would also get mad and bolt

21

outside in the winter in shorts with no shoes. It took a while for him to learn that he couldn't run in and out of neighbors' yards.

Mark and I have the love of running in common, but unlike Mark, I'm not belligerent and have never run away from my parents. I only run in sports. At the beginning of my sophomore year, my parents told me I could only play one sport. Our school does a pay-to-play, and it costs about five hundred dollars per person by the time we pay for the sport, equipment, and a "charitable, one-time check."

Basketball or lacrosse? It was a really hard choice. My parents let us play two sports freshman year with the intent of selecting only one going forward. I love basketball, but almost the first time I picked up my lacrosse stick, something clicked, and I knew this was the sport for me.

When I'm working out or on a team, two things happen. First, I'm much better organized with my time. And second, I'm totally happy and in the zone, hanging out with friends and practicing.

I love sports, but sometimes life just isn't fair. Like, why does Mark have autism? Jill and I kind of joke about it, because for his birthday and at Christmas, two of Mom's friends go out of their way to buy Mark presents. Seriously! What about Jill and me? Plus, if Mark didn't have all his issues, I know I would've been able to play more than one sport. It's not fair.

My freshman basketball team was undefeated. I became really close with my team, and it was tough for me to sit out sophomore year and watch my friends play, since we didn't have the extra money for me to play two sports. Putting a smile on my face and pretending I was "okay" while waiting for my lacrosse season has been hard.

It's also been hard for me to watch my sister, Jill, play on her freshman basketball team. Mom goes to the home games, and I usually go with her. My sister's horrible team has only won two games this year, and they play right before my friends on the JV team. It's absolutely awful that I have to sit there with a smile on my face while my sister plays a sport I love. It's not fair. She sucks, her team sucks, and then Jill comes home and says how much she *hates* basketball and she can't wait to play her sport—soccer—this spring.

And if I hear one more time, "But you were on homecoming court..." I will scream! Even though homecoming court was fun, I found out later that the money we spent on a long dress, makeup, and hair would've almost paid for a second sport. Seriously, if I'd known in advance, I would've said "bye-bye" to homecoming court.

At the beginning of this year, my family asked what I was most looking forward to. Hands down, I told them playing lacrosse with my friends, finding out if I'm on the JV or the varsity team, and getting my driver's license.

Well, guess what? This is now officially the *worst* year of my life!

Our lacrosse team was supposed to find out this Friday what team we made. But, no... on Wednesday, March tenth, our teachers were kept home in case we went to distance learning. Even before the weekend, we were told we would be off school for a few weeks—at least two.

Not only is my lacrosse season on hold—who knows if we're going to get a season? I've been waiting to get back out on the field with my friends, and now I have a bad feeling they are going to cancel it. And the worst news is my driving test for Saturday was canceled. No one understands how horrible this is for me. I've been waiting to play lacrosse all year and get my driver's license. I just want to scream at the top of my lungs!

Every time I get upset or start to cry, Rex jumps on me. He won't stop barking until I pick him up and cuddle with him. Rex is a people dog. He loves everyone in our family and acts like a killer attack animal when anyone comes to the house. He thinks it's his "job" to alert us if someone is outside. As soon as we let the person in, he stops barking and tries to lick them to death.

I'm really glad we have Rex. He kind of belongs to Dad and me more than anyone else. Rex loves all of us, but he follows Dad everywhere. We all laugh, because Dad was the one person in the family who didn't want a pet. And now he's stuck with a two-year-old dog that adores him.

Chapter Four
Patti

March 10, 2020—I wish my Jenni would talk to me, but Jenni and I don't have the same close relationship that Lori and I have. I'm crossing my fingers that will change during Jenni's visit in a few weeks—I'm looking forward to spending some quality time together. It's been forever since my Jenni and her family have visited us... four years is a long time!

STARTING IN JANUARY, WE BEGAN to hear about this horrible virus that was hitting the West Coast, and I worried about my Lori and her Wallace. They travel a lot for business. On our daily calls now, I ask, "Have you seen the news?"

Lori assures me she is taking precautions, using hand sanitizer, and making sure to take the supplements that Jenni recommends to keep her immune system healthy. She's taking lots of extra vitamin C and vitamin D, and she brings melatonin to help her sleep on overnight trips. She's started wearing a cloth mask when she flies and told me she's going to order some N95 masks to wear on the airplane. The CDC is recommending that people save masks for medical personnel that need it, and I told her I don't care what the CDC says, I want my daughter safe. I feel like she needs a better mask than a cloth one. Some people are making masks, since there's a shortage. I'm just not feeling like a homemade mask with a coffee filter is appropriate protection.

Lori came to visit us in Florida for a long weekend in January and another in February. She is the Marketing Director for a cosmetic firm. Every winter, Lori brings bags full of my favorite makeup for me and my friends to sample. I always schedule a special outing with the ladies who are interested in experimenting with a new look.

Lori is easy to talk to. We both like makeup, art and craft shows, and shopping. Let me tell you, that girl can shop! It feels effortless and comfortable with her. She fits in nicely with all my friends. And she calls me every day on her commute to the office or on the way home.

Every year, she and Wallace schedule at least one international trip. They've been everywhere, from Italy, to England, France, and even to Egypt. And since they live in California, I can't count the number of times they've gone to Hawaii. Lori keeps wanting me to go with her, and someday I will, but Joe doesn't like to fly. He keeps promising me we'll go, so I'm waiting for our trip. Trust me, that man has every excuse under the sun to get out of booking a flight!

Lori has it all together. She is smart, after all, but a mom still worries. Lori and her brother and sister will always be my babies. It doesn't matter if they are forty years old. I guess they won't understand until their kids are older.

I just wish Lori and her husband Wallace would have children. I'm afraid they will regret their decision and, by the time they change their minds, it will be too late. I'm so thankful my Jenni and Clint have given us grandkids. I went through too much to have my three children and I just don't understand *why* Lori and Wallace don't want kids. I believe part of the reason is she has seen what being a mother has done to her sister.

Jenni was an extremely successful executive. Things changed almost overnight, as soon as they got the autism diagnosis for Mark. I still don't understand why my Jenni decided to stay home. She had so much promise. We paid for her to get her BS in Business, and then she went on and got her MBA at the University of Michigan. She had the world at her feet... and then autism struck.

I know this isn't a very politically correct thing to say, but it's true and it's how I feel. I've watched my daughter give up her life for my grandson. Jenni's mother-in-law, Debra, is a wonderful woman. The salt of the earth. She's stepped in, and she's given our Jenni and her husband a lot of babysitting help through the years. I couldn't bring myself to. For years, Joe and I tried to convince Jenni to go back to work, so they could hire extra help for Mark.

My vibrant daughter channeled her energy into finding a cure, a recovery plan for her son, but Joe and I were concerned about changes we saw in our Jenni. She looked tired and exhausted, more so each time we saw her. When Mark was home sick from school for several years, she stopped exercising—started eating a lot of comfort food. My Jenni, who used to run and lift weights, gained a lot of weight. It seemed like each time we saw her, she looked rounder, more tense, and more depleted. Of course, if I even mentioned an exercise program or a diet, she would give me the death stare or pick a fight and flounce off.

I have to remind Joe every time we see her, "Do *not* tease Jenni about her weight." I always get blamed for it. I know she feels terrible about her weight gain; she tells her sister, and Lori tells me.

Lori is the same exact size she was the day she graduated from high school. A perfect five feet two inches, with 105 pounds of sheer muscle. Lori has a personal trainer named Roderick. She works out with him twice per week and, when she's visiting, she shows me her exercise routine. My girl looks amazing, much younger than thirty-nine years old. She's a mini-me, a petite frame with auburn hair and sparkling blue eyes.

Jenni is beautiful as well.

It's been a long time since I've seen the actual *real* color of my hair, but it used to be the exact same shade of dark brown that Jenni and Kylie have. Jenni inherited the non-graying gene, but my hair has been gray since I turned thirty. I decided when I went gray, I was going red. Why not?

I wish Jenni could see me like her friends do. They think I'm fun. Jenni gets this look on her face like she's bitten into something nasty whenever I talk about my parties and friends. I believe she misses having her own. My girl is just like me in one big way. She doesn't know a stranger. I remember her dinner gatherings when she was first married. She learned how to put on a good party from me, and she does a nice job.

I know she misses her old, carefree life. She can't hide it from me. I'm her mother and I know her. She thinks I don't see her, but I do. I see her weighted down by responsibility.

I miss my old, carefree life too. It's March 10, and the phone rings as Joe and I are sitting on the balcony, enjoying the Florida breeze. It's our granddaughter Kylie. Oh, how I love our chats.

"Granda—I can't decide if I'm happy or mad. They've canceled school for us on Thursday and Friday. They're saying we might have to go to online teaching, and they have to get the teachers ready." The words come out in a rush.

"Whoa, slow down, honey. I've got you on speaker, so Grandpa can hear. What's going on?"

I hear Kylie exhale in a big whoosh. "Granda and Grandpa—they've canceled school. I'm so mad. We were finding out which lacrosse team we made this Friday, and now I have to wait to find out if I made JV or varsity."

Joe raises his eyebrow to me, silently asking, *Who, is on the phone?*

"Honey... you know Grandpa Joe is a little deaf. I don't think he can hear you very well."

"It's Kylie," I silently mouth, and then take the phone off speaker. I don't have time to keep repeating. I'll tell him later. I wish he'd get a hearing aid, then I wouldn't have to constantly repeat conversations.

Kylie continues, "Everyone has been emailing our coach, and she said for us to just relax... It's killing me. I want to know which team I'm on." And then her voice slightly shakes. "Granda, what if they cancel our sports season?"

I can hear the fear and the threat of tears in her voice. "Honey, I'm sure this virus will blow over, and you'll just enjoy a long weekend," I assure her.

I talk to Kylie, Jenni, Clint, and Lori through the weekend. Jenni is a little preoccupied when I talk to her Thursday night. She and Ben planned a weekend getaway to a conference in Traverse City in two weeks, and she has an event with friends this Saturday. She doesn't get out very often. I'm hoping for her sake that her events stay open. My Jenni needs some downtime.

On Friday, Jenni phones. Her Saturday event is canceled. And she tells me about all the various community events being shut down. Many groups are canceling activities "out of an abundance of caution."

What a nightmare. I'm finding myself very glad my Joe and I are in Florida. We can still walk out our back door, across the bridge, and access the beach. Our HOA community is continuing to have swimming, yoga, pickleball, and other events.

Each night, Joe and I watch the news in disbelief as we hear about more and more people infected with the virus, and the concern, worry, and fear because there aren't enough kits to test people. People are being told to go home and quarantine. Some are developing respiratory problems and dying.

It started in the West Coast and is now throughout the country. Early in March, Florida still does not have very many cases or deaths, but with our older population, we're considered high risk. I'm scared. Joe and I are older.

On March 17, 2020, our Governor Ron DeSantis shuts down all Florida bars and nightclubs for thirty days. Restaurants are restricted to half capacity to limit the spread. Beaches are still open near us, but we're hearing they are shutting down beaches in other counties in Florida.

Three days later, Governor DeSantis orders that all restaurants, "Suspend on-premises food and alcohol consumption." I'm very happy that he is allowing the restaurants to continue operating with delivery and takeout services.

I've been hearing from Jenni that people are running out of toilet paper in Michigan, so we stock up on a large amount at the grocery store. It's kind of funny, every time we place a delivery order, our favorite restaurant gives us a free roll of toilet paper. I'm saving all the extra rolls and will give them to Jenni and Clint when we get home.

And they also close down all fitness facilities. This means our condo fitness center and indoor swimming pool are now shut down. The HOA has to meet and decide if we can keep the outdoor pool open.

Jenni phones when she hears the latest Florida news. "Mom, you and Dad need to think more seriously about coming home. I know the weather is nice there, but we don't want you to get stuck in a shelter-in-place where you can't leave. Please think about it."

I promise her I will. I know as soon as she gets off the phone with me, she will likely call her siblings and they will *all* start in on us.

I feel good about our governor's decision to keep the beaches open. I like what he has to say. It's nice to have a governor stand up for his state and his people. Though I do question one of his statements. Why on earth would a married couple walk six feet apart outside on the beach? I ask Joe, tongue in cheek. Are they supposed to stay six feet apart at all times?

I'm glad to be in Florida, but we're hearing rumors that Highway A1A is going to be closed, as well as the Florida border, to keep away people from New York. We are hearing some other states will also be closing their borders.

This feels like some weird Twilight Zone episode. We have an emergency HOA meeting and vote to cancel our March progressive dinner, as well as other in-person events until further notice. Our friends are leaving Florida in droves. Joe, of course, wants to get in one or two more rounds of golf. But I'm getting scared. In just a few days, three families in our building have packed up and said, "See you next year."

Life has continued somewhat the same. We continue getting up and having our coffee on the deck, taking pictures of the sunrise and sunset, and walking on the beach. We still hold hands while we walk, forget that stupid six-foot rule! The anxiety and worry are palatable; you can almost taste it in the wind as you walk the beach. Sometimes, people cover their face with a mask as they walk or run past you.

By the twenty-fifth, our three kids are encouraging us to pack everything up and come home. They want us to spend Easter in Michigan with them. And, as each day passes, the news becomes more ominous. There are concerns that millions of people will die from this virus. In my daily talks with Lori, I've started to ask her to leave California and come to Michigan and stay with us. But she's calmly told me, "Mom, I have my home here. Wallace and I are staying put."

By the next day, we're hearing rumors that airlines will close as well. And besides, flying isn't a viable option. We have too much stuff to bring back.

Usually, I've always packed in a very organized fashion. Not this time. I'm feeling anxious, worried, and unsure if we'll be able to make it home. They are starting to close beaches in Florida, trying to stop the spread of this horrible virus. Fortunately, our beach remains open and we're still able to get outside and walk along the ocean in the fresh air.

Joe and I sit on our balcony and laugh as we watch the spring breakers descending upon our beach, as far and wide as you can see. They are packed in like sardines. We have never seen so many kids here. It's unreal!

The boys strut around and show off for the girls, but the girls are lost in selfie land. They parade back and forth, sucking their stomachs in, fluffing their hair, making those pouty lips, and constantly taking photos.

"What, do they think they're going to be on the cover of some fashion magazine like *Cosmo*?" Joe roars the first time he sees them posing.

We sit on our balcony and have front row seats to the college students. One group in particular gives Joe a real chuckle.

"Patti, do you see them over there?" He points. "They've been in the same place, taking selfies all day long. We've gone about our day and they are still there. It's been more than six hours since I noticed them."

We both laugh. What a world it is. Kids going to the beach and spending all day posting on social media. What happened to enjoying the surf and being in the moment?

Speaking of being in the moment, like much of America, every night I'm glued to my chair in front of the television. With everything canceled, all I do is watch. I sit in rapt horror as more news of the virus and the infection rates seem to be skyrocketing across the country.

One of my favorite new people to watch on TV is that cute Dr. Anthony Fauci. He makes the daily COVID briefings fun. He's a short little man with a shock of whitish gray hair, sometimes wearing oval glasses, and his face reminds me of a wrinkled, tan apple. He's become a major television star for all the right reasons.

I like him—I think he is someone we can trust. He has been in President Trump's briefings for the last several weeks. As people panicked and starting buying up face masks, he told us to save the masks for people who needed them in the hospitals, so they have enough to take care of people. He also said we didn't need to wear masks.

Good—I don't want to wear them anyway, especially in eighty-plus degree weather. And besides, hardly anyone wears them on the beach or in the grocery store when we're out and about.

The only thing that has me worried is he stepped in front of President Trump on March 20 and said using hydroxychloroquine as a cure for COVID was only "anecdotal evidence." The President seems to be convinced hydroxychloroquine is a game changer. I sure hope so, but I guess time will tell. I wish they were both on the same page. I really like Dr. Fauci.

My Joe and Jenni, especially Jenni, tell me to stop listening to the doom and gloom. I can't seem to get the energy to make a decision about our travel plans. And Joe is happy to be golfing, walking the beach, or reading. I don't know what to do. Should Joe and I go home or stay in Florida?

My Jenni's phone call jolts me out of my thoughts... "Mom, get outside. Get some natural Vitamin D—go for a walk on the beach!"

I promise to go for a walk. I will be sure to walk early in the morning, just as the sun is coming up, long before all the spring breakers descend upon our little beach.

On March 28, we wake up early, and Joe and I both agree it's time. Today will be our last full day in St. Augustine. We will have one last, early morning walk on the beach before tomorrow's departure. I'm so going to miss the beach in the early morning. We've waited as long as we can, but it's time to return to Michigan.

A lot has changed in only eighteen days. We have gone from just learning about the virus to hearing about it twenty-four hours a day on the news. People older than sixty are considered the most vulnerable, and we are in our early seventies. We're being told we should stay home and let others get our groceries for us. And we need to stay away from our younger family members, as they could be carriers. People in nursing homes or assisted living complexes are being completely locked down and unable to see or hug their family.

We have some food in our refrigerator and in the freezer. Most of my friends have left, and I don't want to see it go to waste, so I phone Muriel.

"Muriel, we have some extra food. Would you like it?"

"What kind of food?" Muriel asks.

Gee, I think, *nothing like being rude when someone wants to give you a gift.*

I take a breath and then I start listing it off. "We have three gallons of really good ice cream, three packages of frozen chicken, some frozen ground beef, and some tomatoes and bananas. Do you want them or not?"

"What brand of ice cream?" asks Muriel.

33

At this point, she's on my last nerve. "Ice cream, we've got ice cream. Do you want it or not?"

"Patti, don't get your panties in a wad—I just wanted to know what kind. Geez. John and I will go for a walk in a half hour. How about we stop over on our walk and pick it up?"

"Sure." One more thing I can check off my list. We're giving our goodies to a good home. Well, kind of. We're giving them to Muriel and John.

It's March 29. We finished packing everything and loaded our car last night. I am so anxious and excited, I can't sleep. Joe is out like a light. After tossing and turning for hours, I finally can't stand it. I get out of bed at three o'clock, and make some coffee for the road.

And I might, just saying, *might* be making some extra loud noise to wake Joe. We planned to leave at 5:00 AM to beat some of the traffic on the highway, but I'm in a hurry and just want to be on the road.

Joe wakes up at 3:15 AM and staggers into the kitchen. He finds me sitting on the deck. My University of Michigan flag has been put away, and I'm having my last cup of coffee in the quiet darkness before we leave.

"Okay, Patti, we might as well get going," yawns my tired husband.

Since the car was packed the night before, I just have to grab the thermos of coffee, the small cooler with our chilled bottles of water, snacks, plus our two empty coffee cans. We don't know if we will find restrooms on the way home, so in case of emergency, we are bringing our own coffee cans, along with a roll of toilet paper.

Jenni and Clint have told us about the grocery shortages, so we stop at the store and pick up extra packages of toilet paper. We've separated and wedged the rolls in various places throughout the car. Our beautiful, white Buick Enclave is filled to the brim. We are ready to go!

While Joe drives, I keep watch for cops and also watch our phones to see if any messages come in from our kids or grandkids. If we feel up to it, we're going to try to drive all the way through. In the old days, it took us about twenty hours with stops for gas, potty breaks, and stretch breaks. We're hoping to do it in about eighteen hours. "Michigan or bust" is our mantra.

Many restaurants are closed, with just a few open for takeout, so we've prepared sandwiches and food to keep us going. For the first few hours, I-77 is empty. It's eerie, kind of like a ghost town. We are literally the only vehicle on the road for the first three hundred miles, then as the sun comes up, we start to see a few cars here and there. Atlanta has always been busy, no matter what time of day or night, but not this time. We sail through. We see two police cars once we've been on the road for about four hours or so.

Joe drives the first five hours and gets us to Columbia, South Carolina. We fill up, use the bathroom, and stretch our legs. I am so grateful we don't have to use a coffee can. So far, so good.

Will we make it all the way home, or will we be forced to turn around or, worse, be denied entry into Michigan? We have a map and printed directions in case our GPS or Google Maps has any technical issues. We have no idea what to expect. Not knowing is scary. This trip is definitely an adventure, but not the happy, blissful adventures we had when we were young and just starting out.

To be safe, we've withdrawn several hundred dollars in cash. We also called our credit card companies to let them know we're on our way home from Florida and there might be charges on the way back. In addition to the food in our cooler, we have filled two gas cans. It's a bit of a risk, traveling with gas in the back of the car, but we feel getting home outweighs the slim possibility we'll get in an accident and have our car explode.

Our plan is to drive until we are either too tired to keep driving or we are forced to stop. And we're praying a lot. Joe and I always pray before a road trip, and this time, we have our friends in St. Augustine praying for us too. We didn't tell the kids we were leaving Florida on March 29. We don't want them to worry about us.

We decide we need to stop one more time in West Virginia to fill our tank up, just in case there are problems getting gas after Charleston.

It normally takes about five and a half hours straight through, but my Joe is driving with the pedal to the medal, and we make it in five hours. The fuzz buster only goes off one time, and we have plenty of warning to slow down.

It's now two o'clock and we have roughly six hours left. Joe agrees to switch, and I drive the next three hours. We are surprised at the lack of cars on the highway. The I-77 interchange is a virtual ghost town. Even as we go through Columbus, Ohio the roads are nearly empty. We switch one last time, and Joe drives us home.

Even with four stops to fill up and use the bathroom, we manage to make it in a little over fifteen hours. This is definitely a record. Just as we are rolling into our garage in Grand Blanc, my cell rings. It's Jenni, wanting to talk.

"Jenni, we're home!" I exclaim.

"You're what?!" she says, her voice shrieking on the other end of the phone.

"Your dad and I decided to leave early, and we just pulled into the garage. Got to go—we need to unload and get some sleep. It's been a long drive. Let's talk tomorrow, okay?" I say, then quickly hang up.

I don't know how Joe is standing up. He drove most of the way, probably on pure adrenalin.

We have a mixture of feelings. Exuberance we've made it safely, tiredness, but also feeling energized to see family and friends. Tomorrow is another day, another adventure. But for now, we just need to get the gas, our cooler, and our overnight bag out of the back.

We are finally back home—safe.

Chapter Five
Jen

April 2, 2020—Our life is changing. We have a completely new normal, and it seems like every day there is a major change. It's only April 2—how did this happen?! How did we get here? It's been a few years since Ben and I had time away. We've had to cancel two trips that I was really looking forward to. So many unknowns are scary. Will Ben continue to work from home?

TODAY IS A GORGEOUS DAY. The sky is blue and the sun is shining. I've had two early morning walks, one with Jill and Rex and the other with Kylie and Rex. It's now three o'clock, and I'm halfway through a walk with Mark and Rex. So far, in this "new normal," the family dog is making out the best. His people are home and he gets multiple walks every day.

Just as we pass the small subdivision park, my cell phone rings. It's my mom. I debate: should I wait, phone her later? I pick up.

"Jenni—did you hear the news? The governor has closed in-person school through the end of the school year." Since the beginning of the pandemic, Mom has become a news junkie. She sits at home, listening to the news all day, every day.

"Oh, no! Mom, thanks for letting me know. I need to go. Mark and I are walking Rex. I need to get home before Kylie hears the news. "

"Okay, honey. Call me later."

Mark sighs. "Do we really have to go home, Mom?"

"Yes! Let's get moving. I need to be there when Kylie finds out." I know my daughter is struggling. This news will be devastating.

Within five minutes, I enter our house. "Kylie!" I yell. "Kylie, where are you?"

We are too late. Kylie has heard.

"Mom, it's just not fair! We're going to be doing online school until the end of the year," she wails as tears roll down her face.

I gently touch her shoulder. Kylie turns toward me and allows me to hold her. Kylie isn't a hugger, and I'm one of the few people she accepts them from. As a hugger, it's really hard for me to hold back. She is exactly the opposite of her brother and sister. Mark and Jill come up and give and receive multiple hugs throughout the day. Not Kylie! Sometimes I wonder—how did we end up with a child who doesn't like hugs?

I joke that you need twenty hugs a day for growth. Kylie is quick to state, "I guess I didn't get enough hugs! But I'm good." She will say this as she puts her hand up in a "stop" motion before I can slide in for a sneak attack.

I have felt so alone and powerless since we received the March "Stay Home, Stay Safe" executive order. We're being told to stay in our homes unless we are essential workers—which includes front-line healthcare workers and truckers and grocery store employees. It's become a little scary to go to the store. There are lines out the door as they slowly allow people inside, and many people are wearing masks covering their noses and mouths.

Ben and I are both exhausted and desperately need a vacation. We were planning a romantic getaway to a national special needs conference in Traverse City. Our conference, like many other events, has been canceled.

It's one more thing, one more loss of something I was looking forward to. Because of COVID, we canceled our spring break trip to Florida. It was going to be our first family vacation that did not involve a medical detour to see doctors. And because of the restrictions and concerns over getting or passing along COVID-19, we haven't seen my parents or Ben's mom. My Vision Board Conference with friends for my favorite charity is canceled, as well as school, church, and seeing friends.

Seriously, just stick a fork in me and call me done. The getaway, after canceling our Florida trip, is the last straw. Now we're all in lockdown. Everyone is going a little stir-crazy. Fortunately, we're staying healthy.

I'm used to working from home, so this isn't a huge change for me. Having Ben and the kids home, wanting help with online classes and questions every day, has been a challenge.

Meanwhile, Ben is a rock. He's stoically putting in extra hours to help the kids with homework. Every time he walks upstairs (from his office), I look at his face. Most of the time, it's a medium shade of red. This is an indicator his stress level is high, and probably his blood pressure as well. His company has had three layoffs this year. He thinks his job is safe until this winter, but he's starting to put feelers out.

We have a private joke. I have a warped sense of humor and will laugh at physical pain. If you bump your foot or arm, I laugh. If I'm watching a sad movie and tear up, Ben laughs. I've even found him a t-shirt that says, "It's not funny until someone gets hurt." Yup, that's how I roll, and we get each other.

Weirdly, I'm finding myself grateful, as we will be receiving a government subsidy for this time off and it will help us pay down our credit card debt. I've been at my job for almost a year, and we need the money. Because of Mark's health issues, I quit work to stay home and manage his medical care when he was seven years old. Keeping track of his medical appointments and his educational issues was a full-time job. When our team of doctors explained that he had severe immune issues and would need monthly hospital treatments, my husband and I knew something had to give.

Ben offered to stay home and take care of our son, but we decided I needed to be the primary person managing our son's medical care. I'm a super networker and a Warrior Mom and Mama Bear who will go to the ends of the Earth for my kids. I joke with Ben that he is the "nice" one. Me—not always, and heaven help the person who does something mean to someone I love or care about.

I left the job I loved and began the journey of a special needs mom fighting to get treatments and education and the right specialists for our child.

It was a long road, and fortunately, Mark's health improved and he was able to return to school full time this past year. Once we knew he was stable, it was time for me to go back to work. An environment working with adults was something I craved. Part-time sounded perfect, as I didn't want to go back to crazy town working eighty-plus-hour weeks. A friend told me about a fractional Chief Marketing Officer (CMO) opportunity where I could work from home for twenty to twenty-five hours per week at a medical recruiting company.

I'm ecstatic and feel like I'm back in the land of the living, the land of the capable. My spirit is soaring. My job is helping pay down our immense medical debt, restock our retirement account, and save for an amazing cruise for our daughter Kylie's senior year in high school.

Able Enterprises is a small recruiting company, and the owners are older. Hiring me as their Chief Marketing Officer (CMO) was not exactly in their comfort zone. Any day, I'm expecting to get laid off. I know placing medical personnel has gotten tough since March.

It will be nice to have a few months off. In fact, if I weren't working, I could be more present for my family. It would help me to relax, slow down, and get some time for me. As much as the extra money is helpful, I won't be horribly upset if I lose my job.

No one seems to understand this, but the only time I get for myself is between eleven PM and two in the morning. It's the only time our house is quiet. Everyone is in bed but me and our miniature goldendoodle Rex. He refuses to go to bed until all of "his" people are in bed. He thinks it's his job to stay up with us. It's actually comforting to look across the room and see our precious Rex waiting for me, his "mom," to go to bed. He lies in front of my office door, ready to alert me to any sounds outside the house.

Our kids are struggling—and, truthfully, so am I. If I hear, "Mom, I've got a question," one more time, I'm going to scream! There aren't enough hours to get everything done. Working from home and doubling as a tech problem solver and teacher has significantly added to my stress. Monday through Thursday, I start my office day at seven o'clock, and then segue into home and family projects around one-thirty or so every day.

I almost always end up working more than the twenty hours per week I'm paid. I'm responsible for putting the marketing strategy together and making sure our recruiters have beautiful copy to send to our clients. I usually spend at least an additional ten unpaid hours per week making little tweaks here and there. Before I know it, it's five o'clock and I need to make dinner.

I love to cook and come up with new dinner ideas to tempt my family's palate. Growing up, my mom cycled through the same eight or nine different meals. We would have a barbeque dish, a fish dish, meatloaf—usually on Thursday night—followed by spaghetti on Friday. I love spaghetti, but using leftover meatloaf in the sauce is not my idea of a gourmet meal. My mom is great at putting together dinner parties and planning menus—much better than the actual cooking part.

As I think about it, it's Mom's meatloaf spaghetti sauce that prompted me to learn how to cook. I knew when I graduated from college and got married that I wanted to explore different food options and have a minimum of thirty different dinners I could make for company.

But I need to get better at stopping work in time to make sure dinner is ready. Ben works every day until five, so we usually meet in the kitchen and call the kids from various parts of the house to help. Ben and I work together really well in the kitchen. We take turns with meal prep and figuring out what we'll make for dinner. We joke and have fun. Whoever's recipe we're using leads the charge, while the other spouse chops and mixes. It's almost like dancing, but we take turns leading based on whose recipe we're using.

I want my children to remember our stay home during the pandemic as time we learned new things, played games, watched movies, maybe even slowed down, walked, and had fun together. We're always so busy with work, sports, homework, cooking, cleaning, and house projects. I don't want my kids to remember their mom being absent, stressed, and working around the clock.

I want to stop and play with my kids—to enjoy them and calm their fears—and I'm finding I have to do it in between projects and day-long conference calls. My motto—"If the door is shut, don't enter my office"—has become a daily reminder. I see them missing me, with their teenage noses pressed up against the glass. I close my eyes and I'm instantly back in time, with my three little ones pressing their noses and hands against the door.

Stupid door and glass pane keeping us apart. I feel regret, as I remember a telling conversation with one of our babysitters when the kids were small. Emma, a college student, kindly made an observation about how kids come home and just want to spend time with their parents. What she said struck a chord. Usually, when the kids came home from school, all day I was on a conference call.

Ben has always been super good at being a present, amazing dad. We both work from home, and he is great at managing his day to be available when the kids get home from school. After talking with Emma, I stopped scheduling calls for the first thirty minutes our kids returned. I started having snacks available to coincide with their arrival. I greeted each of them with a big hug, and we'd have a snack and talk. Sometimes, they only wanted to talk for five or ten minutes. But I quickly learned those were the most important minutes of the day, and I had missed them before. But no more.

Fast forward to today. Now, with the concern and fear from the pandemic, I'm learning it's time for another change. My kids are better if I check in more frequently. The only problem is time. And I'm back to not sleeping again. I have to stay up late to get my projects completed, and I'm running on empty. I used to love to read a thriller or murder mystery before I went to bed. Unfortunately, now I'm working until my eyes glaze over and I begin to fall asleep. I don't have the time to read like I used to. Something has to give.

Pre-pandemic, Kylie and I had a weekly date where we went for a walk and talked. Now we have the "Stay Home, Stay Safe" order, my vibrant, raging extrovert needs to check in almost daily. If I wait more than two days, we have a mini-explosion, as anything will set her off. Bens tried to engage, but he's not a touchy-feely kind of guy.

I don't have time to think about myself or my needs. I'm too busy trying to survive and figure out how to keep going forward. But like a typical mom, I just keep chugging along, putting one foot in front of the other.

Right now, I'm struggling to get everything done. Mark wants to go to the park and swing, but our HOA closed our two neighborhood parks and put yellow tape around the playground equipment to prevent use. Mark *loves* to swing and listen to music. It helps him to self-regulate and calm down. When the park closed, we encouraged him to start riding his bike. Riding his bike lasted about two weeks, then it broke. The bike shop is closed—not an essential business. And it's become impossible to get your bike fixed or buy one. Bikes have sold out online, and it's going to take several months to order a new one.

Jill is the only one who is semi-okay through this "new normal." She's typically an extremely organized kid. She comes straight home from school and does her homework. The ability to sleep in, and not have homework for a couple weeks, has been good for her. It's calmed down her brain and gotten her into a good place.

The time off has done just the opposite for Kylie. She told me, "Mom, *all* my friends are getting together at Paige's house for a bonfire. I don't understand why I can't go. We'll be outside, sitting around the campfire."

I honestly don't get it. Why are parents allowing their kids to have hangouts at their homes in the middle of a worldwide pandemic? Pure stupidity! I wish there were a way to give these idiotic parents a ticket—a hefty ticket. We have so much to learn about this virus, and when you turn on the news, all you hear is doom and gloom. And these parents are having a party in their backyard.

I panicked for the first twenty-four to forty-eight hours after I first heard about the coronavirus. Mark has a compromised immune system, and I was instantly terrified for him. His neurologist wrote out a lifetime medical exemption to vaccines a few years ago and strongly told us to be diligent with our son, as he is highly allergic to so many substances.

Everyone has a pivotal moment that transcends and changes the trajectory of their life's path. My moment was when Mark received a series of shots during a wellness visit when he was twenty-two months old. He cried and screamed at the top of his lungs, completely inconsolable. I remember phoning our doctor's office for the third time after hours. The phone rang five times. "Hello, University Pediatrics."

"Hi, this is Jennifer Blake. I was in earlier today with my son Mark, and I've..."

"Can you hold, please?" And before I could answer, the sound of music filled the air.

I banged the phone on the counter as I screamed, "No, you can't put me on hold," and yelled a few choice words to the person who had left me hanging. My child was seriously ill! I didn't have time to hold.

Ben came running when he heard me banging the phone.

I kept thinking how much worse Mark was going to get if we didn't get help. Motrin and Tylenol and cold cloths weren't working. He was burning up. The screaming had been going on since we'd left the doctor's office, and it was now two in the morning. I slammed the phone down and jumped out of my chair. "Ben, we have to leave for the hospital. We've got to go right now."

Fortunately, Grandma Debra happened to be visiting, so we didn't have to wake up Jill and Kylie and put them in the car for a rushed trip to the hospital. Grandma Debra shooed us out the door and told us she would take care of the girls while we took care of Mark.

It took forever to buckle Mark into his car seat, and the ten-minute ride felt like a lifetime. The ER nurse wrote our insurance information down, and then suddenly Mark's body began to shake and jerk. Staff members in blue and white and green came running and whisked our baby away.

Ben held me as I started to cry. We begged the nurse for answers. She patted my arm and said, "He's in good hands now. It's a good thing you brought him to the hospital."

Later, we found out that his fever had gotten so high, he'd experienced a febrile seizure. He was in the hospital in intensive care for four exhausting days before we could bring him home. I stayed at the hospital the entire time. The only time I slept was when Ben would come up to the hospital after work. Ben would sit and gently read or talk to Mark while I attempted to nap in a stiff, uncomfortable chair.

On day three, the nurses directed me to a family shower. I felt instantly light and amazing after showering for the first time in days. The nurses were wonderful, always checking on Mark and me and seeing if there was anything we needed.

On the fourth day, our doctor said we could take Mark home. I waited impatiently for the paperwork to come through, and then Ben and I laughed as they put me in a wheelchair and had me hold our squirmy toddler as we left the hospital.

Before Mark's life-threatening reaction, he was a happy, funny, bright toddler. He was extremely mischievous, into everything, and talked constantly. He was even starting to read and point to words and letters in his favorite picture book. And he was insatiably curious. His favorite word was "Why?"

After his seizure and getting out of the hospital, he would line up his cars in perfectly straight rows, refuse to make eye contact and completely stop talking—no words. Unbeknownst to us, he had many of the classic signs of autism. And, like many families, we were on the river named De-Nile... not our child, not our Mark. This had to just be a blip. There had to be something else going on.

After the fever broke, so did something in our son. After several months of no improvement in his behavior or attention, our gut told us something was horribly wrong. We had to figure out what was wrong with Mark.

When Mark was three, we took him to a group of specialists to run a series of tests. I remember sitting in a cold white room, Ben and I holding hands nervously. We were both silently praying, hoping for good news, hoping for answers. We got the answer we were expecting but didn't want to hear. Mark had autism.

Ben and I both went numb when the doctors told us that our son had a lifelong neurological disorder and there was little we could do. I'd never felt such devastating anguish and despair. I felt like throwing up. I couldn't put my thoughts together, and all I could think of was how very unfair this was. Why our son? Why Mark? My mind refused to process the word "autism." And to this day, eleven years later, I still haven't been able to read the entire neurological report.

We felt numb and incredibly sad. We allowed ourselves to grieve, and after two days, decided we needed to get off our butts and start helping Mark get better. Ben and I went into major research mode. We refused to accept this diagnosis was the end. We became experts on figuring out what Mark needed to improve his quality of life. We didn't listen to the naysayers. Instead, we looked at our son, we remembered what he had been like before he got sick, and our goal was complete recovery.

Today, at the age of thirteen, we are safely on the other side. Mark is doing so much better, but it's difficult to think about the early days. Sometimes, I still want to cry because the sense of hopelessness tries to take over again. And if Mark even sniffles, my mind takes me back to when he was so very sick as a baby. I can't and I won't let the fear and hopelessness take over again.

Knowing how far Mark has come, I start going into panic mode when we are told the only cure for the coronavirus is a vaccine. Our doctors told us that another vaccine might kill our son, and we are terrified. Is he going to have to become a boy in a plastic bubble for the rest of his life or can we find an alternative? We have to keep our son safe and healthy. COVID-19 scares the crap out of me.

Fortunately, the panic and debilitating fear only last a few days. Then I kick into warrior mom mode to figure out how to keep our family safe. I phone some of the really smart people I know, begin researching, and talk to several of our doctors.

Whenever someone in the family sneezes, I immediately offer them extra Vitamin C and extra supplements with concentrated fruits and vegetables to keep them from getting sick. I get teased pretty much by the whole family. Of course, I don't think it's very funny. I've been focused on keeping Mark healthy for too long to back off on this issue.

When Ben sneezes five times over the course of an hour and says he is fine, I'm not willing to accept the "it's dust" excuse.

"Sneezing is a precursor to getting sick. Our doctor's office is closed right now. *Please* take extra supplements."

When I put it that way, Ben laughs and says, "Okay, I'll take the extra supplements."

Chapter Six
Kylie

April 3, 2020—If Mom and Granda tell me one more time, "Well, at least you were on homecoming court," I'm going to scream! We've been off school since March 11. Mom and Jill keep telling me to *chill*. Why doesn't anyone *understand* how hard this is for me? Paul was just starting to show me some attention. Paige saw him at the lacrosse field and he asked about me. He *asked* about me! We've got to get back in school or he's going to start dating someone else.

IT'S DAY ELEVEN OF THE quarantine. Or should I say one million or so? This has been the worst year of my life!

Because my parents told me I could only play one sport this year and I picked lacrosse over basketball, I'm missing the chance to play *anything* my sophomore year. I was hoping we'd somehow still have a season, but sports have been suspended for the rest of the school year.

I know a lot of people will be writing and talking about how the pandemic has changed our lives, but let me tell you something. As a sixteen-year-old, it really sucks. I miss my friends. I miss seeing them every day, talking to them, spending time with them, practicing and playing sports, and even eating in the nasty cafeteria. I was waiting to find out if I made the JV or varsity team. The suspense was killing me, and now that sports and in-person school have been canceled, we'll never know what team I would've made.

The end of March, we were told we had to stay home, per our governor. And we're supposed to maintain a six-foot distance if we leave the house to keep from getting the RONA. This is crazy! The thought of being stuck in my house, with just my family, makes me want to scream.

At first, I was really angry and cried. A lot. Seriously, I think I cried four hours one day. I was so looking forward to my spring season, and now the season is gone and my older classmates will be gone as well. I feel so horrible for my senior friends. Their last year has been wasted.

And, yes, I haven't been the nicest. I took it out on the rest of my family, had a bit of a panic attack, and screamed at them, "Everyone in this house sucks!"

Yup, famous last words I had to eat later. I really felt horrible. I don't hate my family. I hate the situation. I hate being stuck at home.

And my mom... well, let's just say her attitude doesn't make it any easier. I mean, seriously, *who* wakes up in the morning singing at the top of their lungs? The perky happiness in the morning, when everyone else wants to sleep, is crazy annoying. And Mom is always, *always* the first person to try to problem-solve and give you a big hug. She struggles with keeping her hugs to herself. When I'm mad, the last thing I want is someone touching me or telling me everything will be fine. Hugs are not magic!

I'm not afraid of getting sick. I just want to hang out with my friends. I asked my mom and dad if I could still go to the high school field and practice lacrosse with my friends. But no, they've keeping me inside, *imprisoned*, only allowed to go for a walk.

Once, in the beginning of the recommended stay at home, I was allowed to go to the grocery store with my mom. I never thought I'd spend twenty minutes holding our place in an extremely *long* line while my mom ran around the store picking up groceries like toilet paper. Yeah, seriously, TP has become a big thing. Most places sell out pretty quickly, and you have to be there first thing in the morning if you're going to get any. And good luck finding any hand sanitizer. Most stores have been out for weeks. I never thought my life would come to this, actually being excited to go to the store to buy stuff to wipe my butt!

My parents feel bad for me, but Mom doesn't seem to get how I'm feeling. I've been looking forward to turning sixteen and getting my license for a long time. Most of my friends have their driver's licenses. God only knows when I'm getting mine. I was *one* day away from freedom and all the amazing plans I've been dreaming of when everything got canceled. I was looking forward to being able to grab the car keys and go visit my friends, go for ice cream, even run errands and help out Mom and Dad. Now, I have to wait.

One of my biggest disappointments is I won't be able to drive by myself to visit Granda and Grandpa Joe. Granda and I have been planning a big luncheon celebration for after I get my license. The plan was for me to make my first forty-five-minute solo drive to their house to spend the night, then Granda Patti and I would go to lunch all by ourselves.

We were going to go to our favorite place. It's a little diner in Flushing called DJ's Diner, and it has windows facing the small airport. We love to watch the planes take off and land. Granda loves the cheeseburgers and chili, and I've actually gotten her to eat wings with me. She is a very particular person, not the type you will expect to eat wings with her fingers. She carries a huge purse, which is filled with everything: gum, mints, snacks, makeup, a brush, and her ever-present hand wipes and disinfectant. She wears white a lot, so image my surprise when she tried barbecue chicken wings.

On one special trip, Granda put a large napkin on her lap (she was wearing her favorite white winter suit) and put another napkin around her neck. She surprised me as she tried to eat with a knife and a fork before she giggled and said, "Nope, this is not how you eat wings." To my surprise, she picked up her chicken wing and began eating off the bone.

Ever since, we plan little trips, just us girls, to go have wings and chili and French fries. We sit and watch the airplanes, and we laugh and joke and share stories, as well as dream about where the people are going. It's the only time I've ever seen Granda let loose and talk to me about real things. It's Patti and Kylie talking, not Granda Patti and her little granddaughter. Granda always pays for me, and this was going to be my chance to drive and pay for lunch. Now we have to wait.

A couple months ago, before life completely changed, I told Mom, "It's going to be so much fun to drive around with my friends and listen to music!"

Of course, my mom had to get her two cents in. "Wait a minute. It is not okay for you to just aimlessly drive around. I want you to have fun with your friends, but that's not a good idea. If you want to listen to music, then go sit somewhere and listen to music. But do *not* drive around listening to loud music and wasting gas. You need to focus on *driving* when you drive, especially when you're a new driver."

I couldn't help it, my eyes kind of rolled backward all on their own. "Mom, we're not going to get in the car and go crazy. Why do you have to take everything so literally? I didn't mean I was going to drive down the road with the radio blasting and get into an accident. I'll be safe."

See what I have to deal with? My mom can be overbearing and controlling. I can't even go to a party or spend time with friends without her asking if there is anything she can have me bring. She is the only one who still calls to make sure we are having adult supervision. I can't complain too much or then she'll amp it up and have a sit-down with the parents. Seriously! It's embarrassing. I'm the only one that has a mom like this.

My parents have a list of questions we need to tell them before we hang out with friends. The list is on the front of our fridge. Jill and I keep telling my parents that the list needs to go. And when they're not looking, either Jill or I take it down and throw it away. We have the stupid list memorized.

- *Where are you going? Are you staying in one place?*

If we go to a place and decide to go somewhere else, we have to let them know. If we forget, we're in deep trouble. Let's just say I wouldn't want to deal with Mom and Dad if they need us and we're not where we said we'd be.

- *Do we know the parents?*

Mom or Dad have to meet the parents in person or talk to them on the phone. And, trust me, this is a biggie that took years to modify. They used to have to meet the parents in advance, so Mom could get a feel for them and decide if we could hang out with the kids. Who does this crap?

- *What is the parent's phone number? When is a good time for Mom to call the parents?*

She talks to the parent or we don't go.

- *What is the address? Do you need a ride both ways or can you carpool?*

If I'm spending the night with girlfriends and guys are coming over for part of the party—but obviously *not* spending the night, just staying for the party—you can bet my mom is calling to make sure adults will be there. In general, she wants to know that parents will be available.

And then her final question:

- *Is there anything we can bring?*

Obviously, her question about bringing something is just to get her foot in the door. She usually chats the parents up so that half the time they invite her to come over as well and can't wait to meet her. Dad says Mom doesn't know a stranger. It pisses me off.

I'm tired of it. I can't wait until I can go away to college and get out of this town and away from my controlling parents. Don't they realize I'm going to really cut loose and have fun when I leave here? I'm just done. But since no one knows what to expect with the "Stay Home" orders and constantly changing RONA numbers, my mom and dad are being crazier than usual. Mom said until we know more about the pandemic, we have to be careful and we can't have our friends over or even think about having a party at our house.

Meanwhile, my friends are still hanging out. I just can't. We're doing school online. And my parents are stressed. But we're all stressed, and no one seems to see me and how much this is hurting. I had to watch my sister play a sport I loved—listen to her moan and complain about it—and I had to grin and put a mask on my face of pretending everything was fine and life was good.

Life isn't fine, life isn't good, and I'm pissed. Why is this happening? I just want to spend time with my friends. My friends get me. They're all still having bonfires, having parties, and I have to stay home. After you invite someone a couple times and they can't go, you stop including them. This is going to happen, and I'm going to lose all my friends.

Paul was at a bonfire this last weekend. Paige said he told her to say hi to me. Paige didn't want to tell me the rest, but she said I needed to know. "Kylie, there was a girl there from another school. I'm pretty sure it was Ann's cousin. Paul sat next to her and she flirted with him. She even sat on his lap."

Great! Just what I need. I'm stuck at home while some gross girl is moving in on Paul. It's not fair!

My mom needs to realize I'm almost an adult. I make good decisions and I never get into trouble. Besides, if she doesn't trust me here, what is going to magically change when I go away to college? Or when I turn eighteen? Is she going to come with me, check out the dorm and my roommate, and tell everyone to be extra nice to me? She probably won't let me go away to college either—she'll probably find some reason or excuse why I can't go. We've started to look at colleges, and my parents really want me to stay in Michigan.

I want to be free. I need to take my driving test, and Best Driving doesn't know when they're going to open back up… and the secretary of state's office is now closed too. We need to go there to get my picture taken and show them my segment one and segment two paperwork, the paperwork showing I passed the test.

I'm really sick of this year. When is it my turn to have things work out?

JULIE CADMAN

Chapter Seven
Patti

April 8, 2020—I can't get over the difference between Florida and Michigan. Not just the weather and chance to go walking along the beach early in the morning. It's like people are more afraid in Michigan. There's something in the air. It's weird—especially since there is a much older population in Florida. I don't get it!

JOE AND I HAVE MADE it home to Michigan in time to have Easter with the kids. Shortly before the holiday, I go to our neighborhood grocery store to buy all the makings for our feast. I am surprised at how different it is inside grocery stores here. Almost everyone I see is wearing masks in the grocery store—much different than what we saw in Florida.

After promising we will spend the holiday together, our kids are refusing to come and see us! I don't believe it. We haven't seen them and their families since January. I'm their mother, and Easter at the Clarke home is a family tradition.

I receive phone calls from both Clint and Jenni, and almost verbatim, they say, "Mom, we love and miss you and Dad, but we would feel really horrible if we came to your house and gave you COVID."

Jenni doubles down, saying the Michigan Governor just issued an executive order effective the day before Easter. "Mom, according to the order, Michiganders can't see friends and can't go to their second homes. We can't come visit you right now, and you and Dad can't go to the lake house in Charlevoix."

I try to tell her, "Jenni—it clearly says an exception is to care for the elderly. Your dad and I are elderly."

Jenni all but laughs at me. "Mom, you and Dad are in great shape. You don't fit the exemption. If you need something, we'll help, but Easter is not going to work this year."

My caller ID is ringing, and I can see it is Lori on the other line. I know she will commiserate with me. I decide to quickly get off the phone and talk to my Lori.

"I have another call coming in. I need to get this call." I switch over.

"Mom, I'm so sorry you and Dad will be alone on Easter. If I lived in Michigan, I would be there in a heartbeat. Even if I had to stand outside." Lori laughs and says, "As soon as it's safe to fly, I'll come for a long weekend. We'll go shopping and go for some long walks."

I instantly feel better after talking to my Lori. She is so good to me. I know if she lived here, she would find the time to see us. She wouldn't use the excuse that she's afraid of getting Joe and I sick.

In preparation for Easter, I cook a delectable roast beef, cheesy potatoes—some with onions and some without, for our pickier eaters— hot rolls and butter, green bean casserole, macaroni and cheese, a vegetable tray, salad, and a decadent chocolate cheesecake. Everything but the dessert is homemade. Joe helps me lengthen our dining room table, and then I select a special tablecloth and our best china, silverware, and stemware. The table looks lovely.

I nervously begin to pace. Even though they said they weren't coming, I know my son will not disappoint me. Clint will be here. He has never missed an Easter dinner.

Noon comes, and then one. It's now two, the time we usually eat. The rolls are done, the casserole and potatoes are warming in the oven, and the meat is resting.

Joe comes into the kitchen. "Patti, honey, everything looks great. But sweetheart, the kids told you... they aren't coming. They don't want to take a chance on getting us sick."

I can't help it. My eyes fill with tears. We left Florida early, left all of the fun dinners and friends and walks on the beach and fabulous restaurants, to return to cold, frigid Michigan. I've been hoping to see our kids and grandkids. I really expected them to show up.

Joe sits at one end of our formal dining room table and I sit at the other, with five seats on each side between us. Normally we sit next to each other, but I can't muster the strength to move my seat, and I think he's afraid to get too close to me. We eat in silence. After dinner, I go into autopilot mode and put some of the food in the refrigerator and some in the freezer. I seriously just want to throw it all away and forget this day ever happened.

Each day that passes is just like the day before. It's cold in more ways than the temperature. Joe reads or watches old golf videos or Westerns all day while I walk listlessly inside the house... you can only clean a house so many times. I wonder when did my husband get to be such an old fart? I so want to go out, sit inside a restaurant, and have someone serve a dinner that I don't have to cook. But we can't.

All the restaurants are closed for inside dining. Joe refuses to order takeout. Does he think the food is going to prepare itself? He never learned how to cook and he says, "Patti, I feel safer if we stay in. I really don't want to order takeout." Meaning I do all the cooking, and he puts his plate in the sink. I have to keep reminding myself I'm a lady; there's quite a few words I'd like to say to him right now. I'd rather plan dinner parties, order take-out, or go out to eat—cooking is not my be-all and end-all.

I've had it. I'm bored out of my head with nothing to do. It's about as exciting as watching paint dry.

I decide to go to the grocery store this morning. And wouldn't you know it, Jenni phones me right before I leave the store... and I lead her to believe that her dad is with me. I've escaped and am all by myself, loading the cart with ready-made meals. If Joe won't get takeout, then I'm bringing frozen dinners home! I'm pretty sure Jenni and Clint will be phoning later tonight to give me an earful. I shouldn't have told Jenni that I'm bored and had to get out of the house. I'll never hear the end of it.

I've put my winter coat and boots on and gone for walks through the subdivision. I've seen quite a few neighbors out walking their dogs, so at least there's been an opportunity for a little bit of human interaction. If dogs weren't so messy, I might consider getting a dog, but I really don't want to take care of another thing.

I am so bored that I actually call Muriel Rogers. And for the one hundredth time, she tells me about her granddaughter Cloe being crowned homecoming queen this past fall. Usually, I can be tactful and polite. But I'm so tired! And I don't feel very nice. Muriel is a nasty show-off and she loves to brag. She knows perfectly well she's told me repeatedly about Cloe. I've finally had it.

"How wonderful for Cloe," I purr—now, mind you, it is the beginning of May and I've been hearing about Cloe's amazing homecoming queen feat since we arrived at our Florida condo in January. I can almost repeat the story word for word. I am *done*. Done with a capital *D*!

"Yes, it's so wonderful having a fellow queen in the family," Muriel chortles. We are on Facetime, and I can see her preening and patting the heavy gold necklace at her throat, ready to launch *again* into the story of Cloe's homecoming coronation for the one hundredth or maybe one millionth time.

"So, Muriel," I interrupt, "it's so wonderful about homecoming court. It must be so hard on Cloe, a senior, missing school right now. What else has she done this year?" I am on the edge of my seat, ready to finally shut down the subject.

"Yes, it's been really hard for Cloe. She's missed so much of her senior year because of COVID. But what do you mean, what else has she done? She was homecoming *queen*," Muriel proclaims.

I immediately interrupt, "I ask because our granddaughter Kylie was on homecoming court for her sophomore year this fall, plus she plays sports, and she's active in church. She loves working with little kids, and she's got excellent grades." I continue, "What else has Cloe done besides getting elected to homecoming court? What is she putting on her college applications?"

Muriel snaps, "She wasn't just elected to homecoming court, she was the *queen*, but I guess you wouldn't understand since you weren't …"

"Wait just one minute, Muriel. You seem to forget, I was homecoming queen my senior year in high school." I've stepped out of my normal one-up dance with Muriel and gone for the throat. "I'm not sure what Kylie wants to do, but she is definitely a future homecoming queen in the making. *And* she does soooo much more than just sit on a float and wave at people, looking pretty. My Kylie is an independent, beautiful, smart young woman who is going places. In fact, she already has colleges looking at her for academic and athletic scholarships."

I manage to keep from saying the rest of the sentence, the part I want to add: "…unlike Cloe." Instead, I sweetly state, "Muriel, I am just trying to understand *what else* your granddaughter Cloe does or is doing for her senior year. She has to be doing something besides just being on the homecoming court? It's so important for college students to be well rounded."

I finally silence her, and hopefully I will not hear any more homecoming *queen* stories. I mean, seriously—five months and counting! It is time to stop. If she wants to talk about homecoming, then I can pull out pictures of my beautiful Kylie. My mini-me! Kylie has wavy, dark brown hair and my blue eyes. She is petite, and when you look at pictures of her, I swear you would think it was me at sixteen. She's stunning!

Muriel blows the air out of her mouth in a hiss. She waits a fraction of a moment and then launches into the latest gossip about mutual friends. A friend of ours, Kathryn, just lost her husband to the virus. Al was in the hospital for a month. They thought he was going to make it—he'd been on a ventilator, was removed from it, and then put back on.

The family was not allowed to see him until the very end. At the end, they allowed a compassionate care visit, and the family said goodbye—wearing special, white, anti-infection suits. Muriel is full of news about how the family is waiting to have a memorial service. Kathryn and Al have four children and several grandchildren, so just with immediate family, they are well over the ten people that Michigan governor's executive order has limited funerals to. Muriel and I are both quiet as we each think about how horrible it would be to die and have ten people or fewer at your funeral. How sad it must be for the families experiencing this.

I know Kathryn very well and I liked her husband. Suddenly, the virus is very real. It isn't just the news and our government warning everyone to stay inside and stay safe. As Muriel and I talk, she tells me how quiet it is in our condo complex. Most everyone has left. Joe and I had literally gotten out of Florida the very day they announced a thirty-day stay at home in Florida and started to close the highways.

Muriel is enjoying the weather and daily walks on the beach. I am envious and kind of wishing we stayed in Florida, away from the cold. And Joe won't even consider going to our lake house in Charlevoix. He is content to stay put in Grand Blanc. I am seriously needing and craving some beach time, even if it means walking along the cold Lake Michigan shore.

Muriel tells me several of the older members of our community, those who are more vulnerable and have underlying health conditions, are getting the virus and ending up in the hospital. The sickest are being placed on ventilators, which seems to be a precursor to death. And the worst part is their families are not allowed to visit. If they are lucky, they are allowed to see and talk to their families through an iPad or through their cell phone, using an app to show their faces.

Dying by myself is my worst nightmare. This conversation with Muriel is getting really depressing, and I've had enough. I bite the bullet while Muriel is in mid-sentence.

"Muriel, sorry, I really have to go. I promised Joe I would go for a walk with him, and it's almost time for our walk. Bye-bye now." Click.

I get off the phone deep in thought. I started out thinking, *This stupid virus won't touch me or my family.* And then Jenni told me of a woman her church is praying for. A nurse in Troy, who got the virus after taking care of a COVID patient. The nurse was told to go home and quarantine. She ended up in the hospital on a ventilator, fighting for her life.

It makes no sense to me. Why are people being told to go home and quarantine? Why are they being told, "It's a virus and it needs to run its course?" Isn't there something we can do to prevent ourselves from getting sick while we wait for a vaccine?

I've never been so scared in my life. I'm afraid that Joe or I will get it, and even more scared that one of our kids or grandchildren will get sick. I've survived multiple miscarriages, and the last thing I want is to see my children dying before me. All I can think is, we need a vaccine to make us safe from this disease.

There is no one I can talk to. My daily choice is to walk aimlessly around the inside of my house, safe from the virus outside, or watch the news. My Jenni is right—I should stay away from watching the doom and gloom on TV. But I can't help myself. I find myself drawn to the various news stations, clicking through the channels, desperate for information.

This "new normal" we keep hearing about isn't working for me. Life has slowed down to the point that I feel like my head is going to spin right off. If they don't let us out of quarantine, I'm going to say "forget it" and drive up to Charlevoix to check on our house. I feel stifled, like I can't breathe.

Joe is off in his shell, dreaming of playing golf, and I feel like the life I worked so long and hard for is over.

JULIE CADMAN

Chapter Eight
Jen

May 4, 2020—The world is going crazy. My parents are acting like ten-year-olds, and now this? I feel like I was sucker punched today. I really want a do-over... Can I please go to sleep and have this *just* be a dream???

MY OFFICE HAS GOTTEN OUT of control again. I find myself wishing I could blink and have our house clean and clutter-free. We live in a two-story colonial with two and a half bathrooms. My office is on the main floor, just to the right of the entrance. We have a finished basement, and Ben's office is in the right-hand corner of the basement. He manages to work in the basement while at least one of our kids uses the other end for their online school.

Our bedrooms are upstairs. Each of the kids have their own bedroom, and Ben and I have a master bedroom with our own bathroom. The kids share a bathroom at the end of the hall, and our half bath is on the main floor across from our kitchen. We also have a living room that is filled with a mishmash of furniture. Our furniture matched twelve years ago when we moved in, but through the years, we added a couple not-so-lovely, but comfortable, pieces from local estate sales.

Each piece has a memory, a unique story. I'll always laugh when I look at our computer router table. After we bought it, we discovered it was too big to fit in our car. Ben, my amazing spatial expert, figured out how to tie the table to the top of our medium-sized vehicle. We drove with our flashers on, barely going fifteen miles an hour to make it home safely. Our beautifully ugly table, with its bleached white wood top and green legs, has followed us through all our moves. My mom calls it that ugly, green-legged thing. She was supremely happy when it was moved downstairs to the computer room.

Our living room offends my mom's "sensibilities," as she puts it. She keeps trying to give us some of her white decorator objects or get me to go shopping for new furniture with her. I've given up telling her, "Mom, don't you understand? Our family can't handle *white* furniture." That color would last all of two minutes in our house.

Sleep continues to elude me, but I was finally able to sleep seven hours last night. Even when I put a pad of paper and a pen next to my bed and take a melatonin, my mind won't shut off. I end up getting up and working on research or projects or other "stuff" until two AM or so... and then get up by six to start my day by seven. I feel like my body is on the edge of collapsing. I don't know how much more of this I can take.

Speaking of getting sick, my dad is seventy-four and my mom is seventy-three and they are *still* making frequent trips to stores. They *need* to stay home! Dad is an asthmatic with type 2 diabetes. He especially needs to stay home. We keep hearing that people over sixty with comorbidities need to stay home. Conditions like diabetes, asthma, being overweight, just to name a few. I still can't believe my earlier conversation with my mom.

"Hi, Mom. I phoned your landline and you didn't answer. Where are you?" I asked as she picked up her cell phone.

"Your dad and I are at the grocery store," she trilled in her peppy voice.

"Mom, you and Dad should have more than enough food. *Why* are you there? It's not safe for you."

"We got bored, so we decided to drive to the store."

I couldn't believe it. My older, at-risk parents had driven to the store to pick up a few groceries because they were bored. "Mom—come on.

'Stay at Home' means you *stay at home*. It *doesn't* mean you go shopping!"

I am definitely going to phone my brother Clint and see if he can talk some sense into them. People with COVID are being told to quarantine. We're being told it's a virus and there's nothing we can do but let it run its course. People quarantine, and then they are suddenly unable to breathe and end up on ventilators in the hospital. There has to be something we can do to mitigate the risk and prevent it from going from the sniffles to a ventilator to dead. This is so scary!

I'm not the most technically fluent and today is a mess. Usually, it's the kids having problems logging in or staying on their video teleconference calls. I swear, I've got at least one of them close to tears multiple times per day. We're only a few weeks into this, and I've learned to say, "It's okay. If you can't get in, send your teacher an email and let them know you tried. Just let them know."

We have a great internet connection, but it's really hard to have five people trying to video conference at the same time. And today, everything that can go wrong—does.

First, it takes me three hours, *three*, to get the video teleconference to work for my meeting this evening. I put a ticket in, phone the company, and let them know I have an urgent request and cannot get the audio to work. But they do *not* return my call. I work on it for one and a half hours before giving up and asking Kylie for help. She and I work together (mostly her) and finally get it to function. I'm so proud of how technically efficient Kylie is, and I really appreciate her help.

I am still concerned I will have an issue, so at six o'clock, a full hour and a half before the call, I do a test to make sure the audio is on.

Surprise—no sound again! Ben, my incredible husband, takes a look at my computer and discovers one of the boxes is not checked. It takes him less than ten minutes.

Seriously! I wasted three hours today dealing with the video teleconference not working on my computer. And the company never returns my phone call.

My video teleconference issues happen after having problems with the University Hospital app for Mark's neurologist. Mark is thirteen, and they have this stupid rule: if you are twelve or older, you are in charge of your medical records. Yup, parents continue to pay the bills and take care of their kid's medical needs. But somehow our insurance company has determined that kids are in charge of their health information! Love to know who decided this. We spend over an hour on the phone with the University Hospital representative to help set up my phone and get the app working. It is a horribly long day of constant challenges. I'm so grateful that Ben and Kylie are good at solving technology issues.

Just when I think I am getting things under control, Ben comes to me with news. He's been working from home since March 10, and he's been told today he has five more weeks before he is laid off. He's survived three of the first four layoffs. His company will have him finalize the project he's working on and then give him seven weeks of severance. This translates into twelve weeks to find a new job.

All the air leaves my lungs in a big whoosh. For a couple seconds, I can't breathe. I feel lightheaded and like I've been punched in the chest. All I can think is, *We're going to lose our house. How will we manage on unemployment? How will Ben find a job? He's almost fifty and we're in the middle of COVID.* I am inwardly screaming as I silently say, *Breathe... breathe... breathe... Stay positive.* Believe *things will work out.*

My mind and body are swirling with a myriad of emotions. Anger, pain, fear... Ben's manager told him a month ago that his job was safe and encouraged him to stay at his company. Famous last words.

Ben looks me straight in the eye, his face flushing, and says, "I know this isn't the best news, but we'll be okay."

I resist the urge to wipe the lint that is sticking to his forehead as I silently give him a hug. I am trying hard to look and act supportive, when I want to cry and fall apart. How is this happening? Ben looks dazed and shell-shocked as he rubs his eyes and rubs the back of his hair, lightly touching his bald spot.

Ben pushes his glasses farther up on his nose and immediately goes into problem-solving mode. "We will have to tell the kids and make sure they know we will be cutting back our expenses."

I nod my head, barely able to focus. He told me after dinner, when the kids are otherwise occupied. This happened one other time, a few years back. Ben was laid off from his position as Director of Communications and IT. We endured thirteen long months of job hunting. We sold everything that was not nailed down, cut our expenses to the bone, and were within two weeks of having to sell our home. We can't go through another experience like that. I am beyond terrified.

Later that night, I surf the web, unable to sleep. I run into an offer that seems too good to be true. A business executive with a large recruiting firm is offering, for the entire weekend, a series of videos on finding your perfect job. The first three videos are free, to give you a taste of the program. There is a charge for the complete program, but it comes with a guarantee. If you don't find your dream job within ninety days, you get your money back.

I'm skeptical, but decide to listen to his free videos. Despite my initial reservations, I am impressed. He has good, actionable information, and I feel it will help Ben. And the best part, Ben will have a specific plan. This sounds like a huge win-win for us.

The next morning, I excitedly tell Ben I feel we should invest in this program. I tell him how it also includes a weekly coaching call with the executive answering questions that come up during your job search. Ben is resistant. He doesn't want to spend the money and feels like he doesn't need help.

Now, for my quandary. I'm his wife, I've worked in recruiting for several years and know how to research and interview. I know what he should be doing. I don't want to be in the position where I will be asking my husband every night, "So how was the job hunt today?" I can see nothing but problems if we go down that path.

I back off slightly, but continue to press Ben. "Honey, I think this is an excellent program. It will give you the steps you need. And if something happens to my job, I'll be able to use the videos to help get a new position as well. And the best part—there is a money-back guarantee. Please look it over."

Ben doesn't want to—I can see it in the stubborn set of his jaw. While we sit there, I am silently praying, *Lord, please let this be the answer, and let him agree to do this.*

After a few seconds, Ben looks at me. His eyes are initially squinting, and I can almost see the wheels spinning in his brain. He opens his mouth, and then closes his mouth and his eyes, seemingly deep in thought. It's all I can do to keep quiet. Ben opens his eyes and the tension is replaced with a smile. "All right. I'll check it out, and if this is good stuff, we'll invest in it."

I manage to keep from bugging Ben about the program for about three hours the next morning. At 11:30 AM, I bring my computer into the kitchen and flip forward to the website. I finally have to ask, "Ben, have you seen the wonderful videos that Brandon has put together?"

Ben gives me a resigned look as he heats up his coffee in the microwave. "Okay, I'll look at the video. Can you pull it up?"

I am happy to get the video started. And now the hard part is being quiet while Ben watches. I've selected one of my favorites, about how to follow up before you've been offered an interview. Despite himself, Ben is drawn in.

"Okay, Jen, the program looks good. And if you've watched the videos and like them, then let's go ahead and buy them."

Whew! Relief.

The series is really quite good. We have date nights and go through the program together. I'm feeling optimistic, and a lot of the fear is dissolving. It's only been a few days into the program and he's already gotten his first phone interview. This is definitely reducing the stress over Ben losing his job.

Chapter Nine
Kylie

May 28, 2020—YEAH!! **The secretary of state's office is finally opening on June 1. I'm going to finally,** *finally* **be able to get my driver's license and drive to see Granda Patti and Grandpa Joe. I'm also sooooo excited to get out of the house and visit some of my friends. Woohooooo!!!!!**

THE "STAY HOME" ORDER JUST won't end. It was supposed to be a couple weeks, and it keeps getting extended! April and May were both kind of weird. I was used to seeing my friends in school every day. My dad keeps saying, "Why don't you Facetime your friends?" Duh, we don't Facetime—we text or Snapchat—but lately, it's been really hard to not spend time with them. Most of our online classes require us to show our face when we sign in, and then everyone turns their screen off so you only see their names.

My history teacher, Mrs. Raymond, is my favorite. She's young and fun and someone you can talk to. She's been letting me and three of my friends stay on Zoom after class to catch up. She does some work in the background and just kind of checks in with us occasionally. It's nice to see people's faces without masks on. And we have fun goofing around with each other.

We don't have class on Wednesdays. They call it Wellness Wednesdays and our teachers keep sending us emails, checking in to be sure we're doing okay. They tell us how much they miss us and how they are available if we need to talk. I mean, seriously! I want to throw up. My language arts teacher sends the emails too. What a joke. He's a mean jerk, like *anyone* would ever talk to him. When we're in class, he gets off on finding people who haven't done their homework and embarrassing them. It's pretty obvious he *has* to send the emails.

But it's nice to have a day off in the middle of the week. Most of my classes only go for a few minutes. Just long enough for our teachers to give us a huge packet of material and tell us it's due in a week. It's really crazy. I don't feel like I'm learning anything. And I still have to spend almost every night asking Dad to help me with math.

My parents are still not letting us out, other than family walks. My parents have decreed we will walk the dog in the morning and at night—it's good for the dog and it's good for us. It gets us out of the house and keeps us moving. Each of us kids walks Rex at least once a day, sometimes alone, but usually Mom will take a few minutes and walk around the block with us.

Dogs are definitely making out in the pandemic. Rex won't know what to do when we go back to school and Mom and Dad go back to the office. Before the pandemic began, Rex was nice and fluffy. I loved how I could bury my face in his fur, but now thanks to multiple daily walks, he's not such a good pillow anymore. The vet will be happy the next time she sees us.

On a family walk about a week ago, my mom thought we all looked adorable, so she took a picture of Dad and us from behind... and posted it to Facebook. We tease her all the time that she is such a Facebook mom and she laughs at us. I think it kind of bugs her... but at least she doesn't post pics of our family *all* the time, like some moms do. She says she only posts important things. I'm still trying to figure out how taking a sneaky shot of your family walking—from *behind*—is an important picture!

I won't admit this to my parents, but there have been some nice things about having time off. The biggest thing is school starting later. We're online at 8:30 AM instead of in class at 7:15, and that extra hour of sleep has been huge. It's great to be able to go to bed a little later and not have to be out the door by 6:50 every morning. Normally, we go to bed by 8:30 or 9:00—we just police ourselves, something Jill and I started years ago because it's so hard to get up in the morning if we stay up late. Jill is super funny that way. She will seriously put herself to bed by eight o'clock at night. Way too early for me.

We've also started cooking together. Surprisingly, cooking with the family hasn't been that bad. We've tried a bunch of new recipes, and one day, when my mom had a conference call, I asked if there was anything I could do. She printed out a recipe to make Swedish meatballs in the pressure cooker and set me loose.

Mark and I worked together on the new dish. It's now one of our family favorites. We eat it at least once a month, sometimes more if I have anything to say about it. It's so easy—you mix together two cans of mushroom soup with a can of water, a cup of milk, and then put a package of egg noodles on top of the mixture and put your frozen meatballs on top of the noodles. You close the lid and cook on manual for twelve minutes. When it's done, you add sour cream, and some salt, pepper, and garlic. If we're out of sour cream, we add cream cheese. It's a super good recipe, and Mark and I made it all by ourselves.

My mom loves to think she is *totally* different from Granda Patti, but there's one way she is just like her. My mom is a planner and a list maker. Everyone calls Granda Patti the "list diva," but my mom is a close second.

On March 10, when they announced we would be off school for a few weeks, my mom got busy. She told us, "Everyone needs to make me a list of the foods you like. We'll try to make sure we're fixing food that everyone likes at least a couple times a week. Also, since I'll only be shopping once a month or so, we will be eating more canned and frozen fruits and vegetables."

The only one that had a problem with Mom's announcement is Mark. He quickly got bored and started eating *all* the cereal and chips. After the first week, Mom put the snacks in her office and showed Mark what a "normal" cereal serving looks like. For years, Jill and I have been trying to tell our parents that Mark is a pig. It took the pandemic for them to *finally* realize how much he eats and to start talking about eating "your fair share."

In the first week or so of being off school, my mom decided we needed an art day. I have no idea why, because my mom is just like me—she can't draw a straight line. But she bought some small canvases and paints for a day that we were "bored."

She got all the materials together and told us to paint whatever came to us. Seriously? What was she thinking? I don't have an artistic bone in my body. My painting looked like someone threw up on it. I put a bunch of colors on the canvas and mixed them together. Jill and Mark are both pretty good with art, so their pictures looked good. Jill painted two canvases, one of the mountains and one of the beach. Mark painted a lifelike dinosaur.

Mom cheated. She decided to just paint the word "Joy" and put her favorite colors around it. It turned out pretty good. I wish I'd thought of just painting a word. If I'd painted one word, it would have been "Believe." I need to *believe* that I'm going to pass my driving test and get my driver's license. If I keep saying the word "believe," maybe it will come true.

After Best Driving canceled my test and the secretary of state closed, we rescheduled for May, only to get canceled again. I feel like I'm never going to get my license. Every time I think it's finally going to happen, our "Stay Home" order gets extended.

But today I'm so excited—I have great news! The secretary of state's office is open June 1, I'm taking my driving test the next day, and will get my license on June 13 if everything goes well. Dad and I have been practicing almost every night after dinner in an empty church parking lot. I've become a pretty good parallel parker, but I'm kind of nervous. What if, after all this time, I don't pass? What if I get a mean instructor?

One minute, I think: *No problem, I'm going to do great.* The next minute, I think, *No way, I'm going to fail.* But if I fail, it will be so embarrassing and will take months for me to get back in to retake it. I have to pass the driving test or my life is completely over.

It's finally here! Today, June 2, at 5:15 PM. I'm so nervous. I keep saying to myself, "You can do it. You can do it. You're going to pass."

The driving instructor, Mr. Brown, looks nice. "Hi, Kylie, Mr. Blake. Nice to meet both of you. Before we get started, I just need to see your paperwork."

Dad pulls out the folder and flips through it. Then he begins to frantically flip through the papers a second and then a third time. Dad is patting his pockets, his face red, and I realize something is wrong.

Dad looks at the instructor and says, "I'm sorry, I don't know what happened to the registration. For some reason, I have the old copy. I promise you, the car is registered."

The driving instructor shakes his head and says, "I'm sorry, but I have to go by the rules. We need current paperwork or we can't proceed. We'll have to reschedule the test."

I don't have a stoic face. I've already waited two months because of the RONA to get my license, and now I'm going to have to wait longer. I can't help it—the tears start rolling down my face. I'm not crying out loud, but it's obvious I'm crying. I'm so mad at my dad, I can't even look at him. I furiously wipe the tears away. My head feels like it's exploding. *Why me, why this?*

Dad talks to the instructor and sets up another appointment for July 2—a whole month away. It's going to be another month before I get my license. I'm *never* speaking to my dad again.

We walk back to the car and Dad says, "Wait one second," as he looks in the glove box. This time, he finds the registration stuck to the back of the insurance card. He beeps the horn, and we're able to stop the instructor from leaving. I'm relieved, but I'm still upset and can feel my insides trembling.

I think, *Now, how will I pass my test?* I'm scared.

Fortunately, Mr. Brown is really nice. He smiles and says, "I'm so glad you found the registration."

He has Dad get in the back. I get in the front, and Mr. Brown sits in the passenger seat. It's time.

We begin in the parking lot, and the first thing he has me do is parallel park. I start out a little wide and have to overcorrect as I knock over two cones. I have a horrible headache and all I can think is, *I've screwed up. I've failed, and I'm* never *getting my driver's license!*

Mr. Brown smiles and says, "You know what? I think I'll get out of the car for a second and have you re-park. I didn't see *anything.*" He winks at me.

Whew! I'm getting another chance. The tears have finally stopped and are replaced by a steely resolve. I'm going to pass the driving test today, and I'm going to get my license on June 13. Nothing is going to stop me!

Second time is perfect. I nail parallel parking. I don't knock down one cone, and now I'm ready for the road test.

The road test also goes great. I think I only have one point knocked off for leaving my blinker on as I make a lane change. Whew!

Mr. Brown shakes my hand at the end. "Kylie, you had a rocky start but you pulled through with flying colors. Good job!" he says as he hands me my certificate.

Woohoo!

Dad gives me a big hug. "Kylie, honey, I'm so sorry that we had the wrong registration and that it ratcheted up your anxiety. Tell you what— how about you drive us home, and we can stop for a strawberry shake to celebrate?"

"Of course," I say. It's still too soon to laugh about the situation, but since I love strawberry shakes, that sounds like a good plan. I can breathe again. I passed!

June 13 is super anticlimactic. We wear our masks, answer a few questions to make sure we can enter the building, and then wait about ten minutes for the person to take our money and take my picture. After months of waiting, I have my license!

I can't wait to go see my Granda Patti and finally have our lunch. Mom and Dad are starting to let us out of the house a bit, so I'm also looking forward to visiting my friend Ava.

As soon as I get my license, I drop Mom off at home and make my forty-five-minute solo trip on the expressway to Granda Patti and Grandpa Joe's. I drive the exact speed limit and arrive at their house fifty-two minutes after I left. I make sure I drive straight there, no distractions, no radio or phone, just straight to my grandparents.

I walk into their house, and I'm surprised the first person I see is Grandpa Joe. Granda Patti is *always* the one to greet me. She is a one-person party. She all but jumps up and down in excitement and opens the door wide, impatient, and always says, "There you are! I missed your face," as she envelopes you in a special Granda Patti hug.

This is strange.

"Hi, honey!" he exclaims as he pulls me into a big hug. Grandpa is six feet two inches tall—a whole thirteen inches taller than me. He always swings me into the air. But this time, he bends down and squeezes me. With a sheepish look, he says, "Can't do our usual hug, Kylie. I hurt my back and the doctor says I have to be careful what I lift. Even a little cutie like you!" He pats my head. We hear Granda Patti's voice coming from the back.

"Joe, is that Kylie? Bring her to the bedroom."

I give Grandpa Joe a questioning glance. He shouts back, "She'll be there in a minute, Patti." He then takes me by the shoulder and points me toward Granda's living room.

"Kylie... your Granda isn't herself right now." He runs his fingers through his thick, silver hair. "I'm not sure if she'll be up to going out for lunch today."

"*What?*" My Granda is always up for an outing or "an adventure," as she calls it. "Okay, Grandpa Joe," I say. "I'll talk to her."

Grandpa pats me on the shoulder. "Kylie, you go visit with her, it might help her feel better."

I walk with purpose back to Granda Patti and slowly enter the bedroom. She is wearing yoga pants, a tank top, and a pink, zippered athletic jacket—the kind of outfit she reserves for a walk on the beach or at the campfire up north. She looks smaller than normal, swallowed up by the oversized clothes. She seems like a young child playing dress-up in her mom's closet. Her hair is pulled back into a ponytail and she is wearing Cookie Monster slippers. The slippers are the piece that sets her outfit over the edge.

I look closely and notice her face is shiny—probably wearing moisturizer, but other than bright red lipstick, she doesn't appear to have any makeup on her face.

Wow, I've never seen my Granda look like this. I don't know what to do. I sit down and try to talk with her.

"Granda, I'm so excited. I got my license this morning."

She nods her head and seems to be half-listening to me. Her usual happy, expressive face is missing. Her face has a blank look, devoid of expression.

A bunch of thoughts are swirling in my head. Granda Patti always has every hair exactly in place. She's "perfectly put together," as my mom would say. My Granda is a vibrant, effervescent personality, and this person seems like a pale imitation of her. She's shrunken and reclining on top of her unmade bed in the middle of the morning. The sheets are rumpled and kind of wadded up. My Granda is a stickler for immediately making her bed.

This doesn't make sense. Something is seriously wrong. My "way out there," social Granda is acting lethargic and not like herself. Now I understand what my Grandpa Joe was saying. It's obvious he doesn't know what to do. I have to phone my mom and let her know what's going on.

I excuse myself and say, "Granda, I'll be back in a couple minutes, I need to use the bathroom and get a glass of water. Would you like anything?" I eye her nightstand. There are three half-filled glasses of water and a collection of pills sitting there.

She nods toward them. "I think I'm all set with water. But I would like some hot coffee with just a little cream, dear." She puts her head against the pillow as a small sigh escapes her lips, like it's an effort to speak.

Grandpa Joe told me something was wrong and then proceeded to stay away from us. I'm both irritated and upset, unsure of what to do. Grandpa Joe obviously isn't doing anything to help the situation, so it's up to me. I walk quickly into the master bathroom and pull out my cell. Mom has to be home!

On the fourth ring, I hear her voice. I whisper as loudly as I can, "Mom, something is wrong with Granda Patti."

"What did you say? Speak up, Kylie, I can't hear you," she says, an edge of irritation in her voice.

I try again, this time slightly louder. "Mom, something is wrong with Granda Patti." I describe what Granda looks like. Her clothing, hair, and makeup.

My mom responds, "Are you sure?" I can tell she is having a hard time processing my description of Granda. I hear her mumbling to herself and then she says, "Let me talk to Grandpa Joe."

I run out of the bathroom. Grandpa Joe is in the kitchen, staring out the window near the sink. I hand him the phone. "It's Mom. She wants to talk to you."

I can't hear Mom's side of the conversation as Grandpa gives a bunch of "yes" and "no" answers. After a few more, Grandpa says, "For about a month." Then he pauses and hands the phone to me. "She wants to talk to you."

"Yes, Mom?" I ask, hoping she has an answer for what is going on.

"I want you to see if you can get Granda Patti to get up and get dressed. See if she will go to lunch with you. And if she won't, then get some photo albums out and go through old pictures with her. Or offer to watch a movie. Call me later and let me know what happens and how things are going."

I get off the phone with Mom, armed with a plan. I will figure out what's going on. I grab a mug and pour Granda's coffee, then I briskly walk back to her bedroom. She is lying on the bed, listlessly looking out the window.

I try to take control of the situation. "I'm hungry. Are you ready to go to lunch?"

Granda gives me a half-smile and a little sigh. "Oh, honey—we can probably eat a meal out of the freezer and just visit. I'm kind of tired."

I look at her and know I have to take action. "I've got my license. Let me show you my temporary permit."

Granda puts her glasses on so she can read the smaller print. "That's really nice, honey."

Before she can say another word, I go for the guilt factor. "Granda Patti, I'm ready to go out for chicken wings. This is my chance to drive you. We've been talking about me driving forever, and I finally have my license! Are you ready to go to lunch?" I silently hold my breath.

Granda looks at me and starts to shake her head no. But Grampa Joe has snuck up on us. He's standing in the doorway. "Come on, old girl. Patti—you need to get out of bed. Kylie drove all the way up here, her first solo drive, to take you to lunch."

A rush of emotions fly across her face. It looks like she is getting angry and ready to yell at Grandpa, then she looks at me and her face visibly softens. "Okay, Kylie. I'll get ready. We *have* been talking about this for a while."

Granda Patti takes her time getting ready. She walks into her powder room and puts on her foundation, then she sprays her face with a scented spray and starts on her eye makeup. Thirty minutes later, she is finally done. Her hair is curled and she's wearing a pair of black capri pants and a lightweight lavender sweater with some lavender slip-on shoes.

Grandpa Joe comes into the kitchen as we are filling our water bottles. He takes one look at Granda and gives a long, low whistle.

"Beautiful. My girls look absolutely stunning," he pulls me into the compliment while giving Granda Patti a hug.

Granda is a bit like her old self. "Joe, stop, don't mess up my hair." She kind of pushes him away.

Grandpa is in a silly mood and he swoops in to give Granda Patti a big kiss.

She laughs and playfully wipes her lipstick off his mouth. "Serves you right. Now you have bright red lips."

"Have a good time." Grandpa palms a fifty-dollar bill and tries to hand it to me.

I back up, with my hands raised in the air. "No, Grandpa Joe—I'm taking Granda out for lunch. It's on me."

The trip to lunch is uneventful. I drive carefully, but notice Granda is especially quiet as she stares out the window. When we get to the restaurant, she perks up a little bit and is excited to see a two-engine plane land. Initially, she just wants to order a baked potato with butter and chives.

I override her and tell the waitress, "Please bring us a fifteen-piece order of barbecue chicken wings, and my Granda will have a cup of chili." I look at her. "Granda, what do you want to drink?"

"Water will be fine."

I order a soda, and we sit in silence for a couple minutes as we watch airplanes taking off and landing.

Granda Patti brightens as we see a two-engine, sky blue airplane. "Isn't it a pretty color?' she asks, enthralled.

I hold my breath for a second. Maybe I can get her to talk. But her quick enthusiasm is short-lived. Granda is always the life of the party, but now it feels like pulling teeth to get her to talk. I'm really worried about her. Instead of dreaming of the people taking off and landing, and laughing about what possible adventures they are having, we sit in virtual silence. Every time I bring up a subject, she answers in short sentences or just looks out the window. I feel like I'm with my brother Mark, not with my vibrant Granda. We drive home silently.

It's after four by the time we get back from our midday lunch. I ask if she will look at photo albums with me. I love it when she shares childhood stories about my mom. Maybe a walk down memory lane will get her talking.

Granda tells me which bookcase contains the photo albums. It's fun seeing pics of my mom as a baby and a little girl and seeing how much we look alike. Granda points at one picture and lovingly says, "This is when your mom won a baby photo contest. She was twenty-six months old. The prize was a year's worth of pictures from the photography studio."

There is my mom as a teenager and dressed up in fancy dresses for high school dances. I find a small album filled with pictures of Mom starting at the age of two or so. A loose picture falls out. My mom looks to be about three years old or so, and she is snuggling against Granda Patti. There is a big smile on my mom's face and Granda Patti's thrown her head back in joy and with what looks to be a huge belly laugh.

Granda gets a faraway look on her face as she gently touches the photo. "I had forgotten about this picture." There is a small pause and she continues in a soft, frail voice, "This was taken a few days before I lost the baby."

"What? Did you say something about a baby?"" This is the first I've ever heard of it, and I'm full of questions. She says the word "miscarriage." Then like a torrent, the words flow out of her mouth, so fast I can barely understand what she is saying.

"I had two miscarriages before we had your mom, and then another one between her and your Uncle Clint," she says as she gazes past me out the window. She's talking to me like we're friends. But this is scary adult stuff. I'm only sixteen and I don't want or need to hear that my Granda had three miscarriages…. I've *never* heard this story. This is alien and different. In so many ways.

My mom and dad told us how they had experienced a miscarriage a year before I was born. I would've had a brother. They named him David and he died when Mom was five months pregnant. He had been small and perfectly formed. They said it was about two weeks before he could've lived outside Mom. Mom told me she felt like it was her fault, and to this day, if you say anything about miscarriage, Mom will get tears in her eyes.

All these years later, Granda's eyes are filling with tears. My Granda—who never, ever cries—is getting emotional. I didn't know my grandparents experienced multiple miscarriages. I wonder if my mom knows.

But Granda isn't really crying, just kind of teary. Another thing about my Granda—she is a strong person. She doesn't cry. I've heard stories of her yelling at my mom and Aunt Lori and Uncle Clint about crying when they were little. In her world, Clarkes are perfect—Clarkes suck it up.

Granda tells me the pandemic has forced her to slow down to the point she realized she had gone years without grieving the children she lost. She tells me, "Kylie, I was young. Instead of dealing with my grief, I buried myself in my work, then in my kids—their athletic events and band competitions. When Grandpa and I retired, there was always something to do, something to plan. An event, a fundraiser, a family event, or a party. With the virus shutting everything down, I've been forced to stop. For the first time in more than forty years, I've had nothing but time on my hands, which makes me think about the babies I lost. Babies that I never allowed myself to mourn. I just kept going forward. So here I am, an old woman stuck in the past."

I don't know what to do. This is big stuff, big news. My mom needs to hear this. And in the midst of this revelation, I find myself thinking, *If you had all those miscarriages, why haven't you been nicer to my mom? You finally had a healthy baby. Why don't you treat her nicely?*

I desperately want the answer to this question, but the question isn't mine to ask. It's between my mom and my Granda.

Granda Patti is gazing at the picture we found and she smiles, seemingly lost in thought. Her eyes are no longer filled with tears as she says, "Honey, I know this is a big ask, but please don't tell your mom what I told you. I need to tell her myself. And hopefully I can speak to her in person. I owe her my story. I've needed to tell her for a while, but I just haven't been able to talk about it. I thought I was doing a good thing by keeping the pain to myself."

Whew! Who knew my first solo drive would result in a big family revelation? Possibly the answer to a question that I've wondered about for years: *Why is Granda so loving to me and my brother and sister and so mean to my mom?*

Granda Patti and my mom are like oil and water. They instantly separate when they are brought together. They are usually at each other's throats within a few minutes of being in the same room.

Granda begins to talk so quickly, I can hardly keep up. She tells me how she and Grandpa Joe were only children and they both wanted a large family. She dreamed of having five or six children, only to suffer three miscarriages, maybe four if you counted one particularly heavy cycle.

I want to put my fingers in my ears. What teen wants to hear about their grandmother's menstrual cycle and miscarriages?

Granda is winding down after telling me her story and seems to be more like herself. She takes me into the guest bedroom and shows me a special trunk filled with tiny yellow and green clothes. These were purchased for her babies that didn't make it. She carefully put them away and still keeps them safe in the trunk all these years later. She has never been able to use them or gift them. They were a part of her life she has never been able to release.

I don't know what to think. I feel like I'm talking to a stranger, and I have so many questions. While I feel badly for Granda, I'm also angry with her. Why choose now, today, to share a burden she has carried for years? And why me? Why not my mom?

To bridge the sudden silence, I touch the soft baby clothes that were never worn. Now that I know the story, it almost seems as though sadness and loss are permeating the room.

All I can think is, *Wait until my mom hears this...*

Chapter Ten
Jen

June 14, 2020—What a difference two months can make. In April, my biggest concern was if Ben would continue to work from home, only to have his company tell him they were laying him off. And then *I* became unemployed June 1. There has to be a way to make lemonade out of this situation.

I've also found out my mom has kept a big secret from me. I'm so angry, and I don't know if I can help her right now. I want to yell, *What about me?*

I AM WOMAN, HEAR MY roar, hear me scream! I am not invincible, and I'm feeling so completely overwhelmed.

We've almost made it to the end of our school year, a year that has been online since the end of March. Every time I think I've got a few minutes to do something for *me*, someone needs my help. Everything from the kids having issues with their online classes to tutoring them in the evening to working twenty to thirty hours a week.

A few minutes ago, I heard some retching, only to discover our goldendoodle throwing up outside my office. Of course, he never throws up on the wood floor; it's too easy to clean. Instead, it's on the carpet. The girls made pizza rolls for lunch and left them on the counter to cool… turns out, they didn't agree with Rex. Stupid dog! Good thing he's so cute and loving.

On a positive note, I've been working hard at getting in ten thousand steps a day, and I've now gone fourteen days in a row meeting my goal. I've lost one pound in two weeks. Gone are the days I can quickly drop a few pounds. Now I have to fight for every single ounce.

It would probably be easier if I could break my salty snack habit. I'm still eating way too many chips. Getting rid of them is next on my list of things to do. And if I weren't so incredibly stressed, it would be easier. I don't want to have the issue where I'm looking at the COVID-20, as in twenty extra pounds thanks to the pandemic. I'm hearing about people gaining a bunch of weight during the stay at home, and I get it. It's hard to stay away from the kitchen.

Things have been getting really crazy here with the kids gobbling through snacks. We've had lots of conversations about not eating a whole bag of chips or candy just because the bag is there and it's full. Considering the uncertainty of COVID transmission, I've stopped going so frequently to the store. I now go about every three to four weeks. Fresh fruits and veggies are kind of off the diet, unless it's the first few days after the monthly trip. And I'm also trying to teach the kids if they eat through all the "good" food, the food they like, they will have to wait until the next grocery store trip. It hasn't completely sunk in, which is why I started putting snacks in my office closet.

The stress of COVID, the concern and fear that someone in our family will get sick, is hard. I've been busier than usual because I found out mid-May that I was getting laid off from my job in June. I had to wrap up last-minute projects so I could leave my company in a good place. Some people would say, "Forget it!" and happily go into unemployment. Not me. I love my job, and I'm sure when we get past the pandemic, I'll be called back. So instead of whining and crying about it, I've been looking at the silver lining. I will have more time to focus on the kids and help all of us get through this. Plus, I won't have to use all my vacation time for our upcoming trips in July and over Labor Day. I'm not sure how long I'll be off work, but thinking it will be at least six months. Who knows? At least Ben got severance and we've got some money saved. Much better than the last time Ben got laid off. It's just super scary to have *both* of us laid off during COVID.

I'm usually pretty level-headed—and able to calmly think through things. But when we were first told to stay home, I have to admit I had a mixture of emotions. Why weren't we being told on the national news the things we could do to fight COVID? Why were we only hearing the doom and gloom?

Now, whenever I listen to the news, I have a serious anxiety attack, so I've decided to stop consuming hours of news each day. Instead, I've turned to the internet and friends to find out, "How can we combat COVID-19?"

I've bought extra food and stocked our pantry. Seriously, toilet paper and hand sanitizer are hot commodities. What spoiled people we have become. We go to the grocery store, and any time of the year, we can get fresh fruits and vegetables. There has been no need to worry about having enough food. Only now, with the pandemic, there are suddenly empty shelves. People are ranting and accusing others of hoarding.

Unsure of what to do with shortages, I looked up on the internet how to make hand sanitizer, as there is no sanitizer or bleach to be found. I've learned how to make my own disinfectant with alcohol and various essential oils. We set up a makeshift station in the garage and *all* the groceries have to be sprayed and wiped off before they enter the house. The things we don't need right away are packaged separately and left in the garage for forty-eight hours before bringing them inside.

Prior to COVID, I learned to rinse off cans before opening them from my mom. My kids made fun of me, but now with the pandemic, we are all learning the horrible phrase, "This is our new normal." Suddenly, their mom and Granda's weird habit of wiping off cans isn't so odd anymore.

I had a funny experience, involving a grocery trip during late March. Our family of five was down to our last two rolls of toilet paper. I was gloomily looking at the empty rows where the toilet paper should be when a little old lady stopped. She looked to be in her eighties and had deep laugh lines grooved into her face. I still chuckle when I remember her looking at me like a co-conspirator. "Last I heard, you weren't getting the runs with COVID!" she said over her shoulder.

Some people have taken advantage of shortages and begun selling toilet paper in local Facebook groups at marked-up prices. By contrast, other locals are offering toilet paper and cleaning supplies free to anyone in need. People just have to stop by for a porch pickup. We've seen every type of behavior, from the people who shared to the videos of people trying to load their carts up... seriously, physical fights have occurred.

After an unsuccessful visit to one store, Kylie and I scored at another one. We were each able to purchase a four-pack, and we also picked up wipes and Kleenex. When we got home, I told the family if things get really bad, we will start using old pieces of cloth. We will throw them away if we go "number two" and save and re-wash the cloth used for urine. Just thinking about this still makes me want to hurl. But, hey— we are not going to let a little thing like TP get us down.

Now that I'm out of work, I've had time to ruminate and truly begin to feel my age. It's funny, even though I'm in my forty-eighth year, I feel like an older, wiser sixteen-year-old. Sometimes I find myself looking in the mirror at the new wrinkles on my forehead and around my eyes and mouth and the extra rolls around my middle, and I wonder what happened. What happened to my athletic body, to the young girl who could eat anything and never gain weight—what happened? Where did the time go? It really seems like yesterday.

In so many ways, I still feel like I'm not much older than Kylie. I don't know what the right decision is because there's a part of me that feels like my whole life is still ahead of me. Other times, I look in the mirror and see shadows under my eyes turned into dark smudges. If I look closely, I can see my first three gray hairs. They popped through, right in the very front of my head. My mom and younger brother constantly tease me. They think I'm coloring my hair. I'm not, but it gives them something to talk about.

I say, "I guess you will know for sure, since no one can see their hairstylist right now." Salons in Michigan were closed until today, June 14. I've been putting my hair in a ponytail until I can get a salon appointment, even though we are hearing on the news that people were crossing the border into Indiana to get salon services.

I laugh gleefully. I seriously can't wait to see my brother Clint, younger by four years, and see how he's wearing more hair product to hide his gray. I'll proudly show him my three gray hairs—the same three I had the last time I saw him.

As I continue to ponder my face in the mirror, I realize I still smile easily. I still laugh. I have a loud laugh that embarrasses my children. I can see them grimace and almost hear their thoughts, *There she goes again*. I sing loudly and boisterously when there's a song I like, much to my husband's appreciation and children's chagrin. I tick off my family because I have an amazing way of singing the wrong words. It seriously irritates my kids, especially Kylie. Life is meant to be enjoyed, and let me just say this: it doesn't matter if my kids appreciate it or not. I *love* to sing, and I'm *going* to sing.

I quickly learn songs that Kylie loves—only to watch her roll her eyes and say, "Stop, just stop." And I laugh, because I can remember doing the same exact thing to my mom. Yes, I'm in my forty-eighth year, looking ahead and realizing not only do I likely have fewer days on the other side, but so do my parents.

My parents are strong and vibrant people with big personalities. Sometimes it's hard for me to see them as seventy-three and seventy-four, to watch as they start to slow down. My father worked out his whole life, ran, hiked, loves to play baseball and golf, and is an avid outdoors person. To see him develop back pains and a stiff-legged walk is painful to watch. He refuses to take medication until the pain becomes unbearable.

It's hard to realize my mom and dad won't be around forever. As I near the milestone of fifty, I find myself reminiscing about the years between sixteen and now. They really have gone in a blur—or a blink of time, as they say.

Today and yesterday is another blur of rough days. Lately, I've been surviving on four or five hours of sleep. I help Ben research companies and review his cover letters and thank you letters, plus run point on the kids. But with both of us now unemployed, I'm scared. I keep praying and trying to do meditation exercises and yoga to reduce my stress. My body feels like it's running really fast, and I know I need to slow down. I'm a hot mess. I can't show my kids or even Ben what I'm feeling. I get a few hours of calm when the house is finally quiet at eleven at night.

But something has to change. Ben's severance runs out the end of July and we need to be sure at least one of us is working. Fortunately, the nest egg we are saving for our family cruise is available if we need it. I sure hope he gets something quickly, so we don't have to go into our cruise money. Our family has spent all of our discretionary income for years on medical bills. With me working, I've been looking forward to helping pay down debt and saving for some fun trips. Ben's and my job loss has changed all that. We're paying the minimum on our bills, we've cut our expenses back, and we're saving my last few paychecks in case we run into financial problems.

On the upside, we are super excited, all of us, because Kylie got her driver's license. Ben and I have been going for walks. Several nights a week, we have a date night and review his job-hunting video series. It's taken a lot of the angst and fear about unemployment away. This is much easier than the last time he was laid off.

But darn COVID. Darn this stupid pandemic! I'm gritting my teeth—*something* good has to come out of this.

Kylie phoned me yesterday to tell me something is wrong with my mom. It feels like the last straw. I love my mom, but how do I say it… she's hard. My whole life, *everything* has been about her. When we were small, she was a major hypochondriac. She would get migraines that appeared whenever she didn't want to do something or go somewhere. I always wondered if she was faking it because she seemed to get better immediately after the event or function was over.

I don't have time for her games. My first thought was: *She's back to her old tricks*. Part of me was concerned and the other part of me wanted to say, "Take a number. Everyone wants a piece of me, and there's not enough of me to go around."

I don't have the bandwidth for one more thing.

Kylie is my eyes and ears on the ground. She stayed overnight at my parents' and will be back later today. When she gets home, I will have a better picture of what's going on.

My dad has been pretty noncommittal, just answering yes and no to my questions. Hearing from Kylie that mom is tired and lounging in grubby clothing, her hair in a ponytail, is a cause for concern. Typically, my mom has more energy in her little finger than most people have in their entire body.

My mom survived breast cancer a few years back. My sister was traveling back and forth to the Far East the whole time Mom was getting treatments. Lori did a great job of phoning to tell Mom she missed her and loved her, but it was me and Clint doing the heavy lifting and making things happen. And because I wasn't working at the time, everyone seemed to think it was okay to pour everything on me.

News flash: I wasn't working because I had a child with some severe medical issues and special needs. He's been more than a full-time job. We've been in autism hell for years, and my mom and dad have acted oblivious or made disparaging comments to or about us. Comments like, "He'll grow out of it." "You take that boy to the doctor too much." "I think you're overreacting."

Okay, stop… I have to breathe. I'm getting ahead of myself. I have to let this go—we have no idea what's going on. I won't know until Kylie gets home. Hopefully, it's nothing major.

I hear the garage door open and Rex begins to bark. I've been standing in the kitchen, pacing back and forth between the living room and the kitchen for what feels like hours, waiting for Kylie. I have to know if my mom is okay, or only playing games to get us to come and see her.

Kylie walks in and begins to tear up. This isn't anything like my daughter. It usually takes a lot for her to cry.

"Mom, I left as soon as I could." Kylie launches into what she has seen. Everything from the personal to the physical. "Mom—you know how Granda Patti always has her bed perfectly made and her house dusted and looking great?"

"Yes?" I ask.

"Mom, she was lying on her bed. The bedsheets were rumpled and dirty. You know how she cleans her sheets at least twice a week? It looks like she hasn't done laundry in a couple months. She just kind of lies there… and she's lost weight. Her pants and pullover were way too big on her. I also noticed there were a bunch of pill bottles on her nightstand."

Kylie is tearing up again. This is serious.

"I'm afraid there's something really wrong with Granda Patti. And there's something else…" Kylie takes a deep, steadying breath. "Granda asked me not to tell you, but I think you need to know." She pauses. "Mom—have you ever seen a picture of Granda Patti with her head thrown back, laughing? Her arms are around you, and you're both smiling."

I shake my head. This doesn't sound familiar.

"There's a picture of you and Granda Patti, and she looks super happy and so do you. And the weird part is…" Kylie briefly pauses and breathes in deeply. "Granda told me this pic was taken right before she lost the baby."

"Wait, did you say… before Granda lost the baby?" Disbelief must be etched across my face. I'm not sure that I heard the words correctly.

"Yes, she wanted to tell you herself. Granda and Grandpa had three miscarriages, maybe four. She never grieved and now that she's been home alone for the last two months with hardly anything to do, she's really sad. All she can do is think about the babies she lost. She's not herself." The words come out in a torrent.

I'm in shock. I'd gone through a horrific miscarriage a year or so before getting pregnant with Kylie. And not once had my mom shared with me and told me about her experience. That would've been a perfect time to pull together, to get closer and tell me she knew what I was feeling. Instead, she'd been noticeably absent. She sent flowers, but had come down with one of her migraines.

Why is it every time I've needed my mom, needed a mom to be there for me, she has not been there? She has been absent.

I know I'm going to be expected to show up and help her get through this latest crisis. I don't know if I can. I have so much on my plate, and my mom has picked now, this time, this moment, to tell my daughter. Not *me*, but to lay her grief on my sixteen-year-old.

I can't even begin to express what I'm feeling. I reach over and hug my daughter, a way of comforting us both. I hug Kylie for a long fifteen seconds. I want to cry, but I have to be strong and not let her see how upset I am.

"Mom, she didn't tell you because she can't deal with the pain. Will you please go see Granda Patti and help her?" Kylie begs.

And here's the rub. How can I show my daughter the right thing to do? How can I honor my mom when I am so incredibly angry with her? What about me and the years and years of hurt that I'm carrying—because of her?

It seems impossible for me to let go of this anger. I don't know how I will get through to the other side, still be a good person, and survive this latest piece of information my mom has conveniently kept from me all these years.

I have a lot to think about. A lot to consider. I want to do the right thing. But right now, all I honestly want to do is take a bath and eat a huge bowl of chili con queso and chips to numb the pain.

Kylie is looking at me, her eyes full of expectation. I can't let my daughter down, but I'm absolutely clueless on how to handle this situation. I smile through my pain, saying the only thing possible. "It will be okay, Kylie….yes, I'll talk to Granda."

Kylie's shoulders release, and I'm surprised as my non-hugging daughter initiates a hug. "Thanks, Mom," she says as she walks off.

I leave to fill my bathtub with water and lovely-smelling lavender bubble bath. I heat up some queso dip and bring the food with me to sit for two hours in the bathtub.

After my bath, I journal my anger, writing my thoughts. When I'm calmer, I try to read a good murder mystery. The irony of reading a murder mystery is not lost on me. I'm so furious, I totally understand how and why people harm their family members. At least I can still laugh at myself.

The next morning, I phone my dad and tell him he needs to take a walk outside, away from Mom, and call me back. He tries to start a conversation, but I will have none of it. "Dad, we need to talk privately." I say goodbye and hang up.

Five minutes later, the phone rings.

"Hi, honey." I hear my dad's jovial voice.

I get right to it. "I talked to Kylie."

I hear the hesitancy in his voice as my dad tries to keep up the cheerful front.

"Jenni, your mom has been having a hard time. You know how outgoing she is. It's been really hard for her to be away from all her friends and family. Nothing a good party or a visit from you kids won't fix."

"It sounds like more than that. Kylie told me mom showed her a picture of us. A picture where Mom was pregnant—*before* she lost a baby."

There is a long pause. "Honey, I wanted to tell you. Your mom couldn't bear to talk about it and she asked me to keep quiet. "

"I understand it was hard for Mom, but why on earth would she sit down and tell my *daughter* something that her kids don't know?"

There is silence on the other end. Suddenly I realize there is more to the story. I ask, "Dad, who else knows about this?"

He quickly responds, "Your mom wanted to tell you... the only other people she told were Lori and your sister-in-law, Sara, back when Sara had her miscarriages."

I grit my teeth to keep from yelling. "I had a miscarriage when I was five months pregnant. With all that is holy, why didn't Mom tell me then? I mean, seriously, she told my sister-in-law and my sister, but not me?"

I can't help it—I'm crying. The tears are rolling down my face as I try to make sense of this. I am in so much pain. "Dad, I have to go. I can't talk right now." I disconnect the phone before he responds. I'm seriously done, and I need to find my husband and tell him what's going on.

I go searching for Ben. He is in his basement office on the phone, and when he sees my face, he instantly tells his caller, "Hey, let me call you back. I've got an emergency here I have to take care of." He stands up and opens his arms. "Hey, what's wrong?" he asks as he enfolds me in his embrace.

I can't talk for a few moments. I'm safe in Ben's arms, and despite feeling his love, all the hurt, the years of pain, are bubbling up. I'm crying too hard to tell him.

When I can finally explain, Ben gently hands me a Kleenex and looks me in the eyes. "I'm so sorry. I know it hurts. It's so hard to know what your mom was thinking. Somewhere deep inside, she loves you."

Having my husband's arms around me is all I need to know everything will be right with my world. We have a lot on our plate, but he is my person and I will get through this. It will take some time, and I know I will be called on to step up and show up—to show up for a woman who has constantly let me down throughout my entire life. When I talk to her about it, she will likely laugh her little tinkle of a laugh and go back to pretending everything is fine.

This is the same woman who missed my son's funeral. While I feel intense anger, I'm seeing her, possibly for the first time. What doesn't make sense is that she was there every step of the way for my sister-in-law Sara, just wasn't there for me when I needed her the most. And according to my dad, she told my sister, a woman who doesn't even want a child.

My mom failed me, first when I lost David, and then when we fought through the pain of autism and hundreds of therapies and doctor appointments for Mark. Instead of being present with me in the fight, she sat on the sidelines, never cheering or helping. Instead, she pretended everything was fine, ignoring the situation and changing the subject any time I tried to talk about Mark's therapies. It's like she was oblivious to what we were going through or just didn't care.

It's going to be hard to be present for her. Clint helps when he can, but everyone seems to expect me to be the one to carry the load. And, meanwhile, Lori is on the West Coast and always says the right words but doesn't come to help. She uses work as her excuse to be too busy to show up. Always placating Mom and Dad and telling them she *wishes* she could be here. It's time to stop wishing and time to start showing up!

What a mystery this is, my real life. My relationship with my mom has been difficult for as long as I can remember. I wonder how different my life would be if my mom had been able to show me love. If she treated me half as well as the way I treat my three children. I've worked hard to break the cycle, but this revelation makes me realize I need some serious space away from my mom.

Chapter Eleven
Kylie

June 16, 2020—Getting my driver's license turned out to be QUITE the weekend—it will surely go down in history as when the "secret" was revealed. I'm kind of wishing I *never* saw that old photo. Mom is noticeably struggling. I'm really mad at Granda for being such a jerk. I wish grown-ups would act their age. Granda acts younger than I do!

I'M ON THE OTHER SIDE of the basement, and I don't want to disturb my parents, but Mom is talking super loud. You can probably hear her outside the house! I don't mean to eavesdrop, but it's hard not to.

It's also hard to be sixteen and see your mom wrecked by something her own mom has done. Someone who is supposed to love and care for her. And I feel responsible for the "secret" getting out. I'm so glad my dad is home. I'm feeling caught in the middle between my mom and Granda Patti.

There's a muffled sound. I suspect Mom is crying because, for about a minute, I can't hear anything. I think Dad is hugging her, and then Mom's voice rises again... a jumble of words strung together. I can't hear everything, just enough to understand she's really upset.

"Ben, I'm *done*. I can't keep dealing with this crazy, lunatic woman." She adds, "The one time—the one time in my life—I really needed my *mom* to show up, she stayed home and didn't bother to tell me she understood what I was experiencing. Instead, I find out from my dad he wanted to tell me. *She* wouldn't let him—always the control freak—so she tells Sara to help her through her seven-week miscarriage." My mom screams, "I lost David at *five months!*"

The sound of someone crying again. Dad is probably hugging her while she is choked up, struggling to get her thoughts out.

"Ben, she told my sister. She told a woman who doesn't want children, who purposefully went and had her tubes tied so she wouldn't have a child. She told *her!*"

I hide on the other side of the basement. I don't want my parents to think I'm next door, purposefully listening. I feel horrible. Did I do the right thing, telling my mom? Should I have told my mom, or should I have waited for Granda Patti to come clean?

When I was at Granda's, I saw real, honest emotion coming from her. I've also seen Granda Patti be extra super nice to my Aunt Lori, my Aunt Sara, and all her friends, and then seen her basically sharpen her claws and go after my mom for no reason. It's difficult to say this, but my mom makes it easy. She ends up fighting over every little thing with Granda instead of picking her battles.

My mom is my mom. Sure, she can righteously piss me off—but my mom *always* has my back. I know there is something really wrong with Granda, and a part of me felt grown up that she had shared her story with me. But seriously, she put me in a bad place against my own mom. It's not right.

This incident has crystalized many such incidents that have occurred over my sixteen years. So many moments where Granda tried to come between my mom and me to make sure I was "her girl," not my mom's girl.

I have some thinking to do.

No one messes with Mom or her family. She will go toe to toe with anyone and she's *nothing* like my Granda. My mom is real. She doesn't pretend to be something she's not. She doesn't talk about people behind their backs; she's more than happy to let them know right to their face when she's upset and they've done something wrong.

If only we could get her to agree that certain things are not appropriate... like singing the *wrong* words to songs at the top of her lungs all day long. It's actually kind of funny. Jill has resorted to saying, "*Stop*—you're giving me a headache."

What does Mom do? She smiles and goes into a different room and sings a little softer. Or to really irritate us, she'll really get her joy on and she will dance some weird dance and *mouth* the words. Of course, it's a big family joke because she thinks she's being silent, while she's actually singing the words out loud.

Yup, that's my mom. She can be majorly irritating. But when you're going through junk, you absolutely want her in your corner. She's really good at the emotional stuff. I wouldn't have her any other way.

My friends always want to come in and say hi to my mom. She loves it too. She will drop whatever she is doing, and depending on the friend, she'll say, "Have you had your twenty hugs today?"

My friend Paige is especially funny. Mom *loves* her to pieces. She will run up to Paige and give her a big hug... only, now with the RONA, she asks my friends, "*Can* I hug you?" Of course, they always say yes.

A few hours after Mom's meltdown, Mom and Dad call a Sunday night family meeting. I am kind of afraid they are going to talk about Granda and her secret, but fortunately that isn't the reason for the meeting. They want to see how everyone is doing and to talk about financial stuff. Normally, we really don't talk about finances, but with Mom and Dad both losing their jobs, they want to be sure we're aware of everything going on.

Dad's severance is running out the end of July, and they want to let us know we need to carefully think through our vacation plans for this summer. Dad scratches his head and says, "We have the time right now, but until we know more about when I'll be starting a new job, we still have to conserve our expenses."

Mark looks at Jill and starts to chant, "No braces, no braces, no braces for Jill."

I look across at my sister and she looks like she wants to hit Mark. She is not happy that she has to wait until Dad gets a new job to get her braces. "Shut up, dumb jerk," she screams.

Mark laughs and continues to chant, "No braces for Jill. No braces for Jill."

"All right, stop it," Mom says and catches Jill in mid-flight as she starts to hurl herself at Mark. "Jill and Mark, both of you stop it. We're having a serious conversation."

Mark continues to laugh and Jill gives Mark a *look*. He'll be in trouble the minute Mom and Dad leave the room.

Mom quickly assures us we are going to be fine. "We have money for several months, nothing for you kids to worry about."

Of course, Jill asks, "How long do we have money?"

Dad tells her and the rest of us, "We're good until March."

It's the middle of June now—I kind of wish he hadn't said that. I count on my fingers: June, July… all the way to March. We have nine months. Nine months before the money runs out. Now, I have to keep from worrying—what if he doesn't find a new job? This is a little scary.

Dad tells us his company has two positions in Irving, Texas.

Jill immediately jumps in and asks, "Are we moving to Texas?"

Dad responds, "No, we're looking to see if I can work remotely in either of these two positions. If there's nothing else, COVID has taught us we can all work remotely."

Mom says, "Dad will be looking to get a position at a new company. He will take this position for the short term while he continues to look for another job. We can't trust this won't happen again in this company."

Dad continues, "You kids are old enough, we want you to know what's going on. Things might be a bit more stressful right now, but we're in a good place, and we will figure this out together."

Crap. Now all I can think about is moving to Texas—even though they said we're staying here. And, of course, my mind is spinning. What if only my dad has to go to Texas? It will be horrible to have our dad there and us here. Jill and I are friends with two girls that had the mom and kids living in Medway while the dad lived in Petoskey for, like, four years. The family only saw their dad a couple weekends a month before they finally were living in the same city.

I don't want to move to Texas, so I'm already thinking of who I will live with if my family moves. I'll miss them, but I'm not leaving my senior year. Hopefully, it won't happen. I have a lot of friends—I'm sure I could stay with one of them.

My parents are putting a nice face on, but I can see they are both tense. I want and need a rebounder for lacrosse, and we need a new goalie net for my sister and me to play soccer and lacrosse. Our old goalie net was rusted and nasty and couldn't be fixed, and we had to throw it away. I'm going to look and see if I can find a cheap one. I don't think now is a good time to ask Mom and Dad to buy us things we want.

During our family meeting, the next big topic we discuss is our family vacation. Jill and I planned on getting summer jobs, but since most of the food industry and businesses are really struggling, it's not going to happen. We've already missed out on the chance to go to Florida over spring break.

We're all wondering if we will miss out on the vacation we were planning. Mom and Dad give each other a look and Dad says, "We're still crunching the numbers. Our plan is to head up to the lake house in Charlevoix with everyone over July Fourth, and we'll drive up to Mackinac Island. It's been a while since you kids have been there, and we're thinking a day trip will be fun."

"Dad?" Jill angrily pushes her wavy blonde hair out of her face. "What about indoor skydiving? We were supposed to stop on the way to Florida and check it out. Can we still go for a weekend, like we planned?" She asks with just the right inflection, hopeful and not too whiny.

Mom jumps in, "We'd still like to do it, but we'll have to wait and see how things are with the job hunt. For now, we're just going to keep things loose. For sure, we're going to the lake house and we'll have a day trip to Mackinac Island."

It's funny how your perspective changes. Before the pandemic, I just wanted to get a job and hang out all summer. I still want to hang with my friends, but after being cooped up in the house since March, the lake house is sounding amazing. I seriously can't wait to get in the car and drive up to Charlevoix and spend time with my family. Walking on the beach, watching the sunsets, eating s'mores, and making a huge Mexican buffet—my favorite food—is going to be a blast. Granda Patti loves to have parties, so we always have more than enough room for other friends and family to come up as well. My Uncle Clint and Aunt Sara will be there with my cousins, Beau and Liz, plus my Aunt Lori and Uncle Wallace, and my grandparents.

I'm looking forward to the day I'm able to bring one of my friends, like Anna or Paige. Now that I have my driver's license, it's going to be a blast to come up for a long weekend. Hmm. I'm going to need to talk to Mom and Dad and figure it out!

I really love Charlevoix. The house is filled with so many wonderful memories. My great grandma and great grandpa passed it to my Grandpa Joe, and Clarkes have been going there for more than seventy years. Grandpa Joe was just a toddler when his parents built it. My mom has been going there her whole life, and so have I.

The house is a huge, gray Victorian with white trim and a teal door with brass accents that has been completely updated inside. It sits on top of a hill with a large front lawn overlooking Lake Michigan with a beautiful, clear view. It's directly across from the beach, which has a long pier to the lighthouse, acres of sand, and some playground equipment.

The house is about eight thousand square feet. There are three wraparound balconies, and each of the upper floor bedrooms has a mini balcony. The widow's walk has two staircases, and there's a gazebo at the top. One of my happiest memories is of racing my dad up the stairs to see who could get to the top first.

It's been so much fun to have bonfires in our backyard, parties on the front lawn, and play hide-and-seek whenever the weather gets a little rainy. The adults would often enjoy cocktails and appetizers on the deck overlooking Lake Michigan, watching the sun set. The lake house is a magical place.

Granda and Grandpa love to entertain and have two full-size refrigerators and basically a kitchen and a half. Granda loves it when our whole family is together and she loves it when we bring friends as well. "The more the merrier" is Granda's motto. Except no one is merry right now in the Clarke and Blake household.

Life is still kind of weird as we recover from finding out about the family "secret." Mom hasn't been herself. Ever since the talk, the stress in our house has noticeably increased.

Can we just say, "Enough drama already!" When Grandpa Joe phones and asks Dad if he can go up early and help open up the cottage, I think Mom is going to blow a gasket.

"No, you absolutely cannot go up. They can pay to have it done—they certainly have the money for it. Don't they know you're looking for a new job?" I suspect Mom is angry about a lot more than opening the lake house.

Dad has been getting some interviews and is waiting to hear back on two opportunities that he thinks he might get an offer on. Mom and Dad say we will go out for dinner to celebrate when he gets a new job. I can't wait! I really miss going out. Restaurants are now open at partial capacity. We haven't gone to dinner as a family since everything closed.

Speaking of jobs, today has been pretty interesting. My parents go for a long walk, and then we are supposed to have a family movie night. Instead, when they come back, Dad has to look into a job opportunity. Our neighbor told Dad his company has an open position and asked him to send over his resume. He will submit it for Dad. My mom and dad review the position requirements, which look good for his skill set. Dad puts together his cover letter and plans to send it to our neighbor. But his computer is locked up and he can't send it.

Mom becomes a little tense. She doesn't say much, but you can just feel her frustration coming off her in waves.

Did I say Mom is quiet? Wrong! It's now 8:30 at night and Dad is futzing around (her words) with garbage, etc. Mom tries to tell him it's more important to phone the neighbor and take care of the situation than take the garbage out. Dad takes the garbage out anyway, and it gets a little heated. Mom and Dad don't normally yell or fight, but this is a loud one.

Her parting shot is, "If someone is willing to help you get a job, then you get the information to them within a few hours—you don't wait until 8:35 at night to *finally* send an email over. And seriously, why send an email when you can make a quick phone call or send a text?"

Dad storms downstairs and Mom proceeds to follow him. *God, you better hurry and bring my dad a new job... or I think my mom will kill him.* She is a major Type A personality and he is the calm one in the family.

His response to the whole situation is, "Well, excuse me, I thought we were having some family time."

Tonight, we're eating our dinner in the living room. When we were little, Mom used to make homemade soup and rolls. We'd put our towels on the floor (in case of spills) and we would watch a movie. We haven't done that in a while, but now with the pandemic, we've started doing soup and movie night again. It's a lot of fun.

I can almost see the steam coming out of Mom's ears and I cringe. She kind of goes off on him. "Just like I told Olivia—" one of Mom's former employees, "—pick up the phone! Things get lost, or it takes too long. Show some initiative. Do I have to do everything for you? You spend so much time doing for everyone else instead of working on the things that really matter."

Yup, Mom is definitely showing some stress. After the mini-blow up, she goes into her office and proceeds to work on some paperwork.

I can tell she's worried about money. The big sign was when she discovered Mark throwing pop cans away. She put something in the garbage and found ten cans. I thought her head was going to pop off. Her face got red, but she managed to have a civilized discussion with Mark as she explained that each can was worth ten cents and he'd thrown a dollar away.

Yeah, I have a feeling life is going to get pretty rough around here, at least until my dad finds a new job.

I sometimes wonder how my parents ever got together. They are so completely different. My dad is pretty laid back and very much a techno nerd. My mom is this super outgoing person and talks to everyone. Most people (except for the school because she's constantly after them to do their job) love her. She's great at speaking in front of people, and my dad is more on the quiet side.

I've tried pretty hard to find things I can talk to dad about and that we can do together. He likes to play games, so a couple times a month, I play board games and sometimes video games with him. Also, he taught me how to drive. He's a great teacher, extremely patient.

Mom wouldn't drive with me until I had at least thirty hours logged in. And then, once she did drive with me, trust me, I *didn't* want to drive with her. Mom was constantly telling me to slow down and pretending she was braking from her side of the car.

My mom always seemed to have some "constructive message" to share with me. I can't figure it out. I love her, but she gets on my nerves more than most anyone else I know. Instead of being opposites, *maaaybe* my mom and I are too similar.

My mom has played baseball with me—she used to pitch. We've gone on bike rides and walks, and she knows a lot about my life. For my last birthday, she bought me a ski helmet and a new pair of gloves and took me skiing.

At first, I kind of hated it. I fell soon after putting on my skis, and couldn't get one off so I could stand up and fix it. I was lying on the ground almost crying and telling my mom I didn't know or understand why anyone would want to waste money on this. I hated it! Mom assured me I would like it better after my first lesson and took me inside to have my skis fixed.

I took the beginner lesson with this little kid who was probably all of five. The kid could turn and do basic stuff but I kept doing it wrong. After a few practice turns and skiing down the hill, I began to get it. My instructor said he couldn't believe it was my first time, and I was the best first-time student he'd ever worked with.

My mom was right. Skiing is now one of my favorite things to do. My mom really wanted me to like it and was so happy when I did.

It was super special, one of my most favorite outings with my mom. So even though I get a little irritated with her, I love her, and most of the time we have a really good time together. I'm geeked about going to the lake house, but also feeling a little nervous. I can guarantee this trip is going to have some drama. I wonder if Mom and Granda will talk?

Stay tuned... inquiring minds want to know.

Chapter Twelve
Patti

June 23, 2020—I wasn't quite myself when my beautiful granddaughter came to take me to lunch. Before I knew it, I was taking too many trips down memory lane. Sometimes my mouth just gets going and I can't stop it. Seeing the happy picture of Jenni and me brought back all the pain of losing my babies… and then my mouth just got moving and didn't stop.

Argh! I wish I could go back in time and tell myself to "SHUT UP!"

I DON'T KNOW HOW I'M going to fix this mess. It wasn't fair to ask Kylie to wait and let me tell her mom. Joe told me that Jenni phoned him and she was hopping mad and hurt. My man, the mouth that roared, let it slip that I'd told Lori and Sara about the miscarriages… and now Jenni wants to know why I didn't tell her.

I don't have a good answer. I've been racking my mind, trying to think of what to say.

The phone lines have been noticeably silent. Jenni and Kylie, both of them, haven't phoned me since the big weekend. I wish I knew what I was going to say to them when I see them. I want to be real when I see them, not some plastic, made-up face.

I know I hurt my daughter by not telling her, and I know I hurt her by not being there when she miscarried. When she lost David, it was one of the saddest things I've ever seen or heard. There was no reason for him to not make it, except the doctor was too stupid to put Jenni on bed rest until it was too late. I developed a horrific migraine and couldn't lift my head off the pillow. I couldn't possibly be at the funeral when I was so desperately ill.

I wish I could wail and cry and hold my daughter, but I can't go there. If I go there, if I tell her I know how hard it was, then my perfectly manicured life will disintegrate in front of her. She will know once and for all that I'm a fraud.

I'm afraid. I'm horribly afraid to go to my daughter and ask her forgiveness. I've tried to forget, but horrible memories of my mother-in-law and what she did come slamming back. Just two days after my third miscarriage, Millie came to me and told me I needed to get my figure back. I was almost six months along, and my doctor refused to tell me the sex because he felt like it would be easier. So, I never knew if it was a boy or a girl, but I always felt our second child was a beautiful boy. I remember dreaming and wondering what he would look like. But I'll never know the answer to that question this side of heaven.

Millie, that beast of a woman, she brought me a pantsuit as a gift in a *size two*. I'd been a size four before the pregnancy, and she knew it. She told me I needed to get myself together. Clarkes didn't cry.

I'll never forget her words to me. "Patricia," she said. "I don't believe in divorce, but if you don't straighten up, I will be the first person in line demanding that my son leave you. You've lost this child. It's time to get yourself together and try again as soon as you are able."

I didn't think I could hate anyone as much as I hated that woman in that moment. She scared me because from the first when Joe and I were married, I was young and naïve. I thought people were good and kind. Millie wasn't any of those things.

After our second miscarriage when we finally had Jenni, she tried to take my child away from me. She came to the house and fired the helper we had and took the baby home with her. She told Joe that she didn't want anyone taking care of her granddaughter but her, and besides, I wasn't myself—I was sad and ill. Nowadays, they call what I had postpartum depression. We didn't know about postpartum depression back then.

Millie took my Jenni away from me and Joe let her. Granted, he was working a lot of hours. Since Joe worked in Clarke Insurance, the family business, he was bought and paid for by his horrible mom. She took the baby up to the lake house and she proceeded to hold court with all her old cronies. And not one of them, not one, asked about me, Jenni's mom. They didn't dare. She told them I'd had a difficult pregnancy and she was helping me and Joe out.

It took me three months to get my strength back, and the minute I felt well enough, I phoned my best friend Lisa.

Lisa was always up for an adventure. She and I were kind of like Thelma and Louise before Thelma and Louise existed. She was always there for me, a true friend and sister. She died young, right before she turned fifty, and I still miss her.

Lisa was there when I met Millie for the very first time. The garden party—the party to end all parties, when Millie first tried to get rid of me. It was quite an experience, but that's a story for another day.

I was furious with Joe, so Lisa and I plotted what we would do. I was going up there to get my baby and Lisa was going to drive the getaway car. We carefully planned what to wear, what time to arrive, everything down to the last detail. I phoned my great Aunt Betsy and asked her if Jenni and I could come and stay. Betsy was old, single, and she loved babies, so she was an easy sell. She didn't know, however, how long I was planning on staying.

Lisa and I got there ahead of time and we kind of staked out the place. We both wore dark clothing and brought diapers and formula to feed Jenni. I walked into the lake house and up the back staircase to the nursery—at just the right time, when the hired nurse had put the baby down for the night. I was determined to get my Jenni back. I knew the only way it was going to happen was if I snuck in.

We had a car seat and outfits ready. I'd even phoned an attorney. I wasn't going to share my baby and my man with his mom anymore. I was leaving Joe. It wasn't the most well-thought-out plan, but I believed it would work.

I was able to get Jenni out of the crib and put her in a sling close to my body. I nearly made it out. Just as I was leaving the house, one foot out the door, I saw Joe. He was sitting on a two-person wooden swing, looking lonely and sad. There was a young blonde woman seated on the swing next to him. I was instantly furious when I recognized her. It was his ex-girlfriend, the young woman my mother-in-law had tried to get him to marry.

Joe appeared to be ignoring her. Hope flared in my heart. Maybe it wasn't what it looked like. And just as I was ready to run out the door, he looked up and saw me.

I froze. Joe jumped up and hurried across the lawn to stand in front of me. He hugged me, pulled back, and looked in my eyes. "Patti, my sweet Patti, I've missed you so much."

He hardly noticed I had Jenni in my arms. Before I could join Lisa, he put his arm around me and said, "Come with me. Let's walk on the beach."

I looked up and there was evil Millie, glaring at me. I stood my ground, and I pushed Joe away.

"I love you, but I'm here to take the baby home. It is not okay for your mom to steal Jenni from me."

I said something like that. It's been nearly forty-eight years and my memory is a little fuzzy. I could *not* allow this horrible woman to have my child.

Lisa had gotten tired of waiting. Just then, she walked up the path and saw me surrounded by the Clarkes. She yelled, "Patti, is everything okay?"

"Yes." I locked eyes with Joe, imploring him to let me go.

Joe looked angry for a second, and then he sighed. "Patti, I don't want to lose you and the baby. My mom was trying to help—but if you don't want her help, then we won't take it. Let's go home." He reached to grab my arm.

I was weak, but I wasn't stupid. "I'm going with Lisa. I will phone you in a few days. I need some time with our daughter, away from you and your mother. I need to think about what I'm going to do. I love you. But I will not ever live like this again. Thanks to Lisa, I'm now off all the horrible medications your mom's doctor put me on."

"Joe, let her go." I looked over and saw an odd expression on my father-in-law's face. Raymond was always my staunchest supporter, and he was looking at his bride with dislike and anger in his eyes. He was quick and to the point. "Millie, leave her alone, and let her leave."

Raymond turned to me. "Patti, dear—I will get to the bottom of this," he said, but in my mind and heart, it was too late.

I went to stay with Aunt Betsy for three weeks and then with my parents, the last place Joe would expect to find me. I was there for two weeks when they sat me down and my dad said, "It's time for you to go back home."

I remember being so furious and hurt, like my parents didn't have a clue how horrible my life was. Then my dad said, "Patti, we've called Joe and I've had a talk with him. He loves you and he promised me that things will be better."

Joe begged me to come back to be his wife, to allow him to be Jenni's father. And I believed things would get better. I believed he loved me and he would protect me from his beast of a mom.

He kind of did protect me, but from that point on, I learned that I would never, ever in my life see one of Millie's doctors again. I was terrified her doctors had drugged me and caused my depression. I found out later they didn't.

To me, Millie was evil personified. After the incident with Jenni, she was not allowed to have *any* time alone with my girl. She had stolen three months from me that I never got back.

Someday, I'll sit down and tell Jenni everything that happened. Hopefully, she will understand that I've always loved her. Being apart those first three months, not being able to hold her, caused an early break that we've never quite mended. She always preferred Millie. Millie was more her mom than I was for her first three months, and Jenni always loved her grandmother more than she loved me. It's hard for me to admit, but it's the truth.

It's the end of June and we're heading up to the lake house in a couple days. The lake house became Joe's and mine after my in-laws passed away. When the old bat died, we completely renovated it, wiping out every vestige of her. I made it an area of light and love by the water. It's where we can gather to relax and get away. I've always felt our lake house needed to be a gift—a place to be used by the people I care about the most. I married into a family with wealth and money beyond anything I grew up with. It's been my pleasure to have our doors open, to share our retreat with our family members and friends.

I'm feeling much better. The kick in the butt was seeing the expression on Kylie's face when she came to visit. My beautiful granddaughter has been as close to me as a daughter, and I hurt her. I realized I was circling the drain. It was time to pull out.

I phoned my friend Susie and asked her if she had a recommendation for a therapist who specializes in depression. I didn't tell her it was for me, but I think she figured it out. Susie is a dear, gracious friend. After my best friend Lisa passed away, Susie stepped into the void. She loves without reserve and can always tell me what I need to hear. She kindly gave me the name of her therapist and said I could meet online. I knew I had the right one when Susie told me her name is Grace.

I contacted the therapist and set up my initial online session. I was a little nervous, so was very happy when she assured me that our sessions would be private. Grace talked to me about reducing my stress and anxiety. She taught me how to do an exercise called Heart Math, meditating in one-minute increments throughout the day. Grace told me to slowly breathe in through the center of my chest. She said, "Put your hand on the heart, right in the center. Breathe in for five seconds as your stomach and chest expand. Then slowly breathe out for five seconds."

I was surprised at how quickly this calmed me. After a week or so, I was able to get out of bed and start getting my life back to normal.

She also told me, "Think of a time that you are calm, or if I you can't think of a specific time or place, then think of a color that calms you." I love the blue of the ocean, so I kind of combine the two and think of the ocean in front of our condo in Florida as I breathe in and out.

Grace recommends I do this a minimum of four times per day and work up to six times. "Don't sit around waiting for your mood to change. You need to start thinking different thoughts to get back to feeling happier and more cheerful." She talks a lot about seeing myself doing something and succeeding at it. She says if my mind has a positive goal, my body will follow.

It took the pandemic for me to realize how sad I was underneath all of my busyness. I don't really like to read, I hate puzzles, and I get bored watching television. The only things I really like to do are create menus, plan parties, organize, and go shopping. I guess I could've been planning future parties and practicing on menus, but it's not fun to cook for just two people.

Grace gave me the assignment to think of one or two new hobbies I would like to try. I went home and thought a lot about it and decided I want to learn how to play the guitar. I found Lori's old guitar that was in storage and I started looking at tutorials online. It's taken a little bit, but I can play a couple different chords. I'm going to keep practicing and surprise the kids next summer and play some songs around the campfire.

I also love art and art shows, so I ordered some paint and canvases online and I've started to use them. It's amazing the number of things you can learn online. I'm having fun learning how to paint abstract art. I feel like I have my own private instructor. Watching a video that I can start and stop makes it much easier.

I've started to journal more of my feelings, my deep, real feelings. I told Grace I'm not a person who wants to go back to childhood and "explore" things. Having older parents who were cold and distant was tough. My mom was in her late forties and Dad was in his early fifties when I was born, and both my parents died shortly after Jenni was born. My kids never really knew my parents; they were old for me and really old for my kids. When I think of them, I think of two people who were tired and almost seemed to have given up with the idea of being a mom and dad.

I've been packing and getting ready to go to the lake house. Joe told me Jenni and Ben and the kids are coming up July second. I'm afraid to phone her.... I know I owe both her and Kylie an apology. I know I should talk to them. But how? What will I say?

I don't want to go back to being fake and pretending everything is fine. Maybe I will practice what I need to say with Grace. I hope she can help me. I don't know how to talk to my daughter, and I'm praying for strength. I'm praying we can sit down and have the talk we've been needing to have for a long time.

Chapter Thirteen
Jen

June 28, 2020—We're heading to Charlevoix. I know the whole family is feeling cooped up and everyone wants to get out of Medway… but with the latest blow up, I'm not looking forward to putting on my mask. My mom will continue to avoid the issue. I'm struggling with forgiving her.

I'm not too happy with Clint and Lori either. They *both* had the nerve to tell me that I needed to just get over it. Lori told me it wasn't that big of a deal. I'm kind of feeling like *I* need to get a migraine and stay home! If my family weren't looking forward to going to the lake house, I would not be going up this summer. I'm tired of *always* being the grown-up. It's my mom's turn.

LIFE IS EVEN MORE STRESSFUL than normal. I've talked to Dad a couple times, but I immediately get off the phone if he tries to get me to talk to my mom. I'm angry. I'm actually really pissed. Basically, I'm tired of her crap and I need some time away from her and her issues.

I feel like I'm the last person my mom thinks or cares about. Her attempt to put Kylie in the middle of us has me so incredibly angry. I literally shake when I think about what she did. How dare my mom ask my daughter to keep this "secret" from me? How dare she! If I were to talk to her right now, I would say things I would regret. I would completely eviscerate my mom in a couple sentences.

I'd like to have some type of a relationship with her, but I really don't know if it's possible. I am beyond hurt. Giving her grace and staying away from her has been hard. I want to scream and yell and let her have it. But for once in her miserable, fake life, she might actually be sick. I don't want to make her worse, so I'm staying away. I'm so incredibly angry at her right now that I can't even pray for guidance about the situation. I know I should, but for now I need to take some time and recover a little bit first.

Ben has been incredibly supportive. He's great at listening and holding me when I need it. He's got three businesses really interested in him and has already received a good offer. I've been helping him research organizations, and it's been a lot less stressful since we're going through the Brandon videos. There's a lot of great information on how to follow up and how to keep on top of companies to continue to go forward. I feel like this video program is going to help Ben find his next position.

I'm praying and hoping his next opportunity is closer to home, has nicer co-workers, and of course more money would be great. Time will tell, but I've basically spent the last two weeks getting the house back in order and helping Ben.

I've taken a couple days in the last two weeks to go to the beach with the kids. We're about ninety minutes from Lake Huron. The kids and I love going to the cold waters of the lake and then driving just a little bit farther to an ice cream shop near Lexington.

Bunny's Frozen Custard is a small business that takes care of its people. Four years ago, I went to the beach with our kids and my friend, Bunny. Since we had a real live "Bunny" with us, the trip would not be complete without a picture of her next to the store's custard sign. After ordering our treats, I went to pay with my debit card and was politely told they didn't take credit cards or debit cards.

Neither my friend nor I are used to carrying much cash, and we only had about five or six dollars, not nearly enough to pay for our frozen treats. Much to my surprise and delight, the employee told me, "Don't worry about it. Send us a check when you get home."

I was so pleased at their trust that I sent them an extra big tip and a note thanking them. Ever since then, I make sure I have money on me whenever we go to Lake Huron. And I tell everyone to check out Bunny's Frozen Custard. There aren't many stores with a quality product that have such great customer service. They've won our business forever.

Speaking of companies that have won business forever, my mom has been going to the same salon for nearly thirty years. Mom normally has a standing hair appointment with her long-time hair dresser. With COVID-19, all of the beauty salons have been closed since March, but Mom was finally able to get an appointment for the morning of June twenty-fourth. The day after, they were on the road to the lake house.

For as long as I can remember, we've gone to Charlevoix, which is basically a city right on Lake Michigan. I have so many warm, wonderful memories of times with friends and family. Lots of boyfriends visited, until I settled down and decided Ben was the one. Then there are the memories of our children learning how to roast marshmallows, playing hide and seek, and spending time with their cousins, siblings, and friends at the Clarke family lake house.

I love the restaurants up north as well. There's everything from ice cream and fudge to our favorite pizza and burgers. I'm not a fish fan, but Ben, my dad, and most of the family absolutely love the white fish. We have been very blessed to be able to go every summer.

After the big "secret" came out, the last thing I want is to go up for Fourth of July. However, I haven't seen my sister Lori in almost a year, and since she and her husband Wallace are flying in, I feel like I have no choice. This is an opportunity to see her, spend time with my brother Clint and his family, and my dad.

We're driving up to Charlevoix and stopping off at my wonderful mother-in-law's to spend the night and go to my kids' favorite restaurant: "Grandma's," aka my mother-in-law's kitchen. One of my mother-in-law's specialties is sub sandwiches with homemade bread, as well as gigantic turkey dinners. She makes the best gravy, and don't get me started on her baking. She is an incredible chef. She always has the kids' favorite soda pop available. Because it's at Grandma's, they're allowed to have a soda at dinner instead of their usual water.

Driving to Charlevoix takes about four hours, sometimes a little more. We have a standing joke—I'm not allowed to have anything to drink, otherwise we end up making multiple rest stops. The kids and Ben are always in a yank to get to the lake house.

The kids have learned to ask me ever so politely, "Mom did you go to the bathroom?" right before we hit the road. Regardless, we end up making at least one pit stop on the two-hour drive to Grandma Debra's.

Life at the lake house is definitely different. While it was very nice to have extra money coming in when I was working, I must admit it is also very nice to be able to be present and with the kids after I was laid off. I feel like they're growing up and slipping away more and more each day.

I still remember one of our church services where our pastor, Steve Andrews, talked to us with a huge jar filled with marbles he carefully held in his hand. He pulled out one of the marbles and said, "These marbles represent a weekend in the life of your child from birth to graduation." He talked about how, in just a moment, you've made it through all the school years and you're on the other side. I remember thinking, "*Wow*, this is important… but we have a lot of time still."

That service was about four years ago. Pastor Steve was right. I look at my kids and realize time has gone by in a blink. This coming year they will be in ninth, tenth, and eleventh grades. Our babies are getting ready to fly away. It won't be long before they will be at college, dating, and eventually getting married and having kids.

When they're little, it seems like you have all the time in the world. I can remember wishing the bad and crazy moments away, and now we're on the other side. I have to keep reminding myself to savor these moments, even when they argue or they're upset or they ask me to tuck them in. Tucking the kids in doesn't happen as often as it used to. Since our "Stay Home" order, at least once a week, one of them is asking to be tucked in. This is definitely a new occurrence. With the lockdown and everyone working from home, the kids are feeling anxious and stressed. Usually by this age, kids stop showing overt affection. Our kids have continued to say goodnight and give us a hug and a kiss as they go to bed. I feel blessed.

Ben and I talk a lot about the things we want to impart to our children. I still can't reconcile my teenagers with the memory of three toddlers. When they were one, two, and three years old, I remember the constant laughter, the running, and the early swim lessons. I remember going for long walks. Mark, the baby, would get tired, and Ben would sit him on top of his shoulders as I held the girls' hands and we walked around the block.

Now, we have more time to enjoy our kids. The girls are involved in lacrosse and soccer. Mark is getting bigger and has developed quite a physique. Life has evened out from the constant, never-ending doctor appointments for him. He walks really fast, runs, and rides his bike.

I think about how very much I love my children. I'm grateful that I've broken the cycle—the cycle of being manipulative and controlling. Sometimes I'm filled with such strong emotion for them that I want to ask my mom what happened to her. What made her into the person she is today? I know a lot of her story, but it just doesn't make sense! Who has children and then proceeds to spend her whole life working, going to parties, or putting on events? Who has children and then basically ignores them and has other people raise them?

I remember silently laughing as little old ladies or couples stopped to admire our young kids. I still remember an older woman who told us as she looked deeply into our eyes, "Make sure you enjoy it. Because it zaps by like that." As she said "that," she snapped her fingers twice and said, "I snap twice because I have two children. They now live on opposite ends of the country, and I spend a lot of time regretting that I didn't savor those early years. I was always so anxious to get on with my life." She pointed her finger at me. "The most important work you and your husband are doing right now is raising these three precious children. Don't forget it."

We never saw that woman or her husband again. I always wondered who they were and where they lived. Running into them at our neighborhood park was a message Ben and I needed to hear. Since we have three children, we sometimes snap our fingers three times and repeat, *zap, zap, zap.*

COVID-19 has forced us to slow down. The time we suddenly got back because sports were canceled came along at a good time. Because of it, we were able to obtain extra tutoring for our three teens online. When we told them about their upcoming summer classes, we had a few rough days. All three tried to bargain it away. They would do *anything* we wanted if they didn't have to go to school in the summer. Ben and I held strong and we refused their barter attempts. Right now, I'm choosing to believe their grades will improve afterwards.

Like my kids, I wish I could "bargain" this trip away. I would like nothing better than to lick my wounds and stay home from the lake house and away from my mother and her version of the truth. My mom will play the victim, mope around, and get a migraine. It would be nice if, just once, my mom would completely come clean and stop her crap.

What will we do up north? After twenty-four hours of peace and quiet at my mother-in-law's, a beautiful place in the woods, we will drive to the lake house. Don't get me wrong, I'm looking forward to some serious beach time and games and swimming and boating. But there's the big elephant in the room. And I also feel guilty because I feel like I should make sure my mom's getting exactly what she needs to be better. I guess that's the part of me that helps everyone else. I'm really struggling to figure out how to take care of myself and fighting to put boundaries in place.

The weather has been kind of strange. I've been putting my headset on and listening to a weight loss podcast and walking in the house when it's too rainy or chilly to walk outside. I go back and forth between my office, the kitchen, the living room, up and down the stairs, and across the basement. It's hard to make my goal of ten thousand steps unless I start the day off with a thirty-minute exercise program. Recently, I heard a podcast strongly advocating that people walk fourteen thousand steps per day. I'm struggling to get in ten thousand right now, so that many steps sounds huge to me.

Yesterday, I completed 14,036 steps. I'm super excited and can't wait to get on the scale. I've been kind of stuck on a number that refuses to move.

What? I only lost half a pound! Seriously, are you kidding me? This is really hard. I wish I could lose weight as easily as I did when I was younger.

Today is the day we drive to Charlevoix. My mom is the first one to greet us at the lake house. She gives me a big, open-armed hug as she stretches to her full height to pinch my cheek. She says, "Wow, Jenni. Why is it I keep getting smaller and you keep getting bigger?"

What am I, ten years old? I'm inwardly seething. I look at her and say, "Stop it! Woman, I can get in my van and leave right now. I am not here to get into it with you." So much for the half a pound I lost. Guess it doesn't show.

I glance at my children and think, *Okay, how do I leave and set a good example for my kids? Or how do I stay here and set a good example for my kids?* Either way, this feels like a no-win situation. I knew before we left this was going to be tough. Only thirty seconds in, and I'm already dreading the rest of the week.

Mom kind of gives me a little smirk as she says, "Now, Joe, I shouldn't have made a rude comment to Jenni. I might have been wrong."

I have never in my life heard this woman offer a direct apology to me, my dad, or my siblings. It's like she is incapable of admitting she made a mistake. It's always a half-hearted apology through another person or completely unsaid.

I'm very capable of admitting when I make a mistake, and as I stand here looking at her, I think, *Why did I agree to come here?* I know we're saving our money and being careful because we're both unemployed, but I don't think I realized how difficult this was going to be. This might be one of those big life mistakes I will regret. Pretending like everything is okay when I feel like my whole heart has been shattered.

A million thoughts are swarming through my head as I contemplate my next move. Instead of saying what I want to say, I play nice. "Mom where do you want us?" I ask, while silently asking God for strength to keep my mouth shut. With eight bedrooms and constant company, it seems like every time we visit, we sleep in a different bedroom.

My mom smiles and says, "Lori and Wallace are on the first floor in the green room. Clint and Sara are in the yellow room, and I'm going to put you and Ben in the blue room. Then the girls will have the teal bunk room and the boys have the salmon bunk room."

Ben squeezes my shoulder, grabs the suitcases, and says, "Follow me."

I follow him. We spend about fifteen minutes or so putting our clothing in the closet and in the bureau drawer. The kids go to their respective bunk rooms and put their stuff away. They are ready much faster than Ben and I. They quickly come running down to our room. I hear a knock, knock, knock. Then it's louder: bam, bam, bam on our bedroom door.

It's Jill. She is hopping up and down with excitement, and she has her swimsuit on. "Mom and Dad, are you going to the beach with us?"

I look at Ben, and we both kind of raise our eyebrows and shoulders at the same time. I tilt my head toward the door and Ben nods. Our silent communication, after nearly twenty years of marriage. I answer, "Yep let's go. Just give us five minutes."

Ben and I quickly change and grab some bottled water out of the fridge. We always have water in the fridge, as well as small coolers next to it designated for the beach. I grab a cooler and fill it with fruit, chips, and a few protein bars.

The lake house is literally the length of two houses from the beach. It overlooks Lake Michigan and the lighthouse with the long pier. We can also see the parking lot and part of the playground. It's gorgeous, and after our months of being cooped up at home due to COVID-19, we are so ready to be here.

Today is a perfect day. There's a nice breeze and it's about eighty degrees out. The kids and their cousins are happy and excited. Our extended family all walk together to the beach. Sara and I carefully place our towels down, while Ben and Clint pound two big umbrellas into the sand for cover.

The kids all throw their towels on the ground, pull off their shoes, and run as fast and hard as they can to see who can dive underwater first. This Clarke family tradition began when Clint, Lori, and I were little. We've now bequeathed the honor of vying for the cold-water swimming championship to our kids.

This year is different. Beau and Kylie hit the water at the exact same second. They are both fast swimmers and we declare it a tie. Lori and Wallace are joining us later, so they will be disappointed they missed it. They were both on a conference call. Lori muted her headset briefly to give me a hug and kiss and say, "I'll be out soon. Let's go for a walk on the beach and catch up."

You can see the cement plant from where I stand. If you're on the pier, the cement plant is off to the left of the lighthouse. It's kind of an odd look, but it works. I love the beach almost as much as my mom. Feeling the sand between my toes seems to release all the tension in my body.

After two hours, we start packing our gear up to go home and relax with afternoon naps for the grown-ups. Surprisingly, once we get to the lake house, the kids decide to take a nap as well. Ben and I have a chance to lie down and rest. I desperately need to spend some quality alone time with my husband, away from the rest of the family.

My parents arrived at the lake house a few days ahead of the rest of us. They brought in helpers to clean and air out all the rooms. Mom completely filled the two refrigerators to overflowing and contacted our favorite restaurants to get some dinners catered. Since we're not too sure about dining out due to COVID, Mom ordered meals partially cooked and had them delivered to cook later. Then we can eat together outside on the deck, at the beach, or inside if the weather is bad. She wants to make it easy for everyone to come together.

Mom appears to be back to her old party-planning self. She's moving around the house at the speed of light, straightening items to get the house looking just so, and constantly putting out snacks and making sure everyone is well fed. She is happiest when the house is filled to overflowing with family and friends.

Usually, we can see the July Fourth fireworks from the front deck. We sit on brightly colored wooden chairs, eating and drinking and watching fireworks explode and illuminate the evening sky. It's always one of the highlights of our visit. This year, due to COVID, all the surrounding areas have canceled their celebrations.

It's Saturday, July 4, and we've decided to make our own celebration. Clint, Ben, Wallace, and Dad just returned from buying rockets and sizzling sparklers. The guys are in charge of shooting them off on the beach. We'll be able to see them clearly from the front deck. We're all laughing as we *ooh* and *ahh*.

Our next-door neighbors have gotten into a firework battle with us. Clint doesn't like to lose at anything, so it's gotten pretty funny. We're close enough to hear my brother talking smack to our neighbor George. "See if you can top that!" is Clint's repeated comment. So far, I think he is just barely beating the neighbors.

This vacation is just what I've needed. Time to look at the water, enjoy the beach, and have some downtime. We've gone for daily walks, such as into town to pick up ice cream cones and a slab or two of fudge. And the nights have been fun as well. Ben is a consummate gamer, and he has introduced lots of fun party games to the family. Every year, he brings a new board game up north, and Clint and his son Beau eagerly wait to see what it will be.

A few years ago, we discovered a new game manufacturer, Grandpa Beck's Games, and have purchased just about all of their card games. They are super family friendly, and all ages at the lake house have enjoyed them, from eight years to seventy-three years. Our favorites are Cover your Assets and Skull King. Neither game is cooperative—instead, it's every player for themself. They both bring out our competitiveness. Beau is the undisputed winner at Skull King and Kylie always seems to pull a win out of thin air with Cover Your Assets. I'd say she is lucky, but there's also strategy involved—even though I won't admit it to her!

It's day five of our vacation and I still haven't talked with my mom. Seriously, what can I possibly say to her? I'm still too full of pain and anger to even contemplate a conversation with her. And I'm sick of my siblings telling me to just suck it up and get over it. If Clint tells me one more time, "Jen, you've got to let it go. Remember, she's your mom," I will give him a big "remember" right upside the head.

After last night's Mexican night, bonfire, and "shaken not stirred" margaritas, we wake up later than usual. Ben gingerly steps out of bed, rubs his eyes, and pats his cowlick down. I laugh at the expression on his face.

"Hey, you," he says as he reaches over to give me a big hug. "What do you think about driving to Mackinac today?"

A chance to get out of the house for the day? "Absolutely! I'm in." At breakfast, we open up the offer, "Anyone want to go to Mackinac Island with us?" but there are no takers. Just our immediate family. Mackinac Island is about ninety minutes or so outside of Charlevoix, so the drive isn't bad.

We park the car and stand in line to purchase our tickets. We wait twenty minutes before it's time to board the ferry. The kids run ahead, eager to be on the very top of the boat where they can feel the wind and the spray hitting their faces as the sun blazes down. It's been five years since our last trip to the island. The kids can't remember much, so this feels like their first ferry ride. Fortunately, everyone enjoys the ride and no one gets seasick.

We arrive on the island and, as always, I'm struck by two things. First, there are no cars. Tourists can't bring them over. The only ones allowed are specific to construction or maintenance. People walk, bicycle, or rent horse-drawn carriages.

Secondly, I'm struck by the number of t-shirt and tourist shops. It only takes a few minutes on the island to figure out why the locals call the tourists "fudgies." It seems every other shop on the main street is a fudge shop. And it doesn't take long for us to find an amazing deal. We're bringing back five bricks of it to the lake house. We can't resist a "Buy three, get two for free" sale.

This year, a third item stands out as we walk down the main street. Due to COVID-19, everywhere I look, even outside, people are wearing masks. I don't like to wear one, but I'm actually kind of used to it. Due to his compromised immune system, Mark has had to wear them for years. I remember many times getting on an airplane or going to a public place and having to wrangle a mask on him, so I totally feel for parents in this situation. When the pandemic started, we had two cases of masks for Mark, and we were able to share small boxes with friends until masks became more readily available.

A few minutes after our arrival on Mackinac Island we hear, "Blake family. Hey, Blake family!"

We look—and surprise, there're our next-door neighbors. We stop and chat for a few moments. They have four-year-old twin girls, Amelia and Emma. The twins are beautiful, curly-haired redheads with big blue eyes. They absolutely adore our daughters. Kylie and Jill are their favorite babysitters.

We used to talk frequently, but our girls haven't babysat the twins since COVID-19 started. Seeing our neighbors is a welcome reminder we still have friends outside the isolation of our home. Their mom peels the twins off our daughters.

"Please, Mom. Please, can we stay with Kylie and Jill?" little Emma begs.

Her mom quickly shakes her head no. The girls have one last hug, and our mood is now noticeably lighter.

Kylie, always the major extrovert, proclaims, "That was fun! So, Mom and Dad, what are we doing next?"

"We're taking one of the horse-drawn tours." Mark and Ben walk ahead to the ticket counter. "We're only here for one day, so the best way to see everything is to take the carriage ride."

"I can't wait to see the Grand Hotel," says Jill as she excitedly does a little dance in place.

The weather has warmed from an initial fifty-five degrees and is now seventy-five and perfect. Our first stop on the carriage tour is the Surrey Museum. We don't get out, as we're anxious to visit the Arch Rock. It's made out of limestone, and the pamphlet says this is one of the most photographed spots on the island. I believe it! We previously used a picture of our family in front of the Arch Rock for our family Christmas card and I'm hoping to get another one today.

The Arch Rock is stunning, offering sparkling views of Lake Huron. What a gorgeous place to enjoy the scenery. I catch all three kids in a rare smile. They are standing against a railing with the Arch Rock in the background. After quickly taking multiple pictures, I look and see that there are at least two really good photos. I happen to snap a really funny photo of Kylie when the horse moves its head a little bit too close to her.

We board the carriage and I have to take a quick selfie of all of us *mask*-free. We're in the fresh air, there's a plastic partition between us and the next row, and we're outside. The pictures turn out great, and Mark, our rule follower, immediately puts his mask back on. "Mom, I'm afraid I'm going to get in trouble."

I chuckle to myself, remembering how hard it used to be to get him to wear his mask, and then I look around. There is our family of five, a couple in the very front, and another couple in the very back of the carriage. We're several rows apart. The carriage takes us down a dirt road, past a forest of green trees with ivy and a few wild plants near the road. It's hard to image we're on an island and close to water. It feels like we're in the middle of the country.

Ben and the kids are excited about our next stop. Me—not so much. I'm still recovering from plantar fasciitis. I've put my foot in a walking boot to make the walking portions of the trip bearable. We get off at Fort Mackinac and have the chance to take a tour and listen to the actors dressed in period costumes. Ben is a history buff just like my dad, and he is thrilled to be here. I drag myself up the stairs. I'm hot and sticky and suddenly realize it's no longer seventy-five degrees. I'm steaming and feel like I'm becoming a puddle of yuck. We arrive just in time to see the cannon and the muskets fired. Ben and Mark have the biggest smiles on their faces.

Our last stop, and Jill is vibrating with excitement. "Mom, I can't wait to see the Grand Hotel," she states, "I've always wanted to sit on the deck and rock in one of their rocking chairs!"

And we're here. The pictures of the Grand Hotel don't do it justice. As far as you can see is a huge white building with a wraparound porch filled with white rocking chairs.

As I stand at the base of the hill and look at the beautiful promenade leading to the entrance, I'm surprised to see a sign. The cost to tour the hotel, the grounds, and sit on the beautiful porch is ten dollars a person unless you're a guest. Is it worth it to spend fifty dollars for our family to tour the inside and rock on the longest porch in the world?

Prior to this exact moment, all Jill has talked about is visiting the Grand Hotel. I close my eyes briefly and wait for the explosion. Instead, I'm pleasantly surprised.

"Hey, Mom, did you see that sign? It's fifty bucks for our family to go sit on the porch. That's crazy!"

Wow! Disaster diverted. I smile at my sweet daughter and a million thoughts are colliding inside my head. I've always wanted to stay here, but the hotel is a bit out of our price range—especially now, with both of us unemployed. Maybe next year we can plan an anniversary trip. In fact, what the heck, when Ben and I are back to work, we will save and plan to stay here. Yup—this is definitely one of my bucket list items. Ben and I say simultaneously, "Maybe next time."

We are both pretty determined people, so if we set the goal of coming back here for our anniversary, I know we'll do it. What will next year look like? Will we be able to afford to stay the night at the Grand Hotel and enjoy some time peacefully rocking on the long front porch?

And will Mom and I be in a better place then?

JULIE CADMAN

Chapter Fourteen
Patti

July 2, 2020—I've had a mixture of feelings about this year's trip to our lake house. Dread and anticipation, all surrounding the conversation I need to have with Jenni. I've been dealing with my thoughts and emotions... practicing what to say... I know what I have to do, it's just hard and I don't want to do it. Why can't I go back in time to before I opened my mouth to Kylie? I really wish this mess would just go away!

JOE WAITED UNTIL BEDTIME WHEN it was just us in our bedroom. "Patricia Lynn! What is wrong with you? What were you thinking?"

I flush, since I know exactly what my Joe is asking. Jenni was in the lake house for no more than two minutes when a snarky comment came straight out of my mouth. I don't know what possessed me. I don't know why I said it, but she looked frumpy and horrible and all I could think was, *What's wrong here?*

I didn't say everything I was thinking, but I said enough. Joe is right. It wasn't very kind. I always warn Joe to keep quiet about Jenni's weight gain, and then I blew it. My mouth got in the way. Instead of making peace with my daughter, I started off on the wrong foot again. Another moment I wish I could take back, but I was nervous about what to say and how to talk to her and I don't have a good excuse.

When Jenni lost her baby, I couldn't deal with all the pain it brought up for me. I was afraid I would fall completely apart. The longer I waited, the harder it was to tell her.

Now that she knows, I don't know how I'm going to explain my actions to her. She won't understand. She thinks I have ice in my veins. It's not true. I so desperately wanted to hug and hold her and cry with her. When she lost her baby boy, I had to close myself off. The emotions were too raw and too brittle. Anytime I thought about telling Jenni, my eyes saw spots and I started to get this crescent aura, which told me a migraine was on its way.

The pandemic brought forth a lot of feelings I've purposefully kept dormant. It took a global disaster to make me finally stop and take inventory of my life. I buried my loss so deeply.

My first two miscarriages were very early in the pregnancy. We'd hardly known we were pregnant, maybe seven or eight weeks along. When I had my third miscarriage, I wanted to give up and stay in bed. I was about six months along when I lost the baby. Joe was struggling, trying to be there for me and little Jenni. He was now working at Buick Motor division, having left the family business a year or so prior. My wonderful father-in-law offered Joe the chance to come back, and told him if he returned to the family business, he could take as much time as he needed to help me recover. Raymond was always kind to me and Joe. I still think of him with love.

After my miscarriage, I cried and listlessly lounged around our house. Joe and I had a horrible fight. His words are seared in my memory, "Patti—you're a Clarke. Clarkes bounce back! You need to get back on your feet and help take care of Jenni. She's only three years old and she needs her mama. Now, get out of bed and get your body moving."

If I valued my marriage, I needed to get going. After that horrible day, I got up, cleaned up, poured myself into my family, and had two successful pregnancies and possibly one additional miscarriage. Once all three kids were in school, I went back to work. I purposefully found a job as an executive secretary *outside* the family business. Despite offers from my wonderful father-in-law, I knew it wasn't the place for me. I needed to be far away from Millie. I needed something that was completely mine.

Joe's escape from the family business didn't happen overnight. When Jenni was almost two years old, he decided to work for Buick Motor Division, a Division of General Motors. I was so happy that he was away from his family's business.

Our first few years of marriage started out so promising—two people, best friends, together in love—who enjoyed each other, laughed, and communicated so well despite being from two completely different backgrounds.

Us—me and Joe—unbreakable, together forever. Instead, Joe allowed his beast of a mother to take baby Jenni away from me.

I went back to Joe for two reasons. I desperately wanted our Jenni to have a mom and dad who were together... and I could hardly breathe thinking of a life without him. Without Joe, I felt like I had no one.

But my parents told me it was time for me to go back to him. For years, I've carried that hurt and pain with me. I've been so angry that my parents didn't seem to love me enough to help me. I've never been able to completely forgive them. I've never understood *why* my parents would kick me and my baby daughter out and tell me I had to go back to my husband. They knew what my mother-in-law had done to sabotage my marriage.

As I've gotten older, I've begun to release some of my anger and begun to understand my parents a little better. They were in their seventies. My dad was smart enough to know that by staying and keeping Jenni away from the Clarkes, I was playing right into my mother-in-law's hands and dooming my marriage. Mostly, I'm understanding them better thanks to a conversation that Joe and I had just last week.

I'd just finished my online session with my therapist when Joe and I met in the kitchen for an early lunch.

Joe politely asked, "How was your meeting?" This time, I decided to be real. It was time for us to have a conversation that we should've had years ago.

"Joe. Today was a tough one."

He looked at me with a questioning glance—and before I chickened out, I plowed ahead. "Today we talked about when your mom took Jenni away from me."

Joe looked down for a second. He said nothing, just sat there silently.

"Joe, there was so much pain back then. You and I were in a bad place and I wasn't sure my parents loved me."

Before I could continue, he interrupted. "Your parents loved you a lot and they wanted the very best for you. In fact..." and he paused for a moment before he continued, "I phoned your parents looking for you, and your dad initially refused to let me talk to you or tell me where you were. He said I had to go to their house and sit down and have a conversation with him and your mom."

"He what?!" I was astounded. This is the first I'd ever heard this story. My father had always been so hard and stingy with his feelings and his words. He wasn't someone who got involved in my life or even seemed to care about me. The only crack in his steely façade had happened right before I walked down the aisle on my wedding day. He'd offered to drive me anywhere I wanted to go and told me, "You don't have to marry this boy unless you're sure it's what you really want. It's not too late to change your mind."

I was dumbfounded. My dad had talked to him about me and Jenni. I instantly felt a mixture of anger, curiosity, and loss. Why hadn't Joe told me about this before?

As if reading my mind, Joe answered my silent question. "Patti, your parents and I had a really long conversation right before you left Aunt Betsy's to stay with them. We talked for almost," Joe paused again, "...three hours, it must have been. They asked me a lot of questions and also gave me some solid advice.

"Patti, your dad told me if I wanted to be my own man, I needed to leave the family business. He knew it would be hard, but he told me if I didn't leave, I would eventually lose you and Jenni.

"I've never seen your dad so intense. He made me promise to put a plan in place and leave in twelve months. He also told me that it had to be my decision to find a new position. He said if you thought he had put me up to it, you would resent me and be angry at both of us.

"And then eight months later when he was dying, the last thing he said to me was, 'Joe, you've got four months. Don't let my girls down.'" Joe looked at me, a silent plea for forgiveness.

All I could think was *wow*! My eyes welled up with unshed tears as I realized my parents had cared for me. They had truly loved me. My quiet father encouraged my Joe to step up and be the man that he knew my husband could be—the man he needed to be for Jenni and me.

For one of the first times in our marriage, I was speechless. I was shocked to realize that not only was I important to my husband, but I was also important to my parents.

Joe and I have a lot to talk about. We're not finished with this conversation. But a weight seemed to lift from my shoulders. I felt lighter. I wanted to shout out loud, "My parents really loved me. They really, really loved me!"

I wish I'd known that my quiet, taciturn father had acted like a loving father and done everything within his power to ensure that baby Jenni and I were happy. I would've resented him and Mom a lot less. Instead, I've spent the last forty-seven or so years thinking bad thoughts of my parents any time I thought about that time in my life.

It took the pandemic for me to slow down and really take stock of my life. You see, I was always busy during my marriage, and once I retired, I poured myself into being the best retired lady there was. I was always *busy* and there was never time to sit and reflect. If I sat too long, I thought about what was missing in my life, in my marriage, and in my relationships with my children and grandchildren. I kept going. At least, I kept going until the pandemic hit.

It was like something snapped inside of me. I felt like I was walking through quicksand or heavy waters. It was hard to keep going. And when Kylie found the picture of me and little Jenni, it brought back memories of a happier time before everything changed.

I know I owe an apology to my daughter and my granddaughter. I just don't know how I'm going to say it. In our family, we sweep a lot of things under the rug. We joke, we laugh, we have fun together. When it comes to real emotions, we don't go there.

I don't know why there's such a big break between me and my oldest daughter. I wish I could go back in time and I wish I could change some of what's happened, but it's too late and I can't. I'm seventy-three years old. I guess Jenni doesn't have to like me, but I love her regardless.

And it's nice to have the whole family together over Fourth of July. Most of them are staying until Saturday, except for Jenni and her family. They are leaving on Wednesday. I've been dreading them leaving because I know I need to talk to her, but the time just hasn't been right. Even Kylie is avoiding me.

I've noticed Jenni goes out of her way to never be in a room alone with me. The air is frosty whenever the two of us are together. I really struggle with what to say. I grew up in a family where the adults didn't apologize. My mom would say, "Children are to be seen and not heard." Even though Jenni is in her forties, I still think of her as a teenager.

I was an only child and a disappointment because I wasn't a boy. I never wanted my children to feel that way. I can't help but think I've somehow perpetuated the legacy of not feeling loved or wanted onto my children, especially my Jenni. Well, I guess I have some big things to talk to my therapist about next time.

The picture of me with my head thrown back, so full of joy with my sweet little Jenni, brought back memories. It was summer, and our family had a lovely picnic with my best friend Lisa and her family. It was more than twenty years before Lisa passed away.

I haven't thought of her in a while. Lisa was very close to my kids, especially Jenni. If Lisa were here, she would be giving me a whole ton of advice. She would've been able to see when things were going bad and help me before it got out of control.

I really miss my best friend. It's hard to find people you can trust who always have your back. Lisa and I knew everything about each other, the good, the bad, and the ugly. We loved each other anyway. We were dear friends from the time we first met in middle school. We were in each other's weddings. We each had three children. Lisa was there when I had all of my miscarriages, holding my hand and comforting me. She was the lone voice telling me I needed to cry. I still laugh when I remember her comment, "Patti, screw the Clarkes. Millie is a cold, miserable fish."

Age has a way of muting memories. Some are too painful to remember, like losing my babies and losing my best friend. Before the pandemic, I'd gotten really good at stuffing them away and not thinking about them. I learned to compartmentalize. The only problem is, with the painful memories, I also packed away some vibrant, amazing moments.

It wasn't until all these years later that I realize I didn't grieve. When my Jenni miscarried at five months, it nearly destroyed her. I know how hard it was for her, and I couldn't bring myself to tell her. I don't know if I can explain it, and I don't know if Jenni will understand or if she will forgive me.

Before the summer is over, I will make sure I tell her how much I love her, how important she is to me. I don't think she knows how proud I am of her. I look at her and think what an amazing woman she has become. Her dad and I think it all the time.

But before I jump ahead to having a big discussion with Jenni, I need to have a discussion with my therapist. The Clarkes are very strong people, and when I first told Joe I needed help, he had tears in his eyes.

My whole married life, I've always heard how strong the Clarkes are, how they don't "do therapy."

I told Joe, "I love you and our family. But I've been going completely out of my mind since the pandemic started." It took me losing myself for Joe to realize that I needed help.

When the pandemic started, a lot of things changed for a lot of people. Since my hobby is socializing, isolation tore me apart. When the virus hit, the house became eerily silent, just like the lake house when everyone leaves. Suddenly, our feet echoed as we walked across the wood plank floors. No sounds of children laughing and running in and out of the house. No cooking big menus for thirty of our nearest and dearest family and friends. No bonfires or sing-alongs at the campfire as we saw who made the best s'mores.

I wandered around, listless, with nothing to do. I had to wait seven long months before we were able to go up north and begin to see friends and family again.

The first time Jenni and the girls came to visit, right after the virus had started, Jenni walked in and said, "Mom, can I hug you?"

I just opened my arms wide. We both teared up because, as bad as things can get between us, I can't imagine seeing my daughter and not hugging her.

A few weeks ago, there was a social media post about a woman who stated how devastating it was her father had died. She had flown in from out of state and said the worst part of the virus was she couldn't hug her sister. Call me crazy, but if a family member dies, you can bet your sweet butt I'm going to kiss and hug my remaining family members. I am not going to let the fear of a little germ—yes, I know it's a lot more; I have friends who have died from *the virus*—but I'm not going to let the fear that I'm going to get sick prevent me from loving my family.

Wow—as I think this, I'm realizing the only thing preventing me from loving my family is my own stubborn pride. I wonder how many other people have been through this pandemic and have maybe started to realize they don't have enough to keep them busy? And the people

living on their own who are suddenly unable to see friends and family—
I wonder how they're doing, how their mental health is holding up. I
heard on a news program over twenty percent of the US population are
on antidepressant medication.

I'm raising my hand to say, "I'm one—I'm now one of *those*
people." My doctor works with a therapist and a psychiatrist within the
clinic, and they put me on an antidepressant.

Let me tell you, at first, I saw absolutely no change. Joe laughed at
me when I told him. He said, "Oh, no. Honey, you are not the same
when you take this medication. It's revving you up and I'm getting my
Patti back."

How strange is that?

My first step to getting better was changing the sheets on a regular
basis and making the bed. My next step was getting dressed, exercising,
showering, and then putting my makeup on and doing my hair. Once I
started these things, I was ready to pick up the phone and check in with
friends.

The pandemic has brought forth the realization that Joe and I have
really changed. We don't have as many things in common as we used
to. It's tough to have conversations when you can't see your friends, you
can't go to restaurants, and you can't get out of the house. The stay at
home has not been fun. Catharsis never is, I'm realizing, as I have
weekly online meetings with my therapist.

Grace wants me to sit down and write a letter to Jenni. She says I
don't have to *give* her the letter, but I need it to help frame what I want
to say. Grace told me it would be good to start the letter with what I love
about my daughter and then get into my apology. The first part, how
much I love her, is harder than I thought it would be.

At the top of my list will be how proud I am of her. She has worked
so hard to get Mark better. Jenni and Ben are very good parents. They've
given up a lot of time and money, and I know they've struggled. Joe and
I could've helped, I guess. At the time, I felt like it was something they
needed to do on their own. If you were to ask her what she thought,

Jenni would probably say something like, "My parents are mean and have their heads stuck in the sand," and all kinds of stuff. The reality is somewhere in the middle.

I know we spoil Lori a lot. She is the youngest, she is our baby, and she doesn't really need as much when you think about it from a financial standpoint. Lori and Wallace are both working at well-paying jobs and they don't need financial help.

Life goes on. Right now, I need to focus on letting my daughter know I love who she is and what she's accomplished. I need to keep my mouth shut and not make any snarky comments.

I seem to be stuck in a rut. It seems like just yesterday I was Kylie's age. A few years later, I was married, and then a few years later, I had my first child and had to deal with a hideous mother-in-law.

Okay, enough of these negative trips down memory lane. It's time for me to go forward. A talk with Jenni really should happen this trip, but I'm not ready... I'm scared about what might happen. I'm not ready... I need to write a few practice letters.

I know I keep putting this off, but maybe over Labor Day.

Chapter Fifteen
Kylie

August 17, 2020—Everyone wears masks in Michigan—you can't go anywhere without a mask. To me, the stupidest thing is seeing a person sitting in a car all by themself with a mask on as they drive down the road.

I can't believe the difference in Ohio. We live one and a half hours from the state border. Only one and a half hours away from freedom in that direction and a few more hours away from freedom in Indiana.

My friend Mary moved to Ohio a few years ago, and they started back to in-person learning a whole month before we did. But the biggest thing is seeing how much more open their state is. I want to move!

OUR PLAN TO GO INDOOR skydiving has been on hold until Dad accepts a new job. We planned on going on the way to Florida over spring break before we canceled our trip. The RONA basically shut everything down.

I'm super excited—it looks like we're going. I can't wait!

Real skydiving is on my personal bucket list, so this will be a chance to get a feel for what it will be like. I keep teasing Mom. She says she used to be a daredevil back in the day. When I ask her if she would go skydiving out of an airplane with me, she says, "Kylie, there is *no* way

I'm jumping out of an airplane. You'll be on your own with that plan… and, by the way, you can't go until you've graduated from college and are no longer living under our roof." So, I'm not sure if I believe she used to be a daredevil.

Things have been much less stressful these last few weeks. Dad has received two job offers. He's been holding them off, as he thinks he's going to receive a third offer, and then he needs to decide which one is best for him.

It's August and things are opening up. There's a noticeable reduction in tension. Mom and Dad held a quick family meeting and told us the trip is on. Woohoo! I was born to skydive. We haven't been *anywhere* (except the lake house), so driving to Ohio and staying in a hotel is going to be amazing.

We're leaving August twenty-first on Friday morning and going to Cincinnati. We have it all planned out. We will eat fast food for lunch, then check into our hotel and go for an afternoon flying experience.

I'm so excited, I can hardly stand it. Mom and Jill are both a little apprehensive. I guess I am too, even though I won't tell anyone else in the family. What if I'm really bad at the wind tunnel? I'm not very big, so what if the wind tunnel throws me around and I get hurt?

When we arrive, they have us fill out waivers. You know, the standard, "You will not sue us if you die, we are not responsible if you break any bones," etc. You should see the look on Mom's face when she starts reading it. We all have a good laugh.

Next, they give us each a one-piece suit like the astronauts wear to put over our clothes. We also have a helmet and we have to wear masks until we put our helmet on and go inside the wind tunnel.

Our instructor Steve is super hot looking. He's my type of cute. He's got dark, wavy hair, bright blue eyes that crinkle when he smiles, and he's built. He's got strong arms that could really cradle a lacrosse stick. In addition, he's the perfect height for me, about five feet ten inches tall, and he's got dimples! I could sit and look at him all day. He tells us,

"Stand in the doorway and put your hands out and just let yourself fall forward."

It's super funny watching Mom. Mark does a really funny imitation of Mom with her arms and face all scrunched up like a cat. She swears she has her arms straight out, but trust me, they aren't.

Jill and I love it. We can't wait to go again. Steve, our instructor, kind of shows off and does a bunch of flips at the end of our session. I want to learn how to do flips like him. Mom, Mark, and Dad all get headaches. I guess it's a good thing our trip to Florida got canceled. Mom and Dad would've been miserable if they had to drive after indoor skydiving.

Dad says, "Why spend money on something when I won't feel good afterwards?"

After our epic experience, we decide to go to a nearby mall. We eat at a sit-down restaurant that has a whole menu filled with appetizers, main meals, and incredible desserts. We all order different appetizers and entrées and share them. There's this spinach cheese dip with homemade tortilla chips, and crispy potato skins with bacon, cheese, scallions, and sour cream—so yummy—and Jill's favorite mozzarella cheese sticks.

But the best part is we each get a different dessert and everybody gets to taste five different sweets. Dad orders the regular cheesecake with strawberries on top. We are surprised to discover it's a little too plain for our taste. We also try some chocolate mousse, strawberry pie, and coconut cream pie. My absolute favorite is the Reese's Peanut Butter cheesecake. It's one of the best things I've ever eaten.

We're starting to get our rhythm back. The lake house over July Fourth was fun. We were all having cabin fever and it was awesome to get out of Medway. I continue to be the Cover Your Assets champion, and this year, my cousin Beau and I tied in the contest to dive underwater first. He's a foot taller than I am, so he was a little faster, but everyone says we went under at the exact same time. I'm going to beat him next year!

Mackinac Island was fine until Mark got into a fight with Jill. We were literally walking down the street and those two were shouting at each other. It was low-key awful, and I just pretended I didn't know them. In the middle of their fight, we ran into our next-door neighbors. I'm sure the neighbors heard us before they saw us. I had secondhand embarrassment for my brother and sister. Mom and Dad acted like it was no big deal and completely ignored the situation.

The only bad part was the awkward feeling I had around Granda Patti. Granda still hasn't said anything to me. She just went forward like nothing had happened, like everything was the same. Why can't she act like a grown-up and just apologize?

My mom told me, "Kylie, we need to give your grandmother some grace. She is who she is. I can't change her, as much as I'd like to. All I can do is make sure I'm setting appropriate boundaries."

I kind of started when she called Granda Patti "grandmother." We've never called her "grandmother" or even "grandma." I guess my mom calling her that is a way of showing her anger.

I'm feeling caught between them, and all I can do is sit back and feel sorry for these two. I love them both, but when it comes right down to it, my relationship feels strange because of the position my Granda put me in. It really sucks. My mom can be a real pain in the butt, but I love her. It's not right for my Granda to make me choose between them.

After our indoor skydiving and dinner, we go back to the hotel to swim in the pool. Thanks to the RONA, we have to sign up in advance. It's a pain to schedule our pool time, but it turns out okay. We have the pool completely to ourselves for an hour, then it's another family's turn.

We've stayed at this chain of hotels before, and we usually love the hot and cold breakfast they serve in the morning. Breakfast has changed because of the RONA as well. We are given a boxed breakfast that includes a boiled egg, a bagel, juice, and a protein bar. We are all missing the hot waffles we usually make when staying at this hotel. But, waffles aside, I'm ready to move to Ohio to stop having to wear stupid masks! It's been great getting away. It feels almost normal.

144

Usually, we start school the day after Labor Day, but not this year. This year, we start school on September 1, a whole week early! Since school is online, it really isn't a big deal to go up north over Labor Day. Granda Patti's birthday is on September third, so we always celebrate over Labor Day weekend. Aunt Lori and Uncle Wallace fly in as well.

It's a pretty chill weekend. We relax, go boating, walk on the beach, and, of course, play some nightly games with the rest of the family. We have a tradition of making a sheet cake and then putting M&M's on top of the frosting. We're not the best at decorating, but it's fun and it's become a family tradition to have the grandkids make Granda's cake.

Here's where life gets weird. They say you shouldn't listen at the door if you don't want to hear bad things about yourself. I'm not exactly listening at the door, but I certainly hear some things that blow my mind.

I am on my way to hug Mom goodnight—Dad had a headache, so he went to bed early—when I hear something that totally shocks me. I overhear Grandpa giving my mom this amazing compliment. It is absolutely, totally bizarre. I hear grandpa telling my mom how proud he is of her.

I don't know what to do. I'm kind of afraid to walk around the corner and enter the room. I don't want them to think I'm listening at the door. I'm really not, but wow, this is big. I can clearly see my mom and the back of my grandparents. No one notices me.

Granda Patti isn't saying anything, just nodding her head up and down, kind of like a bobble head. I debate if I should enter the room or leave before they see me. As I start to back up, the floorboard creaks. I quickly act like I dropped something and then go forward into the room. As I walk toward my mom, her eyes are kind of glistening. I think, *It's about time her parents tell her how special she is.*

My mom is the person you go to if you're having a bad day. She'll always drop whatever she's doing and envelop you in a huge hug. I'm not much of a hugger, but her hugs are special. Every year for Mother's Day, I always include a PS on the card. I tell her, "This year, part of your gift is a twenty-second hug. Just one hug for twenty seconds, so use it wisely."

Yeah, I'm funny like that.

School is going to be much different from when we first had online learning in March. In the beginning of the pandemic, everyone was scared. No one knew what to expect, and we were told to stay away from our older relatives. Everyone I know was afraid of getting the RONA, and my mom was a space case. When every place sold out of sanitizer, my mom figured out how to make her own. We had Wednesdays off for "Wellness Wednesday" and weren't required to be online for our classes. Teachers weren't even taking attendance.

This has all changed. No Wellness Wednesdays, and it's starting out a lot harder. We're getting much more homework than we did last year. We were given the option of going to school online or in person, and we had to decide by a certain date. There's been a huge big fight between a whole bunch of parents and the school board and administration. Most of the families and their kids want the students back to our normal schedule. The MCS school board had over five hundred letters sent to them requesting we return full time. A lot of parents are really mad because the board voted and didn't appear to take into account what the families want. They unanimously voted to put us on this crazy schedule that everyone hates!

There are rumors that a recall is in the works for some of the members. My friend's mom was fired from her job. She was fired right before Christmas because the assistant superintendent of the school district called her employer and complained that she was posting complaints about the school board on social media. The mom was fired the next day, and she is now suing in federal court.

I pity the fool who ever tries to pull that crap on my mom. She'll eat them for lunch.

It's hard to believe last year at this time I was thinking about running for homecoming court. This year, we're still having issues with the RONA and there won't even *be* a homecoming.

However, students are pretty creative! A bunch of my friends are going to get together and have their own homecoming. A couple different families are having a small "bubble" of friends hang out together—a bubble is where you've got friends that you continue to see and have them be part of your extended family. Some of my friends are going out for a nice dinner or having it catered in their houses. People are decorating their homes and backyards to have parties.

People also organize drive-by birthday parties and open houses. My mom has a nurse friend, Linda, who survived the RONA. She was in two different hospitals, on a vent a bunch of different times, and was finally released to go home. I went with my mom for a drive-by welcome home party. Linda sat in her wheelchair just outside her garage and people dropped off cards, gifts, plants, and even balloons.

There's even RONA weddings in backyards. Our neighbors had one. We were driving to our local grocery store when we saw a flash of white and a bunch of cars. There was a bride in the backyard just down our street. I'm really glad that I'm not old enough to be getting married. It would really suck to have to limit your wedding guests and get married in your backyard.

A bunch of my older friends waited until July or August to have their graduation parties. Even then, they had smaller parties than they would've had before the RONA. I was invited to some. Basically, they just had nighttime bonfires. By now, Mom and Dad are okay with me hanging out with friends occasionally, but it's still nothing like it was pre-pandemic. School has started, we have to wear masks, and all my teachers can talk about is how they can't wait for a vaccine to come out.

I hope this mess is over with by the time I graduate. I just want life to go back to normal and *for sure* I want a big grad party with lots of friends.

My mom and I got in an argument the other day. I told her, "I will take a vaccine if it will get things back to normal."

Totally wrong thing to say around her. She went a little crazy on me. "Kylie, it's too soon to get this vaccine. They've *never* been successful at creating an mRNA vaccine. I don't want the same thing to happen to you that happened to your brother."

Guess it doesn't matter what I want. Around my mom, you can't have a normal conversation. Just because Mark and my mom both have tons of health problems doesn't mean I have the same ones. But because my brother has horrible allergies—the kind that make you stop breathing—she is super cautious and researches everything. She thinks she's so tolerant, but my mom is a pain in the butt.

I wish she would realize I'm an adult. I have the right to be making an informed decision. I really don't want a vaccine, but if it means I get to see my friends and go back to normal, then sure. I'll do it.

I'm old enough to make my own decision!

Chapter Sixteen
Jen

August 30, 2020—We're going up north over Labor Day, our big family tradition to celebrate my mom's birthday. This year has been mind-blowing. This is the first year in probably ten years the whole family has been together for both Fourth of July and Labor Day weekend.

And Mom *still* hasn't apologized or even mentioned how she told Kylie to keep a secret from me.

ONE OF MY FAVORITE THINGS since I was a little kid has been singing songs around the campfire. Ben plays the harmonica and Clint plays the guitar. Each year, my brother comes to Labor Day weekend, and he always teaches us a super long, super funny song. He has a hysterical sense of humor. Sometimes the words are a little bit raunchy, but that just makes it funnier.

Usually, our kids' school year starts immediately after Labor Day. This year, we start on September 1. A lot of families are really upset about it, and our kids are pissed. They don't understand why they have to go to school *before* Labor Day. They're super afraid it will mess with our family tradition of going to the lake house.

We decide we're not canceling Labor Day. We'll bring their books, get their sign-in information, and figure they might as well do school up north. The lake house has enough rooms they can have some privacy.

All we need is a hotspot in case the internet doesn't work. If nothing else, because of COVID, we've learned we can do school online anywhere.

Ben has two job offers in hand and is hoping for a third, so we're expecting he will start a new job the week after Labor Day. This news is making it much easier to plan and anticipate a family getaway over Labor Day weekend.

Labor Day weekend has been more relaxing than I anticipated. It was a good call to have the kids do online school at the lake house. But I have the most surreal experience this evening, our last night before going home. It's so bizarre and out there, it's almost like the expression, "This will happen when pigs fly."

Ben and the kids are in bed. I'm wide awake and decide to watch a little TV. I just settle into my favorite chair when my mom and dad enter the room and join me. Dad looks pretty intense, and he absolutely shocks me with his words.

"Jenni, your mom and I want to make sure you know how very proud we are of you. You are a strong, independent woman and an incredible mom. You have done amazing things with your children. Mark is doing so well, and it's because of the hard work that you and Ben have put forth."

I'm stunned. My dad has never told me this before. I have tears in my eyes. I can see my mom sitting there, silently nodding her head.

Before I can respond, Kylie comes charging in. She is stopping off for her goodnight hug. It breaks the mood, and my parents go back to their safe cocoon of watching television.

Kylie hugs me and my parents, and I rise to leave with her. "Thanks, Dad," I say as I give him a big hug and give my mom a side hug. I don't really want to keep playing the game of "everything is all right" with my mom. I find myself falling too easily into old family patterns and pretending things are fine when I'm with my parents.

Ben is asleep, so I rush into the room, trying to be quiet, but bursting with news of what just happened. He is a bit groggy as he starts awake. "What's wrong, what's the matter?" he asks in a blurred voice, looking at me through half-closed eyes. "Jen, is everything okay?" He partially raises his head off the pillow.

The words come rushing out of my mouth. "Ben, you won't believe what just happened."

I tell him what my dad said, and Ben wakes up enough to hear what I have to say. He pats me on the back and says, "Honey, that's nice. Can we talk about it in the morning?"

"Sure! I just had to tell you this because it's so amazing and so unreal! Ben, do you realize my parents have *never* told me they are proud of me? They've never told me I've done a good job and they are impressed with anything, absolutely *never*."

Ben has drifted back to sleep. I find myself wishing he would stay up past ten o'clock and enjoy life a little. I'm wide awake and want to talk. Mindful of Ben's headache, I decide to sit quietly and talk to God. God is always there and He will listen to me.

My husband and I have different sleeping patterns. He gets up at the crack of dawn. I'm just the opposite. In fact, I seem to really get into my groove at three o'clock in the afternoon and can go until one or two in the morning with no problem. When I was younger, parties used to begin when it was nine or ten o'clock, Ben's bedtime. I find myself thinking for the millionth time, *It's a good thing we didn't meet until well after college. There's no way we would've lasted more than a minute.*

My senior year in high school, I dated a freshman in college. He was a nice boy, but he was already talking about marriage. We broke up, and I gave a huge sigh of relief. I dodged that bullet.

Getting married at nineteen like my mom was not on my bucket list. My mom got married super young, and I didn't want to be like her. I vowed to experience life. Even as a high school student, I knew I wanted to go to college and travel and explore and have adventures.

It took some failed relationships before I was able to open my eyes and really determine what was important in a relationship. Before Ben, I dated a lot of "bad boys." The guys were typically good looking, had money, and thought they were "all that." I was addicted to the adrenalin rush of new relationships, and a part of me wanted to be a bad girl.

There was one problem. I *wasn't* a bad girl. I didn't look like one and couldn't quite pull it off.

I still remember when my friend told me that I was the type he would bring home to his mom. Bill was a good friend, more like a brother than a colleague. He was one of the top sales guys in our automotive group, and the kind of guy who dated five different girls at the same time, never quite settling down to just one girlfriend. We would have serious talks where he told me what guys were really looking for.

My friends all suspected that Bill had a thing for me, but I assured them this was not the case. Bill told me I was the sister he'd never had. And I felt like he was the big brother I'd always wanted.

I remember the time he asked me a series of questions until he was ready to ask the big one. "Jen," he said, "how do I have fun with a bad girl and keep a good girl interested?"

Seriously? I was pissed! No matter how hard I tried, I was doomed to be seen as a good girl.

Bill came to me a year or so after this conversation. I was twenty-six and a half, and Bill was thirty-eight and feeling like it was time to stop being the single bachelor around town. He said, "Well, Jen, I've decided it's time for me to get married. I'm going to marry Tina."

We had a very serious talk, and he assured me that Tina was "the one" for him. I'm not ashamed to admit it—a bunch of us had a pool going to see if he would actually marry her. Bill had been engaged three times previously and had not made it to the alter. Much to my surprise, he got married and I lost that bet. Shortly after, he transferred to our Chicago office and I met Ben.

Ben is the nice, slightly geeky guy I never thought I would date. He is quieter than I am, and he would classify himself as an ambivert. He's a person who needs time alone to recharge, the introvert side, but he's also game for a party and can be quite outgoing as well. We're good together and bring out the best in each other.

Ben and I have a lot of friends in common and became really good friends before we began dating. Once we started dating, it was quick. Within ten months of our first date, we were married.

The weird part of Bill and my friendship is Bill didn't actually meet Ben until three months after Ben and I were engaged. Bill was very concerned that I was getting married to someone he didn't know. I kept reassuring him. But, like most brothers—aka very good friends—he felt like he needed to see for himself.

Bill came into town, we met for lunch, and had a fun time with lots of spirited conversation. Bill, the prankster, acted like a dad by asking Ben, "So, are you able to handle our Jen? You know she has a pretty strong side to her!"

Ben nodded. "Absolutely," he said. The conversation went on for another two hours.

Bill phoned me a few hours later. He was effusive in his praise. "Ben is one of the nicest people I've ever met. You did good, girl!"

Ben and I still get Christmas cards from Bill and Margie, his second wife. Long story, but Tina wasn't the nice girl Bill thought she was, and they divorced. He's now remarried, and at the age of almost sixty, he has teenagers just like us. They live in Colorado and we haven't seen them in a while. Hopefully, we'll head out to visit them in the next year or so.

It's funny how friends become like family. My friends are encouraging and full of more praise than my actual blood. I know if I had a crystal ball and could look into it, I would likely discover my dad is the person behind the "we're proud of you" speech.

We make it through the rest of the weekend. The kids are now officially home doing online school. In the second week, Kylie shares an absolutely hysterical story at dinner. Her history teacher, Mr. Walters, was having difficulty with the internet. He thought he had the class on mute as he screamed repeatedly at his computer, "Mother trucker, mother trucker… work, you mother trucking computer!" Only he wasn't saying the word "trucker."

Kylie said the kids were typing back and forth privately in the chat and wondering if they should tell him he wasn't on mute. The next day he came into class and, with a red face, apologized for yelling and swearing online.

In the realm of exciting, amazing, wonderful things, Ben also started his new job this week. But suddenly, with Ben working for a new company, life is ten times as hard as before. He has a steep learning curve, so even though he's working from home, he's not available to help with school tech glitches unless they happen at noon during lunch. And trust me, it's rare for issues to happen between noon and lunch! The kids have internet connection issues and sometimes get into their teacher's online room with no issue, only to be thrown out.

Then I hear the scream. "Mom, Mom, I need your help!"

Daily, I run from room to room. As soon as I'm finished helping one kid, it's time to help another. I can't get a break, and they are frustrated, sometimes crying or yelling or melting down.

To top it off, my old boss has been calling me, wanting to know if I'll come back. Yes, I'd like to go back to work, but I'm feeling so much pressure, it's like I'm going to explode. I have to keep it together and not get too frustrated with the kids. I honestly don't know how Ben and I can both work from home with the kids doing online school.

I don't dare say a word to my parents or I will get the same old crap. Why don't you go back to work? Why don't you do this? Why don't you do that? Why don't, why don't, why don't? They have no clue.

After Ben's been working for two whole weeks, I receive a call from my dad. I'm a bit shocked. Dad is slightly hard of hearing. If my dad is placing the call, it has to be important.

He gets right to the point. "Jenni, your brother Clint and I are going to Myrtle Beach for golfing in October. I'm calling to see if you can come and stay with your mom for the week we're gone."

My mom has definitely been experiencing some mental health issues, and I understand my dad is concerned about leaving her alone. The last thing we need is for Mom to go off the deep end again. But I'm stymied. This doesn't sound like a request. *You will come and do this,* echoes beneath his words. I know he fully believes my acceptance is just a formality. I want to help, but I'm seriously overloaded with the kids.

"Dad, it's going to be difficult. What about Mom coming here and staying with us? We've got a lot going on right now."

I hear the sneer in his voice. "You always have so much going on. Your mom hasn't been feeling well, and this is the only time Clint can get away. It's better if you come here. Besides, you're not working right now..."

I wince as I take a deep breath. "Dad, I can't come for the whole week. I will talk to Ben and figure schedules out, but the kids are in school. I'm probably only able to come on Friday and leave on Saturday."

"No, Jenni, that won't work. Your mom has really been on edge. It's taken quite a bit for her to get back, and I don't think it's a good idea for her to go to your house. We need you to come here."

There it is, the summons. My dad is asking for a favor, but demanding at the same time. I'm still upset with my mom and can't imagine spending a whole week with her, pretending everything is fine. Given my current state of mind, I won't be able to last for more than one day before we have a blow up.

I try again, "Mom staying with us will make life a lot easier. The kids are in soccer and lacrosse league. Ben just started his new job. Life is really crazy."

I hear my mom in the background. "Ben can take care of those kids. She needs some time off."

There's a scuffling sound and my mom comes on the line. "Jenni, if you come and stay with me, I'll be able to treat you to a spa day. We can get a pedicure and manicure and go out to lunch."

I close my eyes and silently count to ten. A spa day, her answer to everything. My husband and children need me. My mom has never been available for me, and now she is expecting me to be completely available for her. I can feel my face grow hot.

My mom continues to scold me. "Now, your dad and brother go every year, and I don't want to be a burden on them. I'm just not comfortable being alone. Why don't you bring the kids? You can bring the kids, and we'll order takeout every night. They can do their schooling from my house. Then Ben doesn't have to worry about them. It's only for a week. "

Again, I try to explain, but it's like my words are getting lost in the wind. I let out a big sigh. "You need to understand my husband just started a new job. He hasn't even been there a month. The kids have to be online in school, and you do not have good connectivity at your house. They need my help and Ben's at night because Ben can't help them when he's working. We can't afford for him to lose this job."

I'm once again stuck in the middle. My parents' solution doesn't work for us. They don't have good internet, and I can't leave the kids and Ben to fend for themselves right now. And my parents absolutely refuse to have my mom stay with us.

Argh! I've heard the term "sandwich generation" and finally understand what it means. I'm caught between my family's needs and my parents'.

I know Mom doesn't like to drive. In fact, she seldom does. Her car is four years old and only has 3,200 miles on it. Dad pretty much always takes her where she needs to go, and she sits in the passenger seat, complaining and moaning and telling him how to drive.

Almost like he's reading my mind, Dad says, "Did you know your mom isn't really comfortable driving? I don't want to put her in that position."

Now it's her turn to weigh in. "Why don't you have Kylie come and stay with me?"

The conversation isn't going anywhere, so I take the easy way out. "I will talk to Ben and get back to you."

It's two o'clock and my husband still has another two and a half hours of work, but I don't want to wait until dinner to talk to him. His office is on the right side of the basement. I walk to the bottom of the staircase and kind of stage whisper, "Ben?"

A frustrated voice yells back, "Yes, I'm on a call. I just muted it. Can it wait?"

"Sure. Sorry, honey. We'll talk later."

After dinner and after we finish helping the kids with their homework, we sit down to relax over a plate of snacks and a glass of wine. After a couple sips of chardonnay, Ben looks at me and says, "Okay, out with it. What's going on?"

I'm so incredibly grateful for my husband. He is supportive and an amazing father. I really lucked out with this guy! I don't know how I would've gotten through the last ten years without him. We've had our hands full on our autism journey with Mark. Along the way, I've met way too many moms who ended up doing everything on their own or divorced. Thankfully, Ben has been incredibly invested and has always had my back.

I take another drink of my wine to fortify myself. "I got a call from Mom and Dad today."

"Is everything okay?"

"Depends on how you define *okay*."

Ben looks at me and smiles. "It seems like a pretty easy answer."

"You're right. Dad wants me to come and stay with Mom for a week while he and Clint go golfing. The problem is they're not taking no for an answer. When I said, 'Why don't you ask Sara?' her response was, 'Sara is busy.' I almost came unglued. It's like they have absolutely no respect for me. They expect me to drop everything."

The more I think about it, why doesn't my sister Lori come from California and do one of her beauty weekends? Mom is trying to talk me into it, but I'm the last person in the world who wants one. I'm an active sports girl. I wear sweats and yoga pants all the time. A beauty weekend doesn't sound the least bit relaxing to me.

Ben is generally very easy-going, but not this time. "Do you need me to call them? Help them understand I just started a new job, and you need to be accessible here for the kids. I can't stop what I'm doing to deal with meltdowns every day."

"I know you can't. And no, they don't understand. They aren't willing to compromise." I pause and take another drink of my wine, mulling through our options. "Let's look at the dates and figure this out. Maybe mom can get one of her friends to come and stay with her, and I could come for part of the weekend."

I phone my mom the next morning after I've got the kids started for their school day. She's still unwilling to budge and wants me to come to her house. She keeps talking about how it will be good for me to relax. I seriously just want to scream.

I bite my tongue and say, "Mom, I want to help you, but you need to meet me halfway. I can't be as accessible and available as you want me to be right now."

"Jenni, I keep trying to tell you. I see that you're overwhelmed and stressed. I see it and I'm trying to help. Take a few days. Even if you can't come the whole week, you can get away to relax."

"Mom, please stop."

She responds, "I don't ask a lot—I'm just asking if you can come and spend some time with me. You can relax and get away from your family. I know they are stressing you out."

I swallow again. Right now, this exact moment, it's not my family stressing me out. "Mom, I can come on Friday, but I have to leave midday Saturday. I need to help Jill get ready for a birthday party."

"What time will you be here on Friday? I will see if one of my friends can come earlier in the week."

"I should be at your house around twelve-thirty or maybe even one o'clock, depending on how things go with the kid's online classes."

"Why don't they skip school on Friday?"

"Mom, that's really not an option."

She responds, "The afternoon is too late. Why can't Ben work with the kids? I need you here. If my friend comes, she has to leave on Friday morning. Your dad doesn't want me to be alone."

"Mom, I want to help you, but I've got multiple balls I'm juggling. I have to help the kids with their online school, and I will need to leave by three on Saturday for Jill. The party is a big deal and she wants my help getting ready."

I can almost see my mom roll her eyes through the phone. "Jill will be fine. I need you here. I don't understand why you can't stay through Sunday. That way, my friend will only have to stay five days with me." Before I can say another word, Mom curtly states, "I'll see what I can do." The phone clicks as the line goes dead.

I'm not sure, but it kind of feels like I've just been hung up on.

A few hours later, I receive a text from Mom. **My friend Susie will come the entire week. I don't need you this time. I'll need you for the boys' next golf getaway.**

This is what the sandwich generation feels like. Wanting to help while you're caught between two generations of your family. Fortunately, I've been saved by the bell. Mom is all set and doesn't need me now. I'll just wait for the next call.

Clint phones me to commiserate and tells me I should write our parents a letter and explain what I'm dealing with. They don't fully understand I'm already stretched so thin, and he comes up with a couple ideas. He reinforces the importance of getting Mom to come to our house. Heck, with Kylie driving, she could even go pick up Mom.

"Jen, I'm proud of you," Clint says. "Don't let them railroad you. I wish there was more I could do to help."

"Hey, you're golfing with Dad. You're helping him to get some quality downtime, doing something he loves to do."

I can almost see Clint's smile through the phone as he laughs. His parting words are, "Right, but Mom and Dad need to understand they can't expect you to drop everything and be at their beck and call. Seriously, write them a note and let them know you'd like to help them, but you need them to help you too."

Now, it's my turn to roll my eyes. "Seriously! You do know our parents, right?"

Chapter Seventeen
Patti

September 25, 2020—For the love of all that's good! I don't ask for much. I just expect when I need a favor or my children to help me, they will show up. I deserve more respect than what I'm getting. I know my Jenni is tired. That poor girl is always, always taking care of that husband of hers and her three kids. How can they learn to be independent if Jenni is doing everything for them? At what point will she allow those kids to grow up and be on their own?

I KNOW THIS MIGHT SOUND weird because my Jenni has a life. She has her children, she has her husband, and she has done wonders, absolute wonders, with getting her son better. What I don't get is why am I always last on her list?

I call. I ask for help. And it's like crickets. She doesn't care about anyone but her three kids and her husband. What about her dad and I? Specifically, what about me? I'm her mother. It should be enough for her to say, "Let me know what you need, Mom. I'll be there."

For the love of God, I went through two days of labor to give that child life! She's always been the one who made her own plans and did whatever the heck she wanted to do. It makes me angry. She has always been difficult. She's been a pain in the rear since she was a baby.

I have a good plan in place. The plan is for Jenni to get away for a few days, bring some of her favorite mysteries and thrillers, and spend time at our home in Grand Blanc. We'll go for walks and get some beauty treatments. We could go out for lunch a few times and sit back and relax. I'm paying for everything. All she has to do is come and see me. If Lori lived in town, she'd be right over.

I don't know why Jenni doesn't understand. It's really hard for me to ask for help. But every time I ask for a little smidgen of her time, she tells me no. She's either too busy or she's working with the kids or the kids are in school or Ben has a new job... cry me a river. She always has a reason to stay away.

I understand that she's busy. It's just hard to hear she doesn't want to spend time with me. I'm so far down the list in terms of priorities for my daughter that I'm not even on the same page.

Instead, it's like she's a sassy sixteen-year-old again. She is determined to do whatever the heck she wants. I feel like we keep having the same conversation again and again and again. It's like we're somehow stuck in this dance. A dance that never seems to end.

Jenni doesn't understand. I really need her help. I'm not getting any younger, and I would like to have a better relationship with my daughter. Improving our relationship is impossible if she won't come to our house. I'm tired of talking about superficial things that don't make a difference or mean anything. I could honestly care less about all the projects she is working on for the kids. What about her? What about *her* hopes and dreams? What happened to my feisty daughter who was going to take on the world?

I want to have an authentic relationship with all of my children. I'm the first to admit that I've led a preoccupied and busy life. Whenever I look in the mirror, I see the mistakes of my past. Seeing the new wrinkles and gray hairs popping up have me realizing I'm not getting any younger. If I'm really truthful, I'm terrified of going back to the bad place. I'm afraid that if Joe leaves me alone, I'll backslide, and all the bad stuff will come back. I can't go through it again. It's taken a lot to get to this point, and seriously, therapy has been kicking my rear. I shouldn't have to tell Jenni that I'm scared to be alone. That I'm terrified the depression will return.

Jenni told me, "Mom why don't you come to our house? That will work perfectly for us."

Yeah, it works perfectly for her but what about me? I would like to spend some time alone with my daughter. I want to stay in my home. Is it really too much to ask? I spent my whole life taking care of my children, and now, when I ask for a favor, when I sweeten the offer and try to make it nice for Jenni, she's not interested. I'm willing to take her out and spend money on her but my daughter won't let me spoil her.

I've had more time to be introspective. I'm not liking what I'm finding, and as much as I want to change things, it takes two people to change. I can't improve the relationship with my daughter if she won't let me.

I know that Joe's afraid to leave me alone. He's afraid he may come home and I might check out again, or I might do something to myself. I'm not a person who will ever intentionally hurt myself. That worry is mute. We have been through so much over the years. I don't want to worry him, but I'm a little afraid the depression will return as well.

The virus has been hard on everyone. Joe has been especially wonderful to me, taking care of me when I was at my worst. He's thinking about his golf trip. He wants to get out and start hitting those irons and swinging the clubs. But what about me?

I've gone golfing a few times, but it's not my cup of tea, as they say. Joe tried to show me. He said I developed a decent swing. It's not something I enjoy. I would much rather go to the beach and walk on the sand. The feel of sand beneath my feet and between my toes is delicious. There's nothing better than a good walk on the beach, and it doesn't matter what the weather is like.

After my disastrous conversation with Jenni, I called my friend Susie. Susie's husband passed away two years ago and she's a very close friend. She's told me anytime I need company, here or in Florida, just call her. She's up for it.

When we were younger, Susie was my wild friend. I say this with laughter, because everyone has a wild friend. And everyone needs to have a Susie in their life.

I remember when we had just become friends. We were both tiny and petite, but that's where the similarities ended. I dressed in a navy blue or black sheath dress with a jacket over the dress and pushed up the sleeves for easy, unrestricted movement. I swear, when I retired, I had a whole wall of just blue and black suits. My wonderful husband Joe gave me a pearl necklace for my wedding gift, and I wore it nearly every day with pearl earrings to complete the look.

I was working as the administrative assistant for a director of our company when the president, Mr. Stone, approached me. I remember him saying very sincerely, "I need to have a talk with you."

I was terrified I was going to be fired. It seemed like whenever an executive called you into the office, it was not for a good reason. But Mr. Stone had noticed that Susie and I were friends. He sat down and said, "Patricia, I need to ask you a few questions." The first question was, "I've noticed that you appear to be good friends with Susan, is that correct?"

I nervously nodded my head in agreement. "I have lunch with Susie quite frequently. Is there a problem, Mr. Stone?" As I'd called my friend Susan by her nickname, Susie, I gulped. Shoot, I should've maybe called her Susan? I was so nervous I could hardly think straight.

"No, there isn't a problem. I wanted to verify you and Susan were friends before I went further." He shrewdly looked at me. "You dress quite conservatively and appropriately for the office. I've noticed.... let's just say Susan has a tendency to wear more flamboyant outfits to work."

I nodded. Flamboyant was an understatement. Today, she had on a black leather miniskirt with a bright fuchsia silk blouse, fishnet stockings, and her orange and black hair sticking straight up in multiple directions. She also wore those horrible toe-crushing shoes with four-inch spike heels, while I wore sensible pumps. Her hair color changed almost weekly. Blonde, then red, then black, back to blonde, and then a medium brown. Sometimes she had multiple colors at the same time. I found myself occasionally wondering what her true hair color was or if she even knew her natural color.

"So, Patricia—or do you prefer Patti?" he asked.

"Patti is fine, sir."

"Patti, you are a young woman who I believe has strong leadership potential. I would appreciate your discretion with Susan. It's a very uncomfortable conversation for me, an old codger, to have with her," he said and paused. "A bit on the irregular side. But I believe if you were to mentor her, she could be one of our top assistants and potentially be moved into the C suite. I'd like you to think about it."

He seemed to stare off into space. "Susie is the daughter of my late brother. I would greatly appreciate your help. This is a difficult subject and I don't want to embarrass her, so if there's a way you can do this circumspectly, I would be most appreciative."

Shortly after our conversation, I convinced Susie to go on a shopping trip. To this day, I laugh when I think about it. Even though Susie and I were good friends, shopping for a business suit for her was not easy. In fact, it was probably one of my more difficult assignments during my tenure at Stone Corporation. Everything I showed her was too long, too frumpy, too black, or too blue. We ended up buying nothing that day. She preferred her current look of miniskirts and wild hairdos.

Susie has always been a beautiful woman. She met her first two husbands at Stone Corporation, the second one a keeper. His name was Ed Galen. Ed was from our accounting group, and they were complete opposites. How they ever got together I will never know. They had thirty-four wonderful years before he died of a sudden heart attack.

Ed was quiet but able to handle my wild friend. I don't use the word "handle" in a bad way, but I mean he was able to curb her impulsivity.

She wanted to please Ed, so once they got together, she stopped showing leg and cleavage at work. She loved her husband, and he adored her. They were a good match.

Susie's always been someone who understood me. I wasn't surprised when I phoned Susie today and asked if she could come and spend some time with me, and she instantly said, "No problem, my friend. You just tell me when you need me and for how long. I'll be there."

My boys leave in the middle of October for their weeklong trip to Myrtle Beach. It's an annual vacation that Clint and Joe have been taking since Clint was a sophomore in college. Joe is over the moon proud to have a son who is a scratch golfer. Clint was on his high school team, and college as well. He could've gone pro but decided to just keep it as a hobby.

My two guys have always tried to get the girls in the family interested in golf. Lori dabbled in it briefly, and Jenni, oh my goodness, she was hysterical. Jenni had the best swing Joe said he's ever seen, absolutely perfect. I remember the first time she went on an outing with her dad. Joe had taught her, and she marched right up to the tee and lined herself up perfectly. When she swung at the ball, it went backwards and nearly hit another player.

Jenni has her dad's sense of humor and was nearly on the floor, she was laughing so hard. Normally, Joe would laugh with her, but since she almost hit one of his biggest customers, he wasn't laughing. Once Jenni saw how angry her father was, she became serious and ended up golfing one of her best games. She finished eleven under par. This young lady, who could care less about golfing, not only won the women's trophy, she also beat her dad's score.

It was the first and last tournament she entered. Through the years, Joe has attempted to get her to play golf with him again. Initially, we heard, "I don't want to do it. I'm not gonna." And, of course, the snarky teenage response: "You can't make me."

Joe tried repeatedly to get her to love the game. He would beg her to experience it with him again, saying, "Jenni, you've got the best swing I've ever seen. It's a crime for you to quit." But our Jenni is stubborn, and she hasn't golfed since.

It's sad. I sat on the sidelines and tried to explain to Joe what was happening, but he would have none of it. His girl was a natural and he wanted her to play. It's really too bad. Joe isn't very good at teaching or training. He isn't patient, and once Jenni proved she was a better golfer, he evolved into super coach. Super coach wanted a champion. Jenni wanted a dad, but he wasn't interested or willing to let his girl just enjoy the sport.

Other than the golfing, Joe and Jenni get along quite well. She's always been a bit of a daddy's girl, while Lori was more a mommy's girl. Clint was kind of split between Joe and me.

It's been too long since Susie and I have gotten together. Susie will be here shortly, and I'll have the opportunity to talk with someone who knows me very well. Someone I can unburden myself to.

Susie and I are both seventy-four years old. Susie and Ed both wanted children but were unable to get pregnant. They talked about adoption but decided to travel and have fun, focusing on being the best aunt and uncle they could be to their family and friends' children. Our kids benefited quite a bit. Auntie Susie is the fun, crazy aunt who everyone loves.

Just like everyone loved my dear friend Lisa, who passed away at a young age. Losing Lisa before we were fifty was devastating. There's not a day goes by that I don't think about her. There have been so many times through the years that something has happened and I've wanted to talk to Lisa. I miss her.

Susie stepped into the wide chasm that was created. She helped to heal the cavern of hurt caused by losing my best friend in the whole world.

Now, Susie walks into our house like she owns it, no surprise. It's been a while since I've seen her, but she is always a person who owns the room when she enters. Susie immediately gives me a hug, and we both begin to jabber and catch up. She stopped at her favorite little market and picked up several little delicacies for us to sample. We have everything from my favorite wine—I love me some pinot grigio—to wonderful, delicate, homemade croissants. She also brought some organic homemade peanut butter and a whole box filled with gorgeous finger desserts.

"I have the water boiling in case you want tea, and I also have coffee ready."

"Nope, I'm feeling like a glass of pinot. Where's your bottle opener?" she asks. Susie rummages in the kitchen drawers, finding it just as I am about to open my mouth and point her in the right direction.

"Got it!" she exclaims as she holds up the bottle opener. "Now, let's get this party started."

We talk for the next two hours, eating and drinking and catching up. Susie and I can be apart for a year or more and then pick up right where we left off.

At about the two-hour mark, Susie suddenly stops and gives me a questioning look. "Okay, spill it. What's going on with you?" she asks. "There's *something* going on. What's wrong?"

Just like that, she has seen through the fake face I am wearing and realizes something is wrong. My eyes fill with tears. Having a friend that knows me as deeply and as well as her is really affirming.

I tell her about my big screwup with Jenni and with Kylie. I wring my hands as I explain, "The last thing I wanted was to cause more tension between me and my daughter. I don't know what to do or how I'm going to fix this."

Susie nods her head with a slight smile on her face. She reaches out and gives me a quick hug. "Honey, usually I say if it ain't broke, don't fix it. But you don't have a choice. You messed up and you've got to talk to Jenni. And you also need to apologize to Kylie for putting her in the middle. "

"I know," I say. "I know I've got to fix it. And I am feeling like such a coward because I don't know how to do it."

Susie throws her head back and laughs. She laughs so hard and with such contagion that I find myself laughing as well. And she reminds me, "Girl, do you remember the time you had to sit me down and tell me to start dressing 'like a frumpy old lady' because old man Stone asked you to help me?"

"Yes," I say. I must have a perplexed look on my face. "I don't really understand what that has to do with this situation."

"Course you don't," she says as she continues with peals of laughter.

At the expression on my face, Susie stops laughing and puts her hands on my knees. "You need to listen to me. You listen really good. I know exactly what you should do." She leans in as she says, "My friend, *you* know exactly what to do as well."

She is right. I *do* know. It takes an old friend to hold up the mirror and shine the light of truth in my face. Only really good friends are able to hold that mirror up and tell you in a loving, caring way, "This is what you need to do."

Just as I once shone that mirror in Susie's face, she is gleefully shining the same mirror back in mine. The irony is not lost on me, and the mirror is shining a little too brightly into my eyes. I can't say I like it too much.

Susie and I don't see each other as often as we'd like. But we talk at least once a week. If I happen to miss our weekly call, she calls within twenty-four hours to check up on me. She always starts the conversation with, "Hi, friend."

I'm about as conservative as you can get. I'm a staunch Republican. I don't love our current President Trump, but I can't see myself ever voting Democrat. And Susie is so far left that she will barely make a right-hand turn.

I wish more of my conservative friends had a friend like Susie. She always has my back and is closer to me than most sisters. I wasn't blessed to have siblings, so God gave me Lisa first, and then He decided He needed her in Heaven. I laugh as I say that because Lisa would be the first to say, "I'm no angel." But saying God needed her in Heaven is the only way I can process the fact she has been gone for so many years. And then He gave me Susie.

I'm going down memory lane thinking of all of my old friends. The ones still here and the lost ones, the ones I've been missing.

"Susie, I'm not playing," I tell her. "I'm serious. I absolutely need your help and I need some guidance here because I don't know what to say to Jenni. I feel like I have screwed things up so badly that Jenni and I will never get past this. Every time I see her, I act like a fool. I get snarky, say something stupid. I think about the only thing to do is get some cards and write myself a note describing what I can and can't say. But I tend to focus on when I *can't* say. Those are the words that end up coming out of my mouth."

More laughter from Susie. "Girl, you have got to know… the reason why you and Jenni have such a problem is because you two are so much alike."

"We're so much alike?"

Susie raises her eyebrows and chuckles. I find myself instantly laughing as well. Darn it, but I know she is right. My Jenni is stubborn. She's independent. She's successful. She is everything I want to be and more, and she is everything I *have* been and more.

I look at Susie. "Okay, mea culpa, mea culpa. I guess I should've just kept the secret to myself because I hurt my daughter when I told Kylie before I told her."

At this point, Susie's eyebrows come up. "Girl, did you just say what I think you said?"

"What do you mean?"

"Patti, it sounds like you don't fully understand *why* Jenni and Kylie are so upset with you."

I stutter slightly, "Of course I get it. My daughter is upset because I told Kylie first and asked her to wait to tell her mom."

Susie lightly bangs her palm against her head and shouts, "No! That's part of it, but that's not why she's so hurt!" She continues, "Patti, I love you, you know that. But there are times when you can be really thick. Girl—Jenni lost her baby to a miscarriage. Instead of talking about your experience, you shut her out in the cold. You told *everyone* but her. Jenni is devastated because when she needed you the most, you kept valuable information from her that would've helped her heal. Don't you realize that you froze her out?"

Susie is right. I can be obtuse. And I'm kind of angry with her. I had good reasons not to tell Jenni about my miscarriages. It's just messed up how everything came out the way it did. Call me mean, call me dense, but I still think if I could take it back, I would.

Susie continues, "Then when you decided to tell her, you told her teenage daughter first. Patti, I've never had kids. But seriously, if my mom did that to me, I would be hurt and pissed out of my mind. You're lucky she's even talking to you!"

I know my friend is right. I need to pull the Band-Aid off and just get this done. I'm going to talk to my daughter the next time I see her. Probably. Maybe.

Well, I am already waffling… but I am going to try.

Susie surprises me when she pulls out her phone and says, "Did you know your cell phone has a notes section?"

"No, I didn't know," I exclaim.

"Patti—we're putting talking points in the notes section so you have them available the next time you see Jenni."

We don't spend the entire week working on my talking points, just touching them up an hour or so every day. Having Susie to talk with, go out to dinner, and share my pinot grigio is delightful. It is just what I need—my friend helping me see who I am, what I want, and how I am going to get there.

It's not going to be easy. It's going to be one of the more difficult things I've ever done in my life. I don't want to do it, and I know I need to work up to it. But I know, for the sake of my daughter, for our future relationship and happiness, I need to have this conversation with her.

I've basically got about half a year to figure it out. I promise Susie I will do it, and I know this means I have six months—or watch out, because who knows what Susie will do? I wouldn't be surprised if she tries to pull something like locking us in a room with *no* bathroom or food until we talk it out.

I guess I need to make this happen. First, talk with Jenni and explain myself. Then, talk with Kylie and apologize. This time, I need to do it in the right order.

I can't tell you how thankful I am to have a friend like Susie who isn't afraid to tell me what she's thinking, who isn't afraid to speak the truth in a loving way. She lets me know she'll always care for me, but she just wants to light a fire under me to get me moving. And she's right, I need to do it.

The truth is… I don't exactly like myself at the moment. I know I hurt my child and my granddaughter. And I need to fix it.

Chapter Eighteen
Kylie

November 1, 2020—It's November! We've been having mock elections in my government class. It's been really fun debating with my friends. I'm not old enough to vote in this election, but I'm definitely thinking about the candidates. I keep flip-flopping on who would get my vote. Our family is split when it comes to Democrats and Republicans. For me, it's super interesting to watch the two sides get into political discussions.

I FIND IT ESPECIALLY FUNNY when certain family members have an opinion, a strong opinion, they can't back up. Thanks to my parents, especially my dad, I know how to defend my opinion. Each summer, starting in elementary school, we read a news article and then talked about what we learned at the dinner table.

In case you haven't guessed, my dad loves to debate. He's a person who speaks with conviction and researches his facts. My sister, brother, and I are all pretty good debaters, but we learned the hard way. Thanks to Dad, I've almost single-handedly won some important debates in my language arts class.

My earliest chance to argue for something important involved basic communication. *All* of my friends had a cell phone. I was literally the last kid in the eighth grade to get one. Even the really weird girl on my bus had one. It wasn't fair. I decided to put together a presentation showing my parents I was responsible and needed a phone.

I told them if I had a phone, they could get in touch with me more easily, put GPS on my phone, and *always* know where I was. But, most importantly, I needed it for socialization and communication. I was being left out of group chats with my friends because I didn't have a cell. Being the last kid in the eighth grade to get one was branding me as weird. I didn't think my parents wanted me to be picked on for not having a phone.

My parents were impressed with my points and agreed. I got a phone in September of eighth grade, but had to wait for social media until the beginning of ninth. Before getting those apps, our parents made us listen to a local presentation about keeping safe on the internet. Jill, Mark, and I were all pissed, but our parents said, "No Snapchat until you go to the presentation with us."

Seriously! Who does this to their kids?

The RONA happened right after my sixteenth birthday and going out on an actual date has been pretty much impossible. I pity the first guy I bring home. He has to stand up to my dad's questions and show he's not afraid. Hopefully, he'll be able to have a conversation that involves defending his opinion, otherwise it won't go well.

For now, I've been hanging out with some friends online and playing video games. Nothing has really progressed to the point of dating. I really wish I weren't the oldest in the family!

My dad is this closet intellectual. He's super smart. You never want to give my dad a wild opinion or make an assumption. You better know your facts because he will nail you to the wall. Dad is all about backing up what you say. If I had a dollar for every time he asked, "Why do you believe that?" or "What makes you think that way?" I'd be rich.

My mom's side of the family is staunchly Republican. I think my grandparents were one of the first people in the United States to get those MAGA hats. You know, "Make America Great Again." They love Donald Trump.

Notice I said "Donald"—I have a hard time calling him president. He doesn't sound like a very nice guy. I hate how he gets on Twitter and makes a fool out of himself. He acts like a little kid, ranting and raving. I think his numbers would be a lot better if he would just shut up and if someone would take away his Twitter account. And the other candidate, Biden, is an ex-vice president. There's a lot of rumors going around that Biden has Alzheimer's or the beginning of dementia. He wants to get rid of gasoline for our cars and force us to buy electric vehicles. I've done enough research to realize that electric cars are not as good for the environment as Biden and his camp are saying. And he also seems to be for stricter gun control. I'm for stricter gun control in terms of making sure kids can't shoot up schools, but think we need to balance that with not taking away people's guns who are legitimate hunters or marksmen.

I'm trying to figure out who my mom is voting for. She's a pretty strong Democrat except for one thing. She gets on a soapbox for medical freedom. She's pretty concerned that once the RONA vaccine comes out, they will try to mandate it. Ever since my brother Mark almost died from a shot, she's become a research queen.

She believes in women having the right to determine if they will continue a pregnancy. She thinks abortion rights should be extended into medical freedom rights, and she is seriously pissed off at the Democratic Party. She will get high on her soapbox and tell other Democrats, "How can you believe in a woman's right to her body, but you don't believe in a person's right to make a decision over what happens to them medically?"

She's super embarrassing. I would not be exaggerating if I told you, pretty much every single time we go somewhere, she finds someone to talk with about vaccines. Another topic my mom is stuck on is friendship. Mom tells me, "It's important to have good friends to talk to."

Yeah, thanks, Mom. Then she somehow finds a way to go into her other concerns. "Kylie, I know you're getting to the age where you'll go to parties and there might be alcohol and drugs there." She tries to play

175

the fun, nice parent. I'm seriously on to her as she says, "I was young once. I want to be sure you have a good group of friends when you go to a party, and you have multiple designated drivers. If you're ever in a position where you don't feel safe, remember just text me an x or a few x's, and I will immediately come and pick you up."

"Sure, Mom," I respond with a smile on my face, but inside I'm thinking, *Whatever*. If I've heard the speech about the x's on my phone once, I've heard it a million times in the last two years. "Mom, I'm not going to do any drugs and mess up my lacrosse."

I don't know how to get this through my mom's head. None of my friends are into heavy partying. I know people who vape and drink or smoke pot, but none of my good friends. I tell her, "I have friends that have my back." And, if I'm lucky, it stops there.

Most of the time, I'm not so lucky. My mom's friend is a therapist who encourages her paranoia. She scares Mom with date rape stories. Even though I keep telling my mom, "None of my friends would ever do anything like that," she tells me about a girl who was in college, walking back from the bar with her friends, and a guy tried to grab her. Or a girl who was given a date rape drug because she put her drink down where people could get it. I think it's been beaten into my head—*when* you go to a party, *never, ever* put your drink down or accept a drink from someone else.

Mom always ends with, "You can't trust *anyone* when it comes to your health and your body. Stay safe and know that your dad and I will *always* come and pick you up."

Mom also has developed this new habit of texting us initials. Her latest was **KSDS**.

I know better, but I bit and texted back, **What does KSDS mean?**

Keep Safe, Drive Safe, she immediately texted back.

What do you say to that except **K** and just drop it?

One of my dad's favorite sayings is, "If you're not a liberal when you're twenty-five, you have no heart. If you're not a conservative by the time you're thirty-five, you have no brain." It really pisses me off when people say things like that.

I'm smart. I figure if you can't learn from both liberals and conservatives and be able to laugh at both, then you've got a problem. I hate it when anyone tries to put me in a box. It's okay if I have a mixture of liberal and conservative opinions. I mean, geez, have you met my parents?

It's the beginning of November and I'm still deciding on who's going to make the best president. I'm not dumb enough to talk to my grandparents. I swear, they bleed Trump. The only one I can safely talk to is my mom.

Mom tells me she's always voted Democrat—other than when Bill and Hillary Clinton ran. She didn't like the Clintons. My mom liked Al Gore, and she was really pissed when he didn't win the election.

I ask my mom who she is voting for.

She looks at me and says, "Kylie, it's a tough decision. I don't really like either candidate. I don't like Trump or his platform or the way he presents himself. I tend to be more of a Democrat."

Here it goes. Now Mom is off to tell me about her *one* issue and how that is what she uses as a basis for her decision for the election.

"Kylie, I have one main issue…"

See, I'm not kidding!

She continues, "…it's medical choice. And Trump is the only candidate that says he doesn't believe in mandating vaccines." Mom pauses. "The future COVID-19 vaccine scares me. I think it's being developed too quickly—"

Blah… blah… blah… I stop listening the first thirty seconds in. Of course, I know where Mom stands. I've only been hearing about it my entire life.

My ears snap back on as I hear my name. "Kylie, I'm just gonna tell you one thing. With our family history of vaccine injury, it would be stupid for you to get this shot until we know more about it."

I've already decided to wait until more information is available on the RONA shot. I know it's new, untested technology, but she really pisses me off by not giving me a choice or letting me make my own decision. The last thing anyone wants is to be dictated to. I'm sixteen years old. I don't think it's too much to ask that my parents treat me like an adult. They challenge us to express our opinion but there's no talking to my mom about the RONA shot. Usually, my mom can be open and talk about the pros and cons of different subjects. But not this. You talk about the RONA shot and she completely shuts down. It's crazy.

I sometimes wonder how my parents got together. Their personalities are completely different. My mom is a Democrat, while my dad's a very conservative Republican. He loves President Ronald Reagan. Mom hates him. They get into loud discussions over their political differences. After their stupid discussions, they always make up. It's really gross to see your parents hugging and kissing in front of you. I mean, geez, go make out somewhere else, just not in front of me.

All you see on the television is how Biden is going to beat Trump. It seems a lot like the last election, when all we heard was how Hillary Clinton was going to beat Donald Trump. Honestly, who cares? I know it's important for people to use their right to vote and to get out there. I'm looking forward to the next presidential election when I'm old enough to vote. And I'm hoping by the next election, we'll have a female president.

It's finally November third. We've been watching the election results and the race looks close. By eleven o'clock, our whole family is tired, so we go to bed. I guess we'll find out who won when we wake up tomorrow morning.

We have to wait for several days to find out who is "officially" elected. Surprise, it's November seventh and Trump will no longer be president. I think he's acting like a baby. Saying that he really won the election... Of course, my grandparents, the major Trumpsters, are convinced the election was stolen from him.

I'm just a kid on the sidelines looking in and wondering how is it possible we could have voting machines that could be reprogrammed. Wondering if there is any truth to the allegations. I guess this is something we won't know for a long time, if ever. Kind of like the mystery of who really shot President Kennedy. Would anyone actually admit if the election were stolen?

I've been thinking about experiences and opinions that define someone. My mom is completely and totally defined by her concern regarding vaccines. Because of my brother, my mom carries a lot of guilt. And she's so afraid of lighting striking twice that she is super, super careful with all of us now. Trust me, unless you have an extra hour in your day or longer, don't get into a discussion about vaccines with my mom.

Mom threw herself into first finding out everything she could about Mark's autism and his immune issues and then worked around the clock to get him better. She's brought him much further than anyone thought possible. My mom is the kind of person who doesn't give up and doesn't take "No" for an answer. If doctors or people tried to tell her to slow down, she basically blew them off and looked for doctors and medical specialists who were in the fight.

It's kind of weird, but Jill and I both got a certain amount of comfort out of seeing the light on late at night in her office. Many times, Mom would be up researching until two or three in the morning and then get up just before seven to get us ready for school. Now that I'm older, I don't know how she did it. And she did it for years. As irritating as my brother is, I've seen how hard my mom worked to help him, and I know if we ever needed it, she'd do the same for me and Jill.

Some nights, I would wake up to use the bathroom and know everything was fine just by the glow of light coming up the stairs through her office door. Sometimes I couldn't sleep, and I'd creep downstairs and enter her office to see how she was doing. I wanted to see her face and know that she loved me. She would stop what she was doing to give me a big hug.

I've been thinking about my mom and Granda. Both of them are focused on one moment in their life that's paralyzed them. It's prevented them from moving forward and being the person they could've been, if not for that critical moment in time. Kind of deep, but I think that kind of sums it up.

I used to think my Granda Patti was the best. Like most kids, I love my mom but can get really irritated with her. It's taken Granda Patti putting me in the middle for me to realize that I need to give my mom a break.

I don't want to be like them. I don't want to have one life event paralyze me to the point that all I can see is that *one thing*. Granda Patti shut herself off by not being available to her family. Conversely, my mom shut herself off from us by working almost around the clock to get Mark better. When I was little, and sometimes even now, I feel like she loves Mark more than she loves me and Jill.

I don't want to be like my mom and basically run away from my destiny because I have a sick kid. My mom has allowed Mark's autism and immune issues to completely change her life.

A few years after Mark's diagnosis, she quit work and stayed home to help him with therapies for his autism and immune system. Our whole family is completely different because of that one decision. My whole life I've heard, "We can't afford it, we can't do it," and on and on… and it's all because Mark got sick and Mom had to quit work.

But Mom always apologizes when she's hurt our feelings or made a mistake. I personally think it's because she's gone her whole life with a mom who can't say, "I'm sorry." From the time we were little, we were encouraged to step up when we did something wrong.

Granda Patti has been a good Granda, but I see how she hurts my mom. It's been almost five months and she still hasn't discussed "the secret" with her. I wonder if she ever will.

Chapter Nineteen
Jen

December 5, 2020—Happy December! One of my favorite holidays is Christmas. I love singing, going to church—I especially love the candlelight services.

But not this year. This year, due to COVID, we're staying home and celebrating on our own. And this year, I'm worried about Kylie's gift. We know what the perfect gift is but it's so expensive. If we can pull it off, it will be amazing!

USUALLY, I'M SUPER ORGANIZED AND have presents wrapped by Thanksgiving. That way, I can absolutely enjoy the Christmas holiday. Right now, I'm feeling overwhelmed and I'm struggling to get basic things done. It's December ninth and I'm not finished with our Christmas shopping. Due to COVID, I'm getting most of our gifts online. Today's goal is to run through my list one more time, double-check with Ben to make sure I'm not missing anything, and then order everything we need by this weekend.

Everyone is asleep and the house is quiet. Before I go to bed, I'm finishing up the clues for at least two of our kids' scavenger hunts. Each year, the kids have to find their "big" present. It's a tradition we started when they were in elementary school. This year, I'm most excited—and worried—about getting Kylie's gift.

Kylie learned how to ski right before COVID started and she's been telling us *all* she wants for Christmas is a pair of downhill skis. Nothing else, just skis. We limit our budget for gifts and I haven't found a good price for a complete set. It breaks my heart to think about telling Kylie that skis are too expensive this year.

The next morning, I phone my mother-in-law Debra and sister-in-law Annette and tell them we'd like to get skis for Kylie but aren't finding any deals. They both offer to go in on the cost and help us surprise Kylie. Annette completes some research and might have found a really good price in the Ann Arbor area.

I'm heading there for an initial dental appointment with Jill, so we phone ahead and make an appointment to look at skis. I'm super anxious—what if we can't find what we need?

Jill and I meet her new orthodontist and stop on the way home to look at skis. And, boy, do we score! This guy, Craig, has a business out of his garage. He buys skis from resorts out in Colorado and re-sells them. We pick out a red pair for Kylie. They're brand new, still in the packaging with stickers, along with new bindings, poles, and some semi-used ski boots for a very reasonable price.

I'm sooo excited. I can't wait until Kylie sees her present. It's going to be so much fun to see the shocked look on her face.

Other than the gifts, I think one of the best parts of Christmas is writing scavenger notes and then hiding them after the kids go to bed on Christmas Eve. Ben and I have fun putting the scavenger hunt together. We've had the kids jump on one foot, sing a song, and complete other fun and slightly embarrassing things to reach the next step. One memorable year, Kylie had to speak in a British accent before she could get her next clue. This year is going to be amazing, one of our best Christmases yet.

In December, the girls and I make between eight and ten types of cookies. We put together our ingredients, set them out on the cupboard, and then we mix, roll, bake, and sample throughout the day. This year, because of COVID, we can't include my mom.

Usually we let the cookies cool, separate them into boxes, and then we begin to put them on specially decorated paper plates. Each year, we put together four plates of cookies with Christmas cards and bring them to our four closest neighbors. But due to COVID-19, we won't be giving out cookies this year.

Instead, we predetermine the best cookies for freezing and enjoying later. This way, we won't end up feeling too sugared out and like we have to eat *all* the cookies we make. As we finish up baking, I find myself wishing we could send a *huge* plate of cookies into Ben's office, but at the same time, I'm thankful he has been able to work from home and has his new job.

The first week of December has been pretty uneventful. The kids continue to take their classes online and we finally seem to be in a rhythm. I no longer have to rush from room to room, helping them. Life has slowed down to a manageable pace and we are all anxiously looking forward to some time off.

It's Saturday, December 12, and we're going to Grandma Debra's for an early Christmas celebration with her. This is the first time we will see her since March. We've missed her so much! Everyone is excited.

We talk on the phone and go back and forth, trying to figure out if we should go for the day or for a few hours or, like in years past, spend the night. We decide to see her at lunchtime and spend the night. When we last saw Grandma Debra, COVID was just beginning and she breezed in for a quick visit.

For the first time *ever,* she had announced, "No hugs. Let's stay six feet away and keep safe."

This visit is different. The smells of turkey, hot bread, and warm apple pie assail us as we enter Grandma's house. The smells are the physical representation of Grandma's love for us. We are all missing each other, and we're so over the heavy restrictions keeping us away from our loved family members. Before we can ask, "Is it okay to hug you?" she swoops in to give us a massive hug all at once. There are tears in Ben's eyes as well as mine. We've missed Grandma Debra so much. It feels really good to be here.

Grandma Debra grew up in a family of six, three boys and three girls. She usually spends a lot of time with her siblings, as all but one live within a ten-minute drive of one another. They meet for lunch, go to the casino, and frequently get together to spend time with each other.

Because of the concerns of getting and spreading COVID-19, she has not seen us, her daughter Annette, or her siblings in several months. She's happy and laughs as she says, "You can only put so many crosswords and puzzles together before you start to go stir-crazy."

Grandma Debra missed us as fiercely as we've missed her. Talking on the phone isn't the same as a real, live, in-person visit. It's like we can all breathe a sigh of relief. The kids keep hugging Grandma. One hug isn't enough.

Grandma is healthy, we are healthy, and we're in a peaceful place. She's made her famous turkey with gravy and all the sides. We eat until we are ready to burst, and then it's time to open our gifts.

Since Grandma Debra and my sister-in-law are helping with the skis, there is a noticeably smaller pile for Kylie under the tree. A younger Kylie would've noticed the discrepancy in the number of gifts and asked, "What's going on?" or started to cry.

I observe Kylie. She is shrewdly comparing her number of gifts with Jill's and Mark's piles. I take Kylie aside and assure her that Grandma and Aunt Annette have gone in on a larger gift for her and she will get it Christmas Day. Her face brightens, and despite herself, she asks, "Skis! Am I getting skis?"

Before I can say anything, Jill pipes up, "No, stupid. Skis are too expensive. Quit trying to make Mom and Dad feel bad."

I smile to myself. Jill definitely has a future in acting. She's completely convinced Kylie that skis are no longer on her radar. Now we just have to wait for Christmas Day, when she'll go on her scavenger hunt and find her gift. The suspense is killing me.

In our immediate family, only Ben, Jill, and I know. Mark doesn't know. We don't want to take a chance on him telling her what she's getting for Christmas. Years ago, Ben bought me a beautiful, twenty-four-inch pearl necklace. Mark was with him, so as soon as they got home from the store, Mark proceeded to tell me, "Mom, you're going to like your new necklace. It's really pretty."

Poor Mark, he's never lived that incident down. I guess he gets it from my dad, Grandpa Joe. My dad has a hard time keeping Christmas ideas or presents to himself. He's worse than a ten-year-old when it comes to Christmas.

My dad used to love to walk around and shake presents and try to figure out what was inside. To prevent him from guessing, my mom began putting stickers that said FRAGILE, DO NOT SHAKE, RATTLE, OR TOUCH in big letters on the boxes. When it stopped working, she developed a numbering system. She used the numbers one through four instead of putting our names on the gifts and changed the numbering system each year.

One of my dad's favorite tricks is to find the hiding place for his box of chocolates and sneak pieces of candy in advance of the holiday. It's become a game to see how long it will take for Dad to find the box. One year, he found the chocolates super early, and my mom wrapped the empty box and gave it to him for Christmas. She refused to buy him another box of candy.

Another time, my dad actually unwrapped and rewrapped his gifts. Mom found out he had been snooping. She handled the situation beautifully. Instead of confronting him, she gave a bunch of his favorite gifts to other people. One of his most anticipated gifts went to someone else. Mom taught him a lesson by picking up a few random gifts. She bought him an ugly Santa tie, his favorite snack foods, and a few books from our local Dollar Store. He wasn't happy about it.

My dad still snoops, but not as aggressively as in the past. He finally learned his lesson and hasn't opened and rewrapped a present since. He's the only super snoop in our family.

I have no desire to find out what I'm getting ahead of time. I love surprises and the anticipation almost as much as actually unwrapping the gift. One year, when I was small, I guessed I was getting a music box. I made the mistake of picking up the gift and telling my Grandma Millie what I thought it was.

Grandma Millie blew a gasket. She made me open my gift right then. I didn't want to. I wanted to wait, but she insisted. She told me if I didn't open the gift at that exact moment, she would give it to someone who would appreciate it.

I remember sobbing as I unwrapped the gift. It was the music box I had asked for, but the gift was no longer shiny and bright. It had been tarnished by the anger in my grandma's eyes and her shrill demand that I immediately open it. Even now, so many years later, I wonder why didn't she laugh it off, tease me, and say, "Nope, that's not it. Good guess," and continue with the magic of Christmas.

Instead, for me, the wonder and guessing stopped at a young age. I've never since tried to guess what's in a package. I think there's a part of me that is still afraid someone will come out of nowhere and start to scream at me.

Hmm… isn't it funny how experiences can put a mark on you? I'd completely forgotten about that experience until just now.

This year, we are taking the ultimate precautions. We want the skis to be a complete and total surprise. We brought them in the house when we knew Kylie was taking her online classes. Jill stood guard at the base of the stairs and I rushed them into my office. They are now safely in my closet. No one goes in there. You have to first walk past me seated at my desk, then move the chair and boxes of folders Jill set in front of the door. Mission accomplished.

Thinking about Kylie, I smile and feel a strong connection to my dad. Like Kylie, I begged for a pair of skis at the age of sixteen. I also proclaimed the *only* thing I wanted was a pair. The problem was my mom had already bought all our Christmas gifts.

My mom, the list diva, has *always* completed and wrapped all her Christmas shopping by the beginning of July. While it was fine when we were small, it became problematic as we became teenagers.

The year I turned sixteen, my dad insisted my parents buy skis for me. According to family lore, he told Mom, "Patti, this is the only thing the kid wants for Christmas. We have to get them for her."

Thirty-two years later, I still remember unwrapping a small, heavy box with my bindings. There was a note telling me the rest of my present was in the hallway closet. I literally jumped in the air and, in one bound, was holding my new skis in my arms. Still my all-time favorite Christmas gift.

I remember how amazing it felt when I was the same age Kylie is now. I absolutely can't wait for the look on her face. I've been giddy with excitement, and I can't wait to surprise her.

My side of the family, the Clarke side, is known for a lot of Christmas traditions. One of the traditions is going out for dinner on Christmas Eve and making sure we put cookies and a glass of milk out for Santa.

When I was small, it was hard for my siblings and me to wait for Santa to come. My parents started taking us out for a nice *looooong* dinner. We'd get dressed up and eat at a fancy restaurant. I can remember coming in from the chilly Michigan cold, sitting in front of a blazing fire at a table adorned with white tablecloths and a fancy centerpiece. We would eat garlic toasts and breadsticks until I thought I would burst. Then we'd have our soup, salad, and main courses before we went to church. When we were small, we went to the early service, but as we got older, we went to the candlelight or the midnight service.

Now that we are older, my brother Clint and I continue the eating out tradition. We all go to different churches now, so we figure out the best time and our families meet for a midday lunch/dinner.

Due to COVID, all the restaurants in Michigan are closed for in-person dining. We decide to get takeout and bring the food to our parents so we can all eat together.

Our family has stayed home for two weeks, self-quarantining, since seeing Grandma Debra. I am in the kitchen, talking with our daughters, when my cell phone rings. I just miss it, and before I can look at the display to see who called, our home phone begins to ring.

"Somebody really wants to talk to you!" exclaims Kylie.

I glance at my phone and am surprised to see my parent's number in the display. Why are *they* phoning? Has Mom changed her idea on her takeout order again?

I grab the phone and hear my mom's voice excitedly tell me, "Jenni, we won't be able to get together today. Your dad wasn't feeling well, so I took him to a drive-thru clinic. He has the virus."

My mom has this annoying habit of downplaying the coronavirus and calling it "the virus" instead of saying COVID-19. It's like she's afraid to say the actual name.

"What virus, Mom?" I ask. I can't help myself. I have to poke at her a little bit. I'm also secretly hoping it's the flu, not COVID-19.

"Well, the corona, of course." In an exasperated voice, she continues, "Jenni, I don't have time for your lip. I've got to figure out what to do for your dad."

I hear the fear intermixed with anger in her voice, coming clearly through the phone. All joking forgotten, I immediately ask, "What do you need?"

"The doctors sent us home to quarantine. Your dad has a fever of a hundred and three degrees, he's wheezing a little bit, and they said we both need to quarantine for fourteen days. They won't give us any medicine, just told us to quarantine. I asked for that hydroxy stuff the president was talking about, but they said he wasn't sick enough. They told me to stay away from your dad; that I'll probably get it as well."

I can hear the trembling in her voice. My dad is an asthmatic and has Type 2 diabetes. He is one of those people most at risk for getting really sick with COVID and ending up in the hospital on a ventilator.

My mom continues, "We have to do something. What should I give your dad? The doctor said just watch him and bring him to the hospital if he gets worse."

My mom is asking for my help. My mom, who always knows what to do and tells everyone else, is obviously scared. My anger at my mom is forgotten in the fear of COVID. I immediately go into "helper" mode and have a long list of things she should be doing. First, I ask her if she picked up the supplements, we discussed a month or so ago.

No, she hasn't ordered them. Will I order them for her?

Fortunately, we have Amazon Prime and I tell her I will have them shipped directly to her house. It will take a minimum of two days, possibly longer, and tomorrow is Christmas. I quickly look in our cabinet and tell her we will drop off some supplements on her porch later today.

I get off the phone to the worried expressions on the faces of our daughters. It's 8:15 AM, much earlier than normal for our teens to be awake. Ben enters the kitchen along with Mark, which saves me from repeating the story multiple times.

I share the bad news and they're all in shock. Mark is asking a steady stream of questions, Ben has a worried look on his face, and Jill starts crying. Kylie and I are the only two who seem to be in the "What can we do now?" mode.

Fortunately, because of my concern for Mark and his compromised immune system, I've already completed a lot of research. I have a long list of preventative supplements our family is taking, plus extras. I have more than enough to share with my parents.

I review my list to check off everything they will need for the next four to five days. Zinc picolinate, liposomal vitamin C, vitamin A, quercetin, aspirin, melatonin... am I missing anything? Yes, I add in the vitamin k2d3. Now I have everything. I find a pill holder and put two doses, enough for five days, in it. I'm happy we have enough for my parents. I've learned the preparation lessons well.

I phone Clint. "Hi, Clint, did you hear about Dad?" I say, getting right to the point.

"Yeah, I heard. Do you still want to get together with our family for a takeout brunch?" he asks.

"When is the last time you saw Mom and Dad?" I want to be sure there isn't a chance Clint and his family have been exposed.

"It's been more than two weeks. Like you guys, we've been kind of self-quarantining before Christmas. We didn't want to take a chance on getting them sick," finishes Clint.

"In that case, the original plan sounds good. Let me double-check with Ben. Maybe we can meet you guys, eat takeout brunch, and drop off a meal for Mom and Dad."

My dad tested positive. Suddenly, COVID is very real. I insist that he talk to me when I phone Mom back to tell her the plan. Dad's voice is a little gravelly and it's hard for him to talk without getting out of breath. He sounds horrible. I want to cry when I hear him struggling.

"Dad, I'm dropping off some things this afternoon. Please promise me you will check your oxygen levels with the pulse oximeter and that you will take the supplements." I pause, holding my breath, waiting for his response.

He kind of rasps, "Okay, honey. You tell your mom what I need to do. Sorry we're not going to see you for Christmas Eve or Christmas dinner. Here's your mom." The phone goes silent as he hands the phone over.

"Jenni, what is the plan? Are you and Clint and the kids all stopping over?"

Unbelievable. I think my mom is still in denial. As much as I want to see my dad and give him a big hug and a kiss, we will not be getting any closer.

"Mom, we will be dropping off the supplements, along with a list explaining how to take them. I'm also going to drop off some takeout food."

Then I have a sudden thought because they are now quarantined. "Mom, do you have enough groceries and meals for the next few weeks?" I think they are probably fine. My mom is known for having two refrigerators completely full, a full-size freezer, and a pantry. The only food I could think they might need are some fresh fruits and vegetables.

Mom laughs. "Honey, we have lots of food. No worries here. And if we need anything, I will place a grocery order."

"Okay. Tell Dad we'll be praying for him."

"Thanks, honey. Bye now."

Our family somberly gets dressed as I quickly place a supplement order for my parents. It's scheduled for Monday delivery, December 28. I print off the complete list of instructions. In the note to my mom, I also explain how to use the pulse oximeter, a small machine to put on your finger to measure your oxygen levels. It's important to measure, since Dad has some breathing issues. I assure her I will walk her through the process, and if his oxygen level goes below ninety-three percent, they are to phone their doctor.

Finished, I take a deep breath and yell, "Okay, everybody, ready to go. Did everyone use the bathroom?" A last stop before getting in the car, and we are on the road. It's time to meet my brother and his family. Fortunately, the weather is clear and we don't have to worry about snow. Ben drives as I read through the list of supplements, making sure I have written a detailed explanation on everything.

My mom and I are still not in a good place. Despite my residual anger, I don't want to lose her to COVID. She's a tough old bird, in good health, and at a great weight. Not an extra ounce of fat on her, so no worries about her being in the overweight patient category or having comorbidities associated with it. I'm sure she'll be fine.

My dad is another story. He used to be a major body builder, but back issues and arthritis have taken their toll. He's gained weight, along with developing a penchant for fine wines, cheeses, and desserts. His once svelte physique is no more, plus he has exercise-induced asthma and Type 2 diabetes.

I'm having a hard time. My strong, vibrant dad has COVID. Usually, he fights taking medications. He is the guy who will hardly take an aspirin. I'm hoping he will be a good patient and take the supplements and quickly recover. I'm feeling scared—what will happen to him?

Chapter Twenty
Patti

December 24, 2020—My Joe has COVID. The words fill me with fear. When I first heard his test was positive, I literally felt like I was going to pass out. An elephant was sitting on my chest, and it was hard to breathe. My Joe is too young to die.

Then I thought, *Oh, no, I'm going to get COVID too!* And I was terrified. I've never prayed so long and hard in my life.

IF THE TRUTH IS TOLD, I'm pissed as well. We didn't see our family for Easter, Thanksgiving, and now Christmas. Darn it all! I was so looking forward to Christmas Eve brunch, listening to carols, and singing some songs with the family.

Why couldn't Joe get sick after Christmas? I love Joe, but he's gone and ruined my favorite holiday of the year. I've decorated our home beautifully, and now the family won't see the three trees I put up all by myself. I guess I might as well start taking the decorations down.

We planned on leaving for our condo in St. Augustine in January. Now we'll be staying put until who knows when. Will this year of COVID crap ever end?

It's a good thing we have four bedrooms. I was able to sleep last night in the guest room on the other side of the house, far away from the master bedroom. Joe tried to be a gentleman and told me he would sleep in the guest room. But he's the one with COVID, not me. He needs to be in a room with a bathroom, all by himself. I'm sure he will sleep, read, and watch TV, all in that order.

It's a completely different Christmas Day than what I planned. The kids brought over a couple meals from one of our favorite restaurants, and Jenni brought us a cheeseburger rice quiche. I have several weeks of meals in the freezer, and now we've got some nice takeout.

I keep checking on Joe. He's not being a very cooperative patient. All he wants to do is sleep. He isn't hungry and he doesn't want to eat or take his diabetes medication. He takes pills, but he has to have food. He can't keep going on an empty stomach.

When I check on him, I put on two face masks and a face shield. So far, I'm feeling fine. I need to make sure I get enough sleep so I don't end up getting the virus. I've been taking several vitamins, and now with Joe sick, I'm adding the extra supplements Jenni brought over yesterday.

We're six days in and Joe is still not well. He has body aches, coughs, and says he has never been this exhausted in his entire life. I give him food and check back two hours later but he hasn't eaten anything or taken his pills. I've now progressed to standing over him to make sure he takes his supplements.

He snarls and growls at me, "Patti, leave me alone. I'm tired."

He will literally drift off to sleep right then if I don't poke him and make him sit up to eat, drink some water, and take his pills. I'm worried about him getting dehydrated and having a diabetic incident. I talked to our doctor, and the nurse at the office has walked me through how to check his blood sugar. My Joe has always been so healthy. And I'll tell you something, when we get past this virus, he's going to start taking his diabetes seriously. No more soda or super sugary sweets. I want him around for a while.

It's now been ten days. Joe continues to avoid eating and spends most of the day asleep. The only thing he wants or craves is his favorite fast-food hamburger. I've been bundling up and getting in the car to pick him up a burger and a shake every day. Shakes aren't exactly the best nutrition, but he'll eat it. The restaurant is only about ten minutes away, so I find myself praying for Joe all the way there and back. The roads are icy, but Joe has requested a hamburger. And if he'll eat a hamburger, I'm going to get him one.

I'm feeling great. No virus symptoms at all. I'm perfectly healthy, so I've felt comfortable going through the drive-through. I guess my multivitamin and all the prayers are working. No symptoms for me.

I've tried cooking chicken noodle soup, but Joe just sniffs the soup, tells me he can't taste or smell, and goes back to sleep. He normally loves my homemade soup and hot rolls, but not now. Now, it's a fight to get him to eat and take his supplements.

It's day eleven and Joe is being especially resistant. I put his pills on his nightstand and decide to let him sleep for two hours before I go back and make sure he's taking his supplements.

I go into our bedroom and call Joe's name. No answer, so I yell, "Joe," and then a second time, "*Joe!*" even more loudly.

I notice Joe is staring straight up at the ceiling fan as it spins around. He isn't acknowledging me or even seems to be aware I am in the same room. I touch his head—he's burning up. I notice his water bottle is still filled with the ice and water I put in earlier. I unscrew the cap and throw the icy cold water directly on Joe. He doesn't flinch or startle, he just keeps staring straight ahead.

Oh my gosh! Now I'm terrified. I don't know what to do.

I use the landline to call our doctor. *Ring, ring, ring.* Will they ever pick up?

"Hello, this is Doctor Smith's office…"

I interrupt the long message. "Stop!" I scream into the phone. "I have an emergency. I need to speak to the nurse on call."

They connect me, and I quickly explain what is happening.

"Patti, do you have water available and some aspirin?"

"Yes, yes, we have both. What do you want me to do?" I don't know why my hands won't stop shaking.

"Patti, go get aspirin and a glass of water. Get Joe to drink the water, and then once he's awake enough, give him one aspirin at a time. A total of two aspirins. Can you do that?"

"Yes, I can do that," I yell as I run from the room. The nurse talks with me as I gather the supplies. She confirms our address and tells me not to worry. Before I run back to Joe, she tells me to unlock the front door.

"You're doing great, Patti. I'll stay on the phone with you. We've called an ambulance and they will be there shortly. Before they get there, let's see if we can get Joe to wake up for us."

I sit on the bed and gently use my fingers to open his mouth. This man is not going to die on me. He slightly opens his mouth and I pour a little bit of water in. Most of it comes back out, but he gives an involuntary swallow. The nurse tells me to stay with him and keep giving him water until we get him awake.

Where is the ambulance? Why isn't he waking up? The thoughts are screaming inside my head as I struggle to hold it together. I'm not sure what to say, but God *has* to hear my anxious prayers. He has to save my Joe.

Finally, he takes a swallow and his eyes flutter. I breathe a sigh of relief. He's coming back to me.

"What are you doing to me?" he hoarsely bellows.

"Joe, honey, keep drinking this water. Have a couple more sips, then we need to get some aspirin down you."

He resists, but I'm not taking no for an answer. "Drink it!" I sternly admonish him.

I get him to sit up against the headboard. He washes down the two aspirin as ten more minutes go by.

Where is the ambulance? What is taking so long? It feels like I've been doing this for an hour, not minutes.

Joe is finally coherent. "Patti, no ambulance. I just need to sleep."

He's fighting me to lie back down. I won't let him. I'm too afraid if he goes back to sleep, he won't wake up.

I hear the clatter of multiple feet on our wooden entryway and I yell, "We're in here! Top of the stairs on the right."

The paramedics enter and they quickly take Joe's vitals. No surprise, his sugar is extremely high, but he's awake.

The wonderful paramedics load him on a long carry thing and put him in the ambulance. I'm so stressed, I can't remember what it's called. Oh yeah, a stretcher. They load him on a stretcher. They tell me to follow them, but explain I will not be allowed to stay with him in the hospital.

Do I stay or do I go?

No question about it. I'm going!

Thank God for GPS—I load in the name of the hospital and then I phone my kids. It's 2:20 PM our time, which means it's 11:20 in California for Lori. Jenni and Lori answer the phone, but I get Clint's message, which means he's probably in a meeting. I spend less than five minutes each with my girls. I make promises to let them know more information as it becomes available.

As I finish with Lori, we pull into the hospital. It appears they need me to go inside and start the insurance process. Isn't that nice of them? I can't accompany my husband or be with him in his room, but I can start the paperwork. Basically, just sign the papers and leave. Even though Joe was brought in by ambulance, there is a long line to see the nurse and fill out paperwork. I sit and wait.

Three hours later, I finish the forms and the nurse says, "Mrs. Clarke, your husband is safe. Unfortunately, due to COVID, you can't stay with him. I suggest you go home and get some rest."

I can go home or I can sit in the parking lot. Jerks! Joe and I have been married for fifty-four years, and I can't help take care of him. It's too much to bear.

On the way to the car, I pass a trio of vending machines. A bottle of orange juice and a candy bar sound good. I'm feeling a little lightheaded. The adrenalin rush has left, and now my whole body feels like it's trembling. It's hard to explain, but the inside of my body is buzzing, like it's supercharged. The last thing I want is to drive home, but I have no choice.

I walk to the car and sit in the driver's seat. My body still feels like it's vibrating. I stare straight ahead but I can't see. My vision blurs as my eyes fill with tears. My reflection in the mirror looks awful. My mascara is smudged and running down my face, my hair looks like a rat's nest, and my face is puffy with eyes that are red from crying.

I grab onto the steering wheel like it will somehow stop the shaking.

I've never felt so completely alone. My best friend, my husband, is in the hospital. He seems to be stable, but Joe has the virus and his newly diagnosed Type 2 diabetes is out of control. I wonder, would Joe still be alive if I hadn't gone in to check on him? What if I'd taken an afternoon nap?

My strong husband is sick and I don't know how long he'll be in the hospital. I've been lucky so far with no symptoms, but I could still be a carrier. I can't take the chance on getting anyone else in my family sick.

I need to pull myself together. First, I allow myself to cry for a few more minutes. After, I square my shoulders. I put forth the effort to get my key in the ignition and start the car. It's time to go home.

There's a dusting of snow on the ground, not enough to scrape my windshield but enough to use my wipers. I need to sleep and take care of myself. I need to be healthy and able to take care of my Joe.

I pull into the driveway, push the remote garage door opener, and park our white Buick. I drag myself inside, barely taking the time to remove my shoes. If this isn't a night for a glass of pinot grigio, I don't know what is. I put a piece of bread in the toaster oven and grab my wine opener. A little unorthodox, but I'm having wine and a piece of challah bread with butter and peanut butter. The only thing better would be a hot, flakey croissant.

I'm in need of some comfort food and drink. It's been a long day. Other than my orange juice and candy bar, I can't remember the last time I ate. Oh, yeah, it was breakfast, some oatmeal. It's now nearly 6:30 at night and I'm exhausted. I'm too tired to wash my face, so I use the bathroom, put on my pajamas, and eat my small meal. I turn on the tv to numb out and have some noise in the house. It's much too quiet without my Joe.

Before I go to sleep, I say a quick prayer. "Hey, God. It's me, Patti... *Please* take care of my Joe and bring him home to me. I'm not ready to lose him. I promise that I'll be a better person. I'll apologize to Jen and Kylie and I'll..." I can't think of another word, just cleansing tears as I finally release the remaining anxiety and fear from my body. I close with, "God, please be with me and Joe. Please give both of us the strength we need to get through this."

Ring, ring, ring. "What? Who?" For a moment, I forget my Joe is sick and in the hospital. I almost fall out of bed, trying to reach the landline next to my sleeping ear. Everything on the nightstand comes crashing to the floor. I dive for the phone just in time to hear, "Mrs. Clarke, hello... Hello, is this Mrs. Clarke?"

I'm on the floor, instantly awake and terrified. The clock says 7:02 AM. "Is Joe okay? Is my husband all right?" I yell into the phone.

A soothing voice tells me, "Oh, yes, your husband is fine. I'm calling to tell you he's being released this morning. The doctors are requesting that you pick him up."

I'm shocked. As much as I want Joe home, I'm afraid. What if he gets sick again? And despite myself, I ask, "Are you sure it's okay for me to bring him home?"

"Yes, Mrs. Clarke," she responds. "We've stabilized his blood sugar and he will get better more quickly if he's able to sleep and get rest at home. You just need to watch his oxygen and keep him quarantined. Call us if his oxygen goes below ninety." Then as an afterthought, she adds, "What time will you be here to pick him up?"

"I can be there in about twenty minutes."

"Great, we'll see you then."

I get up, quickly brush my teeth, and wash my face. I'm looking the worse for wear, as they say, when I get dressed. I've never left the house in my pajamas or in anything less than full makeup, but I'm honestly tempted. I'm so anxious to see my Joe and get him out of the hospital.

The hospital is about twelve minutes or so from our home. I don't like to drive, and I don't very often. I usually leave the driving to my Joe, but this time, I'm amazed at how calm and in control I feel. There is no anxiety or issues. I keep saying, "I've got to get to Joe, I've got to get to Joe." It becomes my mantra on the way to the hospital, and I drive straight there just as fast as I can.

In ten minutes, I breathe a sigh of relief when I pull into the parking lot at the hospital just before eight. I'm feeling pretty proud of myself. I got dressed in record time and made it here. It's time for Joe to come home.

The hospital tells me I need to learn how to check his blood sugar and give him insulin. He's a brand-new diabetic. Pre-COVID, he was taking half of a diabetes pill, you know, the white one. His sugar is so out of whack he will need between two and three insulin shots daily. The nurse has me practice giving an orange a shot. After a couple of attempts, I've got it down.

I'm willing to do whatever it takes to get my Joe out of the hospital. I'm thinking positive thoughts as I tell myself, "I've just learned two new skill sets that will come in handy in St. Augustine."

As I say "St. Augustine," I almost lose my composure. I'm so homesick for the beach and the heat and warmth of our condo in Florida. I'm completely alone. I'm exhausted. I'm beyond tired. I miss my kids. I miss my family. And I don't know what I'm going to do if something happens to Joe.

After I learn how to give my piece of fruit a shot, the doctor meets with me. My strength and resolve are gone. My husband almost died. The doctor confirms how lucky Joe is to be alive.

The doctor also reiterates *very* strongly, "Your husband needs to eat regular meals. And you will need to check his blood sugar every few hours over the next few days. Mrs. Clarke, are you prepared to give him extra insulin shots if needed?"

"Absolutely," I respond. *Let's get this party on the road,* I'm thinking.

"Okay, then, I guess you can take your husband home. Just be sure to keep checking his oxygen levels and make sure he's eating regular meals."

The doctor tells me to bring the car around and two hospital employees will get Joe into a wheelchair and load him in.

Once we're finally in the car, I look at Joe. I know it's going to be tough to get him into the house. I called the kids earlier, and Clint offered to bring over a wheelchair for us. I didn't think we'd need one, but fortunately, Clint insisted. "Ma, I'll put it in the garage. This way if you need it, you've got it. We don't know how Dad is going to be feeling, and we can't come and help you."

As we pull into the garage and I see the wheelchair leaning against the door, I want to cry. I am so grateful for my son's help. And through my blurry eyes, I notice Clint is standing next to the wheelchair. He is wearing two masks, a plastic head covering, gloves, and a hat. He strides up to the car, and despite our protests, he helps Joe into the wheelchair and then pushes him into the house. He gives me a quick side hug and says, "Ma, let us know if there's anything you need. Love you." Then he's gone.

I can't help it. I'm in tears. This time, Joe is here with me. I don't care at this point if I die of COVID, I have to hug my husband. I sink to the floor and I hold onto his legs as he gently pats my head. "It's okay, Patti. I'm okay. I'm here. Don't worry about me. We're going to get through this."

I'm struggling with my emotions. Caught between the relief of Joe being home and stable and also pissed at him for getting sick. If he hadn't insisted on going to the grocery store, we would not be in this mess. He wouldn't listen to me—no, he had pick up a few more items. I told him we didn't need anything else. He wouldn't listen, and now he's sick and we're away from our family at Christmas. One more reason to cry until there are no tears left.

Joe's sugar continues to go up and down like a pendulum. It spikes and then normalizes. I become adept at checking his levels and doing the math to give him insulin. He's feeling a little better and jokes about me giving him shots in his bum.

On day fifteen, Joe wakes up and I hear his labored breathing from the other end of the house. *He doesn't sound good*, I'm thinking as I quickly run to check on him. I can hear his chest rattling. Joe has let me sleep in. I learn he was up half the night struggling to breathe.

"Patti, I'm pretty sure I've got pneumonia," he says as he bows his head. "We've got to go back to the hospital."

We're both convinced Joe will be away at least overnight. Until I know for sure, I complete the insurance paperwork and then wait in the car, frequently turning the engine on and off to stay warm. Surprisingly, after eight hours, they give him an antibiotic and instructions to phone his doctor. They want him to go home.

Joe is so sick. I want him to get better, and a part of me is afraid he will die if I take him home. I argue with the doctor on call, but it doesn't get me anywhere.

He tells me, "Ma'am, your husband is better off at home. We have an entire wing of COVID patients, and he would be alone with no family or visitors. Trust me. Take him home. He can get some rest and fight this." The resident looks at his clipboard and basically dismisses me.

I'm both furious and relieved at the same time. It's been over two weeks and all we've being given is one antibiotic for his pneumonia. COVID has been here almost a year. Why are they still telling people to quarantine? They have to know more about this disease by now.

I phone Jenni as soon as we get home. She has been busy with the kids, and I've been overwhelmed with learning how to take care of a newly insulin-dependent diabetic. We haven't talked in a few days.

As I catch her up on her dad's pneumonia, I hear her put me on speakerphone. At first, I'm a little upset, then she explains, "Mom, I need to look up some information for you and have my hands free to type on my computer."

She tells me of a repurposed wonder drug called Ivermectin that she heard about in December. Jenni begins giving me bullet points for the doctor. Information about studies, recovery rates, and other information she said I will need if the doctor is resistant to trying this medication on Joe.

Half of my brain listens to Jenni while I fiercely concentrate on taking accurate notes. The other half of me just keeps thinking about my husband. What happens if this doesn't work and there is no cure for him? I keep trying to focus on Jenni and what she is saying, but I can't let go of my concern for my Joe.

Jenni offers to get on the phone with me the next day. I assure her that if she sends me a few bullet points, I can do it.

"Mom, really, it's no problem. Are you sure you don't need me to help with your telemedicine appointment tomorrow?"

"No, dear, I'll be fine. Jenni, I know you told me about this before. Just send me the information, and I'll tell the doctor about it," I say before I hang up.

At our nine-thirty doctor's appointment the next morning, I'm nervously sitting in front of the computer with a list of studies and talking points from Jenni. She must've stayed up half the night. The time stamp on the email is 3:30 AM.

My girl is so smart. I'm impressed how quickly she's able to pull together information about any given medical condition. But, it's no surprise, given the years of dedication she put into finding therapies for Mark. He has come a long way in the last ten years because of her tireless efforts. I'm proud of her.

Our doctor asks a few basic questions and seems to be in a hurry to get off the phone when I tell him, "My daughter wants me to ask if we can get Ivermectin for Joe."

"Oh, yeah, I've seen some of the research on Ivermectin. Absolutely. Which pharmacy would you like to use?"

It's that easy. The doctor calls it in and Clint picks the script up and brings it to our house. I'm not going to tell Jenni how easy it was to get the medicine. She worked too hard and I don't want to hurt her feelings.

I give Joe his pills and ready myself for a sleepless night. He has an inhaler to help him breathe as well as steam in his room, and I've even picked up Vicks to put on his chest. I'm worried. He sounds horrible. I'm beyond overwhelmed, and terrified my Joe will die.

Tonight, I get up every two hours to check on him. After my third wake-up, as Joe slumbers, I notice his breathing appears to be easier. His color is better and he seems to be sleeping well.

I set the alarm for three hours. Three hours later, the same thing. He looks and sounds better. By my count, he's now slept nearly nine hours. I set the alarm for four hours and go to bed.

I oversleep. Somehow, I didn't turn my alarm on. I listen carefully but I don't hear anything. No rasping, no sounds. I'm back to my terrified place. Oh no! What if Joe has passed in the night while I slept the last four and a half hours—what will I do? I'm half afraid to open our bedroom door.

I creep into our room, and Joe is sitting up in bed. He has the biggest smile on his face as he sees me enter. "There's my gorgeous wife," he says as I run into his arms. "Patti, honey, I feel about forty percent better than I did last night." He continues, "I'm not wheezing anymore, and I can breathe a whole lot easier."

Yeah! I can't wait to phone Jenni. Thank God she knew about this drug. I was terrified my Joe would not make it, and now he is feeling so much better. I believe he's turned a corner.

Joe is listening to the doctor and he's staying in bed, resting, watching TV, and reading when he feels up to it. On day twenty, he gets out of bed and declares himself better.

I still don't know how I managed to keep from getting sick. The doctors initially told me to prepare myself, that I would definitely get it. But I didn't. I'm COVID-free. My Joe and I survived the virus.

Chapter Twenty-One
Kylie

**January 15, 2021—Grandpa Joe's the first family member
to get the RONA. I was really scared he was going to die.**

I DON'T THINK GRANDA PATTI appreciates everything my mom does for
her. My mom was pretty incredible during the RONA scare with
Grandpa. She brought lots of food and supplements for Grandpa Joe.
I'm hoping Mom and Granda Patti will finally be able to talk it out and
get to the bottom of their issues with each other.

Granda Patti has this habit of running her kitchen appliances, like
the garbage disposal and other things, whenever she's on the phone. My
mom gave up talking to her with a headset on and pretty much uses her
speakerphone. It's super funny because Granda gets pissed when Mom
puts her on speaker. Thanks to the speakerphone, I'm able to hear their
latest "fight" when Mom phones Granda Patti to see if there is anything
she and Grandpa need before we leave for Puerto Rico.

I can hear Granda using her hurt voice. "Isn't it nice you and the
girls are going to Puerto Rico. Are you really sure that's a good idea?
Have you checked the number of cases?"

Mom responds in a calm voice.

Then I hear Granda. "Jenni, I haven't been feeling well. I survived
your dad getting the virus, but lately I've been having some virus-type
symptoms." Her voice sounds a little mean. I seriously don't get it. I
wish they got along better. It doesn't take much to set either of them off.

Mom continues to speak quietly. "Have you been tested for COVID? If you think you have COVID, you need to jump on this now, not wait."

Granda sounded fine when Mom first called her. Now she is noticeably changing her voice so it sounds a little raspy, like she's sick. I can hear what she is doing, and I sit there waiting for the next comment. This is almost like watching a suspense thriller. What's going to happen next?

My mom is running her fingers through her hair as she removes her ponytail holder. A sign she is frustrated. There it is, the moment I knew was coming.

"Jen, I don't possibly see how you and the girls can go to Puerto Rico for nine days and leave me and your dad here. What if your dad has a relapse... or what if I've got the virus?"

It gets bad. Mom and Granda both say some pretty hurtful things, and my mom is almost shaking when she gets off the phone.

Now is not the time for me to make a snarky comment like, "So, Mom, how's Granda Patti doing?" At least not if I want to make my next birthday. LOL.

We've been planning a trip to Puerto Rico, just us girls, and we leave on Thursday, February 11 through Friday, February 19. My sister Jill loves to travel. This past July, Jill asked Mom about vacationing over winter break. "Mom, if I pay for airline tickets for you and me to go to Puerto Rico, will you pay for the rest? For the car and the hotel?"

Mom talked to Dad and they decided sure, why not? It was going to be just Jill and Mom until Jill got a major bug up her butt about going parasailing. Mom refuses to go parasailing. She says she did it once and, "Once was enough."

That's when Jill started on me. She wants to have fun and have someone go parasailing and into the ocean with her. Mom loves to walk on the beach, but she doesn't stay in the water for very long. Jill needs someone she can play with, which is why she started bugging me to go on the trip.

After a day of babysitting, Jill finally wore me down. I didn't have the money for my airplane ticket, but she promised to help me save. We both figured Mom would be excited to have both her girls on the trip.

She was. Mom just had to double-check there was room for three of us. Mom's friend Annie lives in Puerto Rico. When Mom told Annie she was planning a trip, she insisted Jill and Mom stay with her and her husband, Derry. After I decided to go, Mom talked to Annie again. She said no problem—they can't wait to see all three of us.

Now we're in the countdown to go to Puerto Rico. We're so excited. We've done online school since March of last year, and all of this year. Because we've been online, we babysat three days a week and made enough money for our airplane tickets.

Although we've been out of school all year, wouldn't you know it, we're supposed to return to school the week before we leave for Puerto Rico. Instead, we stay home self-isolating so we won't get sick. I am actually pretty surprised at how jerky our teachers are about it. Most of them give me a huge issue over trying to get my homework in advance of our trip. Only two are actually nice, wish us a good trip, and get us the schoolwork we need. The rest are all pretty rude.

My math teacher, let's just call him Mr. Jerk, accuses me of going to Puerto Rico so I won't have to be in his class. It's all I can do to keep from yelling at him.

I tell him, "We've been planning this trip since the fall. I didn't plan a trip to Puerto Rico just so I could miss your class."

Being the total jerk he is, he says, "That will be enough snark, Ms. Blake. Watch it or I will report you to the principal."

I keep my mouth shut, but inside I am thinking, *Oh, yeah? You try that. See how far it takes you. I've done absolutely nothing wrong.*

When I first agreed to go, I had one condition. I told Mom and Jill I would not have a RONA test where they put a huge stick up my nose. This is important because Mom told us we have to prove we're negative for the RONA within seventy-two hours of our departure. Mom knew I was totally serious, so before we ordered our tickets (in October), she talked to our doctor and was told I could have a throat swab.

I'm fine with a throat swab, only now it's getting close to our trip and no one in Michigan is doing them, just the nasal swab. Mom even calls Ohio before she goes online to find a saliva test.

We make a video appointment for Monday, seventy-two hours before our departure. We have to stand in front of Mom's computer and spit into a tube with a supervisor watching.

It is taking a while, so I tell Jill, "Hey, I bet I can fill mine faster than you can." Just like that, we are racing to fill our tubes.

The supervisor thinks we're funny. Since it takes a while to fill the tubes, she has the chance to hear about our trip. She wishes us a good trip and says they will expedite our results so we have them before we leave on Thursday.

February is my birthday month. We leave today, the eleventh. The twelfth, our first full day in Puerto Rico, will be my birthday, and then Mom's birthday is on February 18. Plus, we'll be there for Valentine's Day.

Dad was cool when he learned we were going to be gone for Valentine's Day and both our birthdays. He laughed and said, "No problem, Jen. I want you and the girls to have an amazing time. We'll celebrate after you get back." My dad is pretty awesome.

I guess I should get used to nothing being easy. We have to leave for the airport at 2:45 AM to make our six o'clock flight. The roads are icy and haven't been plowed. The snow is coming down really hard, and it's hard to see out the windshield. Jill and I are sitting in absolute silence so Mom can focus. I'm super glad Mom is driving and not me. I think we're all wishing we spent last night in a hotel near the airport. Also, we don't have all our RONA tests back yet.

Mom's test results came last night at 7:00 PM, but Jill and my tests aren't done. Mom and Dad have both been on the phone, calling and checking, but by ten when we land in Orlando, we still don't have our results. The customer service rep tells them that our results should be finished by one. Since we are supposed to arrive in Puerto Rico at three, they can send them to both Dad and Mom to make sure we have them for our arrival. Nothing like cutting it close!

Mom has to make a tough decision. Should we spend the night in Orlando and wait to get our results or keep going to Puerto Rico?

Dad thinks we should stay in Orlando. If we go to Puerto Rico and one of us has a positive result, we will have to quarantine for fourteen days. Quarantining in Puerto Rico will get really expensive. But if we wait, we'll have to get re-tested. Our tests from Monday won't be good by the time we arrive if we wait.

We know that we do *not* have the RONA—we've been isolating at home for almost three weeks. We didn't want to take a chance on our trip getting canceled due to sickness or bringing the RONA to my mom's friends.

She goes back and forth as Jill stands there almost crying. Mom finally says, "We're going! I believe everything is fine. If we get a false positive, we'll just test again when we get there."

Yeah—we're on our way to Puerto Rico!

We get on the airplane, and Jill and I listen to music on our headphones as Mom reads a murder mystery. The takeoff is smooth, and before we know it, we're landing in the island of palm trees and balmy breezes.

Mom phones Dad as soon as we get off the plane. We all do the happy dance. Our tests have *finally* come through… both negative.

Next, we have to go through the horribly long line and get our negative RONA results into their computer system before we leave the building. The man in front of us tries to help load the test results on Mom's phone. Neither one of them can get it to work. Mom looks like she wants to throw her phone across the room.

In the middle of the frustration, Dad calls. Mom tries to explain what is happening when Jill grabs the phone. "Dad, we can't talk. Mom can't load the results on the phone." *And she hangs up on him.*

Yup, that's my sister. She can be mean as a snake and right to the point. Mom and I are both stunned speechless. Before Mom can say anything, the phone rings again. Jill is going to be in trouble.

Instead, Mom answers the phone. "Ben, now is not a good time. We're having problems loading the information. We're getting in another line. I'll talk with you later." Mom and Dad say "Bye" as Mom continues to fuss with her phone.

We are finally in the right line, and I seriously think we are the last three people from our flight to leave the terminal. Mom is beyond frustrated and happy when an airline employee loads the test results for us into their computer. It shouldn't have been that hard!

At last, we're standing outside the terminal. I've been to Florida and this airport reminds me of Orlando. There are lots of people, cars are stopping and starting, and there's more Spanish than English in the air. It feels like we're really far from home. Mom points us toward an outdoor bench as she excitedly phones Annie to tell her we've arrived.

Derry pulls up twenty minutes later. He gets out of the car, envelops Mom in a big hug, and turns to look at Jill and me. "My, you two sure have grown since the last time I saw you."

Jill and I both smile. We're used to hearing stories that start with, "The last time I saw you, you were *this* big…"

As we leave, Mom and Derry are talking non-stop in the front while Jill and I sit in the backseat. We are in awe. There are palm trees and large buildings and crazy drivers everywhere. I'm really glad when we pull up fifteen minutes later—*alive*—in front of a condominium building in the Condado area. Derry expertly parks the car in the parking garage underneath the building and we ride the elevator to their floor.

Annie opens the door. "*Amiguita*," Annie says as she reaches to give Mom a hug. Annie is all of five feet tall, Mom is about five feet six inches—so it's definitely a stretch. Mom and Annie met years ago when

Mom lived in Texas. They were both single and became really good friends, almost like sisters. Their nickname for each other is *amiguita*, which means "little friend."

Mom and Annie haven't seen each other in about ten years, and they both have tears in their eyes as they hug and look at each other for the first time. And just like that, they are both jabbering away in Spanish. Hmm... makes me wonder if they are talking about us.

Annie has reddish brown hair that just hits the top of her shoulders. She laughs a lot and has deep dimples. She also has the bluest eyes I've ever seen. She takes a deep breath and kind of sighs as she lets it out and says, "Isn't this the life?" And when I comment that her eyes are pretty, she responds. "Contacts. My eyes are really brown."

Jill and Mom have put together this exhausting list of things for us to do. I just want to go to the beach. Since my birthday is the day after we arrive, we're planning on going parasailing then. I'm so psyched—what a cool way to celebrate. Woohoo! I can't wait.

The other cool thing we're doing on this trip is sailing. Annie asked Mom if we wanted to take a couple days and hit some islands. Mom loves to sail and is so excited. Annie and Derry's friend is the captain of a boat and he will be taking us.

Drum roll! It's officially my seventeenth birthday. Mom starts the day with some bad news. "Kylie, it's supposed to rain off and on today. The website says if it rains, they will not take you parasailing. Tomorrow looks like it will be really sunny and clear. Are you okay with going tomorrow instead?"

Actually, I'm not. I've been dreaming about celebrating my birthday with a day at the beach parasailing and a hamburger for dinner. But I suck it up. "Sure." I force a smile. "What will we do instead?"

"I'm thinking we'll head into Old San Juan. I know you guys want to pick up some t-shirts, and I want to buy each of us a coquí necklace."

Seriously, could it get any worse? Shopping on my birthday? I *hate* shopping. Jill and Mom *love* to shop. Oh, joyful day!

Derry offers to drop us off and pick us up later so we don't have to worry about parking. Mom asks him to pick up a cake for my birthday with just one request: don't get chocolate. I think chocolate cake is the worst.

Derry drops us off on Calle Fortaleza, and Mom and Jill have a blast going in and out of stores. We go to three or four t-shirt shops before they finally make a purchase. They are also looking for the "perfect" necklace for each of us. We find some nice charms but they are more than mom wants to pay.

We go into one more jewelry store to see if they have any coquí charms. The store is having a February sale, and they have coquí necklaces with sterling silver chains for only five dollars each. Mom is so excited.

Now we have our necklaces, it's time for food. We find a restaurant just down from the jewelry store. Mom wants to buy a bunch of appetizers and sample some Puerto Rican food. We order eight different kinds. Mom and Jill love everything we order, but I only like two of the appetizers, the curly french fries with cilantro sauce and the garlic knots. I can't wait to go to dinner tonight. I'm *finally* going to get a hamburger!

We decide to use our GPS on our phone to walk to El Moro, the fort. Our plan is to tour the fort for a few minutes and phone Derry to pick us up. The GPS takes us a completely different route. We're now in the very front of El Moro, right next to the water. Mom has never gone that way. She tells us, "This is fun. I always walked in from the road."

Our directions take us right next to the big black rocks at the water's edge. The water is hitting the rocks, sending spray into the air. Jill keeps taking pictures, trying to catch the exact moment when the spray explodes. It's an impressive sight. It's hard to believe we're half a world away from Michigan. I've never seen water do this.

We keep walking along the base of El Moro until we come to a door. We climb up the steps only to find the door locked. This happens two more times, so we have no choice but to walk back. Everyone is tired, and Mom's step counter is registering over fourteen thousand steps.

We make the long walk back to Calle Fortaleza and sit on the cobblestone street corner, waiting for Derry to pick us up. We're exhausted. The street lights are turning on just as he pulls up.

We drive back to the condo, and Derry has made us a chicken and pasta dish. It's my birthday and I've been dreaming of a hamburger all day, and now we're eating in. And guess what we have for dessert? *Chocolate cake!* Derry tells us he feels horrible because the only cake they had was chocolate. Everyone sings "Happy Birthday," and everyone but me *loves* the cake.

And to end my perfectly awful birthday, we go to bed and *my* bed is the air mattress. I mean, seriously! I know I'm an add-on to the trip, but the least Mom and Jill could do is let me sleep in the bed on my birthday. But *no*!!!

The next day after we wake up, it's time to head to the beach. I'm excited—yesterday was pretty awful—but today is a new day. We're finally going parasailing! When we arrive, we're told to wait next to the water and a small boat will take us out to the parasailing craft. Just as a man gets on the boat right before us, the boat hits a wave and goes super high in the air, nearly tipping over. I love adventure, but this is sick. And the look on Mom's and Jill's face is priceless.

Mom hurt her knee a few months before the trip, so she struggles to get on and off boats. Jill gets in first, and then me and the guy in the boat are both pulling and pushing to get Mom in. For a minute, I think she's going to change her mind and wait for us on the beach, but we get her into the boat. Fortunately, we don't tip over.

The man that went ahead of us is super nice. It turns out he's actually from Detroit, Michigan—not too far from where we live in Medway. He tells us he's visiting his girlfriend and thinking about moving to Puerto Rico.

We listen intently as the captain explains how we will adjust our harness and how, if we get scared at any time, we just need to do a thumbs down and they will bring us in. Sounds easy peasy, but our new friend takes that moment to tell us that he's afraid of heights. Mom says, "Oh, you'll be fine. I went parasailing in St. Croix and we went much higher in the air. They aren't taking you very high."

Of course, I'm thinking. *Sure, Mom. Of course, you went much higher in the air.*

Our new friend goes first and everything seems to be fine until he starts to come down. We can hear him yelling as he's coming aboard, "Sick... I'm going to be sick." As soon as he lands on the boat, they give him a bucket.

Jill and I can't look at Mom because she has the gift of inappropriate laughter. "Totally gross." We are all trying really hard not to laugh.

Now it's our turn. And I have to tell you, as excited as I am about parasailing and as much as I've been looking forward to it, I'm a little nervous. What if something happens to the cord and we break lose? We could die if we hit the water in the harness. It's kind of scary.

But once we get in the air, it's super cool. We're in the air about the height of a condo building. We can see all down the beach and into the Condado area. I have skin that gets really tan, and parasailing with my hair flowing behind me is beyond incredible.

Mom is on the boat to take pictures. The sun is so bright, you can't see when you're taking pictures, so Mom's pointing and shooting as fast as she can. It's really beautiful up in the air, but before we know it, it's time to go back into the boat.

After parasailing, Jill and I have the chance to play in the water and walk along the shore with Mom. It's a perfect day. We're loving the beach and sun while Dad and Mark are home, waiting for an upcoming blizzard.

As we're getting ready for bed, we realize that Jill is extremely red and sunburned. She has really fair, white skin and burns super easy. The seventy sunblock basically did nothing. She is chilled and in so much pain she barely sleeps.

It's day four and we're planning a trip to El Yunque, the rainforest, to hike to the waterfall and go swimming. Because of the RONA, you have to go online in advance and get a ticket for your car to enter, and there are only so many cars allowed per day. We wake up with the intention of stopping at a fast-food place in Isla Verde in the tourist section. Mom has agreed to stop for a burger.

Jill and I are super glad to have Mom with us. Even though this is a tourist area, not many people speak English. Instead of pointing at menu items, we have her to order in Spanish for us. It's really cool to see Mom so happy. Her eyes are shining, her skin is glowing, and her slight sunburn from yesterday has already turned to tan.

Jill is whining about her sunburn. We stop at the local drugstore and pick up some aloe vera, and decide to take her back to the condo to sleep. Then Mom and I are free to go to El Yunque and start our hike.

Mom has a bad knee and she has to be careful. The path to the falls is muddy and steep. You have to be extremely diligent where you step. I'm really sure-footed, and I'm the one leading the way on the hike to be sure Mom doesn't fall and get hurt. She is almost crawling uphill, and on the way down, she sits on her butt and scoots down.

I can't help myself, I take a picture of her from behind. Her shorts are completely covered. I mean, seriously, her backside is encrusted in mud. I don't say anything, but I find myself thinking, *I bet Granda Patti would never do what we're doing.*

Mom laughs at how dirty she's gotten. She just has one thing to say, "Kylie, whatever you do, do *not* put those pictures on social media."

I laugh and promise I won't. It's really fun to have some alone time with Mom.

On day four, we're going to Isla Verde to hang out at one of the hotels. It has five pools and a hot tub. Jill is still pretty sunburned, so we stick her under an umbrella. Jill wears her long-sleeved shirt and an ugly floppy hat and makes sure she has lots of sunscreen on her face. It's a perfect day, we are directly in front of the beach, and we have access to some gorgeous pools.

Immediately in front of the hotel beachside is a food truck. They make everything from nachos to burgers, hot dogs and fries, and wonderful frozen drinks. They are making fresh piña coladas (no alcohol in them), and you have the choice to pay fourteen dollars for a drink inside a pineapple or five dollars for just the drink. We decide to buy one of the pineapple drinks. It's so pretty we need to take pictures.

We Facetime Dad while we are in line to get our food. We are standing on the beach, sand between our toes, looking at the ocean directly across from where we went parasailing. The wind is blowing and the water is about ten different shades of blue. Jill, my sunburned sister, even loves it.

Dad smiles and tells us, "I'm so glad you're having a good time in Puerto Rico! It's snowing like crazy here. You picked a great time to be away."

Chapter Twenty-Two
Kylie

February 15, 2021—Today is the day we're going sailing. Derry and Annie are driving us to Fajardo and we're taking the boat out of the marina. Jill and I have *never* been on a sailboat. We're so excited!

I'VE BEEN SO EXCITED TO go sailing and we're *finally* going! Why are the cars in front of us driving so slow? After what seems like forever, we arrive in Fajardo and find the captain and the boat. The sailboat is fifty-two feet long and much bigger than it looks from the outside. Down below, it has a larger, sun-filled bedroom where Derry and Annie will sleep. It has clear portholes that bring in the sunlight and air. They are going to love looking up at the sky at night.

There's a tiny bedroom to each side of the staircase going upstairs. Mom's bedroom will be on the left and ours will be on the right. Each of the bedrooms have their own bathroom with a toilet, a sink, and a hose to shower with.

Everything on the top deck is a gleaming, sparkling white. The sleeping area and kitchen below are a shiny, medium brown wood color. On deck, once you go up the stairs, there is a table that unfolds for eating, plus there are two benches. Annie and Derry sit on one side and us Blakes sit on the other. The captain stands and steers at the back of the boat. There's also a small kitchen area and a table we could all eat at down below, kind of in the middle of our bedrooms.

The captain will be making our meals all three days we are sailing. We stopped along the way here and bought a few extra snacks and macaroni and cheese, mostly for me. Mom and Annie want to be sure I get enough food because, so far, I'm not really loving everything on the island. I like Mexican food, but the food here has been either too spicy or had a slightly strange texture I'm not fond of... I sure hope I like the food on the boat.

I love sailing. We're sitting on the deck, and there's an awning we can put over us to keep the sun off, our own personal sunblock. I'm amazed at how different the ocean looks from the boat. On the left side, the water is dark blue and churning, a little rough today. On the other side, the ocean is full of a million sparkling lights. The lights hit the water and shimmer like diamonds. Words don't do this view justice. It's really stunning.

We're heading to Culebrita Island. Annie tells us, "Culebrita has regularly been voted one of the best beaches in the world. You're going to love swimming there."

The captain has snorkeling equipment for us to use. Jill bought a special underwater camera to take pictures. This is so cool. It's snowing and cold in Michigan, and we're sailing on the ocean. It just doesn't get any better than this.

About an hour and fifteen minutes into our trip, I begin to wish I'd taken the seasick meds Mom was pushing. I'm not feeling so good. I've got my seasick bracelet on, but it's not working.

I look at my cell phone to check the time, and at exactly 1:32 PM, I jump up. "I'm gonna be sick, I'm gonna be sick!" I'm yelling as Mom and Jill jump out of my way and the captain points to the back of the boat. So much for my breakfast. For the next few hours, I make multiple trips to the back of the boat.

The eighth time I run back, the captain says, "Again?" I seriously want to flip him off, and I have the delicious thought of pushing him off the boat. How would he like *that*? Except I feel too horrible, and who would steer the boat if I pushed him overboard?

It's five long hours on the ocean. I'm sick ten times before we finally reach our destination. It's not fair. Jill and Mom are absolutely fine, and they are loving it out here. I just want to stand on dry land.

We anchor the boat and the captain gives us the option of swimming to shore or he will take us in the dinghy. Mom and Jill swim, while Annie and Derry rest on their side of the sailboat and I lay under the awning, trying to feel better. I'm too sick and exhausted to get in the water.

This time, as we leave for the next island, I've figured out if I listen to music with my earbuds and I wear my sweatshirt with the hood over my eyes, I can survive. I can make it without being sick to my stomach. The next two days pass in a blur, as the only way I can really function is to listen to music and wear my hoodie. The sun bothers my eyes, the rolling of the boat bothers my stomach. The ocean is kind of rough, and I've decided I'm *never* going sailing again.

On our last day, we arrive at Culebra Island. I've been chilling by myself and making this miserable trip work. Our captain anchors the boat about a mile away from shore. He says we will stay here for about three hours and he will serve us lunch in about two. "Go have fun." He tells us we can swim to shore or he will take us on the dinghy.

Mom and Jill get ready for snorkeling and Mom says, "You'll be much better if you get in the saltwater. There are so many beautiful fish. Get in for a few minutes and see how you feel."

All I want is to sleep and be left alone. But I know my mom, and she's not going to leave me alone. "Fine! I'll get in the water for *just* fifteen minutes. "

Mom is super psyched, and she takes lots of pictures. The water is the most beautiful teal I've ever seen. Mom shows me the photos and says, "Look, it's just like an impressionist painting."

Jill is afraid to feed the fish, but once I'm in the water, I feel pretty good. I'm surprised at how much better I feel. No more nausea and my head has stopped hurting.

I feed the fish some hard cookies that Annie has given me. The fish are so hungry they are almost biting me to get the food. And Mom is on deck taking pictures while Jill is sitting with her feet in the water. We're quite a pair. Jill's afraid of the fish but loves to sail. I love feeding and photographing the fish, but hate sailing because I get so seasick.

After a few minutes, we decide to swim to shore. Mom, Jill, and I get our life vests on. It's super far away, and even though we swim pretty well, Mom won't let us in the ocean without a flotation device. I'm still not feeling a hundred percent, so I'm trailing behind Jill and Mom.

We're kind of taking our time, and suddenly Jill and Mom are yelling at me. "Kylie, a shark is gonna get you!" Jill is yelling over her shoulder as she swims as fast as she can.

What? What is wrong with them?

I catch up, and Mom has her hand in the air, cupping something. She is swimming backwards, and I'm barely keeping up with her. "Mom, what are you doing?

She's moving pretty fast and tells me, "Come on, Kylie. We've got to get to shore."

My mom's sport in high school was swimming. She's fast, and she worked as a lifeguard when she was a teen. My sister Jill has her face in the water, and she's swimming along when Mom screams, "Jill, get your face out of the water!"

I have absolutely no idea what is going on.

Mom continues to bellow, "Jill, do not put your bloody mouth in the water! What are you thinking?"

Hmm... it's starting to make a little bit of sense after Mom says "bloody."

We finally make it to shore, and Mom hands something to Jill. I look and see it's Jill's retainer, and now I get the rest of the story.

Jill cut her mouth on her retainer and spit a bunch of blood in the water. Jill said, "Mom, look, I've got blood in my mouth." Mom went into hyper overdrive. She was terrified a shark would sniff the blood and attack us. I mean, every movie we've seen about sharks says they can smell just a drop of blood and will come for it. When Jill cut her mouth, we were exactly in the middle, halfway between the boat and the shore. Mom figured it was safer for us to get on land instead of swimming back to the boat and potentially into an incoming shark.

We walk around the beach for about an hour, getting in the water every few minutes to stay cool. It's a beautiful day, the beach is gorgeous, but we can't quite fully enjoy it. The boat is far away. We don't have a phone, which means we have no choice but to swim back.

It's time to leave. We decide to stretch it out a few more minutes, just to be extra safe. We're all thinking if a shark came this way, it'll be gone by now. Jill's mouth has stopped bleeding. She has strict instructions to keep her face out of the water.

Whew! We make it back safely, Mom pushes me to swim faster and Jill jokes, "I don't have to swim fast, just faster than Kylie."

"Brat!" I scream. "Bloody brat." We are too close to the boat for me to call her what I really want to say. And, yes, it begins with a *B* as well.

We agreed when we were on shore to keep our shark scare to ourselves. But Mom just can't help herself. As we sit down to lunch, she asks the captain, "Is it true that sharks can smell blood from a mile away and will swim really fast to eat a wounded animal?" Jill, Mom, and I sit on the edge of our seat, waiting for the answer.

"No, it's not true," the captain, a man of few words, replies.

We all look at each other and start laughing. I think Jill is going to fall off the bench.

Annie gives us a questioning look. "Please, what is funny?"

The three of us share the story of our *almost* shark attack and everyone gets a good laugh.

The best line is the captains. "There's only been one attack in Puerto Rico. It was in Vieques, several years ago, and it was just a bite. A lot of people don't believe it was a shark. Usually, when sharks take a bite, they leave with something. "

"Good to know," Mom says.

223

Until that moment, we had planned on going to Vieques to visit their bioluminescent bay. In unison, Jill, Mom, and I say, "Let's go to Fajardo instead."

Because of the RONA, a lot of tours and activities are not running, and the captain doesn't know if the tours in Vieques are open. He assures us that Fajardo tours are all open and running.

Picture this. Mom is having problems bringing up the website, so she calls Dad from the middle of the ocean. Dad uses the wonder of technology back in snowy Michigan and texts Mom some numbers to phone the different places.

Mom leaves messages for the Vieques tours as well as the Fajardo tours. Vieques doesn't call us back, which is fine with us. We don't really want to go there, now that we know there was once a shark attack in Vieques.

We do decide to go to Fajardo, and thanks to our captain's connections with the tour owner, he's able to get us on a kayak excursion. Annie and Derry decide to stay back at the boat because they've been to the phosphorescent bay many, many times. And the captain drives us to the drop-off point with plans to pick us up later.

The captain tells us the best time to go kayaking is late at night when it's really dark in the bay, and it's supposed to be especially good when it's a cloudy night. And the captain, now deciding to talk, tells us how he once went when it was raining, and how absolutely magical it was. He says, "Every time the rain fell on the water, it was like a shimmer of glitter. I've never seen anything like it."

I'm finally on dry land, and all my energy has returned. We have a steak for dinner with salad and potatoes, so I'm feeling like I can take on the kayak. Jill and I ride together, and Mom rides in a kayak with a woman from another group. First, our group of over twenty kayaks paddles through a mangrove. We've been told *not* to wear mosquito spray because it will hurt the glow-in-the-dark organisms in the water. Of course, we don't, and Mom is pissed because some other tourists are spraying themselves with insect repellent. And as we go through the mangrove, we all get eaten alive. Lots of mosquito bites.

The width between both ends of the mangrove bank is equal to five kayaks placed next to each other. There are many trees with overhanging branches and limbs that are close to the water.

Our whole group meets in the middle of the bay. Jill and I are both super competitive. At first, it's tough to steer the kayak, but Jill and I quickly figure it out. With my energy back, we want to be first to arrive. So we are. We race some of the other people in the group, and we are right after the instructors.

It isn't dark enough to see the glow-in-the-dark organisms, so we all get in a circle and put a tarp over our kayaks to make it darker. Once we have the tarp over us, they have us lightly splash the water with our paddles. When we put a paddle in, we see these little glowing pieces of glitter hit the side of the boat or the paddle. I've never seen anything like it. It's pretty incredible.

My mom has visited Puerto Rico in the past but never been to the bioluminescent bay. She tells us, "I've always wanted to visit the phosphorescent bay. It's definitely been on my bucket list."

We are all happy, and it is a perfect way to end our sailing trip. We spend the night in Fajardo to wake up to our last day on the boat. We sail today until three o'clock and then arrive back in Fajardo.

I really like to snorkel and feed the fish, but I'm not much of an all day, island-to-island type sailor. I got smarter and started taking the seasickness pills around the clock, but I'm happy to be off the boat.

We drive back to Annie and Derry's condo, and after repacking our clothes and changing, we all head out for dinner. It's Mom's birthday, and we're celebrating at Chili's.

Finally, I'm getting the burger I've been dreaming about all week. It's amazing. The cheddar cheese is melted perfectly, with some lettuce and garlic aioli added to the grilled bun. Everyone is happy and pleasantly tired. We can sleep in the next day because our airplane doesn't leave until midday.

When we get back, we will have to quarantine for seven days, but I'm happy to be going home. I love how tan I've gotten, and I can't wait to see my friends. I'm hoping my tan doesn't fade before we're able to go back to school.

Chapter Twenty-Three
Jen

March 25, 2021—It's hard to believe it's been a year—a year of COVID, a year of being in and out of lockdown, and a year of the kids doing online school. When the pandemic started, our family were some of the few people walking into the grocery store and wearing masks. Fast forward, it's become a necessity. I wonder if it will ever go back to normal?

TRAVELING TO PUERTO RICO WITH my daughters was the trip of a lifetime, and it was important for the girls. They often feel like Mark gets too much attention, and this was a *girl's only* vacation. I'm so grateful for our friends Annie and Derry and their generosity in welcoming us. It was an incredible, much needed vacation.

Jill put all our pictures in the family cloud, so I've been sitting in my home office, looking at our photos and reminiscing. I took many pictures of the water, the sun glinting off the boat, and even some short videos to play when I was home. The color of the ocean as we anchored off the Puerto Rican islands was the most beautiful teal I've ever seen. Each picture was more vibrant and beautiful than the one before. I'm planning on mounting a whole wall of ocean hues to help commemorate this wonderful vacation and remind me of my happy sailing place.

I luxuriated in our three-day sailing trip. It was an experience that I'll never forget. Sailing is my calm place, but because of autism and primary-immune issues, I haven't sailed in years. I feel like all my cares and worries completely disappear when I'm on the water. This trip was amazing in so many ways, from time with the girls, to seeing old friends, experiencing Puerto Rico, and letting go of all our COVID fears while we escaped to the ocean. And I've decided I will be back!

Jill loved sailing as much as I do, but I'll be surprised if Kylie ever sets foot on a sailboat again. I so wanted her to love it. I'm sad her first time made her so horribly seasick.

My door is partially open, which is the signal that it's okay to enter. If my door is closed and my WORKING sign is on the door, the family knows they are *not* to enter my office. Possibly a better phrase is that they are *supposed* to know. They have selective memory if they need something or want to talk to me.

But today is fine, and I see Kylie standing outside, shifting back and forth from one foot to the other. I wave her in. "Hi, honey. Would you like to look at the pictures from the trip with me? Jill just finished loading the rest of the underwater ones."

Kylie comes in and we reminisce about some of the funnier moments of the trip. I haven't seen all of the pictures, so I'm a little shocked when I see one taken below me as I'm snorkeling. The shot gets the front half of my body. Not exactly my best look. We both laugh, and then I say, "Under penalty of death, this picture is *not* to go on social media or be shown to anyone else. *Got it?*"

Kylie is laughing too hard to respond, then she pushes the button and the next photo comes up. It's even worse. "What about this pic, Mom?" she says as she tries to control her laughter.

I'm laughing as well, but seriously thinking it's time for a diet. These last two photos were *not* flattering.

There's a pause. Kylie looks at me, now completely serious. "Mom, I want to talk to you about something that's been bugging me," she says as she stares intently at me. "I'd really like to understand why you and Granda Patti don't just sit in a room until you talk about what happened and figure this out. I know she's your mom, but seriously, I just turned seventeen and I think I'm more grown up than Granda."

She's right. I nod, unsure of where to begin or what to say. This is another result of our trip. The girls and I are closer and less afraid to talk about important subjects. Kylie knows I have her back and I will take her opinion seriously.

Kylie continues, "When we were little, you used to make us sit in the same chair and hug it out until we made up. I'm starting to think we might have to make you and Granda hug it out." She laughs nervously.

I start twisting my hair in and out of the ponytail holder. I'm thinking carefully, as I'm a little nervous about my next words. I take a deep breath. "I've spent a lot of time the last few months thinking about my mom's big 'secret.' I've prayed and talked through the issue with my therapist friend. I took her advice and I've written everything down, including my feelings. Each time, I shredded the paper when I was finished."

I pause for a moment. "I wish it were easy, but it's not. I can't flip a switch and say everything is okay and go forward like nothing has happened. This is messy and uncomfortable and pretty painful. There's a lot of history, not very good history, between me and Granda Patti. And I'll be real with you… it's really hard for me to help her. To show up and be there for her when she has been hateful to me, it seems, my whole life.

"Kylie, I don't like what my mom did. I especially don't like how she tried to put you in the middle. I know she has been having some mental issues and everything kind of erupted at once for her. It's taken a lot, but I am in the process of forgiving her for what she did. I'm forgiving her for not being the mom I needed her to be, while hoping someday she'll forgive me for not being the daughter she needed *me* to be.

"One of the things I am so happy about is how close you and your sister are, and how you both come to me together or separately about things. This tells me that I've been able to change the legacy that's been passed down to me. I'm so glad we are able to have real, authentic conversations."

Kylie nods her head. A feeling of gratitude wells inside of me. I didn't really want to get into a big blame fest, who's right and who's wrong, but I also can't let this teaching opportunity go by. I believe one of my greatest purposes is to help and be there for my children in a way I know my mom is not able to be there for me.

I've done the hard work and it's paying off. Previously, I was afraid to have children. I was afraid of repeating my mom's legacy. I was afraid I would parent like her. Thankfully, I can see that I'm a completely different mom to my kids. Pretty heady stuff to be thinking as I'm sitting in my office with my daughter.

Kylie surprises me. "Mom, what do you think Granda Patti expects from you?"

I pause. The answer is on the tip of my tongue, and I'm weighing how to say it. So, I just come out with it. "Granda needed me to be petite and adorable. She desperately wanted me to be a cheerleader and to go out for homecoming court. But it's not how I'm made. I had completely different interests. I refused to go out for cheerleading. And I refused to go for homecoming court, primarily because she wanted me to."

I think for a second and then continue, "I was too comfortable in the role of standing on my soapbox and telling the world what they needed to do, all in the name of being a feminist. And your Granda Patti just wanted me to dress pretty and go to all the right parties."

We are interrupted by my office phone. *Ring, ring, ring.* I reach to grab it and almost drop the handset as I hit the speakerphone button. Speak of the devil… it's *her.*

"Hi, Mom," I say as I continue fumbling with the phone. "I've got you on speakerphone. Kylie and I are sitting here, talking."

"Hi, Kylie. Sweetheart, how are you?! I've been missing you. I can't wait to hear about your trip… oh, Jenni, your dad and I got our first shot when you were gone. We're so excited and relieved," my mom trills in her little girl voice.

"Wait a minute. What shot are you talking about, Mom?"

"Well, honey, the shot for the virus, of course. Your dad was really sick, and I don't want to take a chance on him getting sick again."

I'm seriously irritated. My mom told me that she and Dad were not going to get the shot, especially since Dad now has natural immunity. "Dad just had COVID the end of December, beginning of January. He should have immunity."

But my mom doesn't want to talk about the vaccine. She wants to talk about our trip and a whole host of other things. Every time I try to ask her more about their decision, she cuts me off. Finally, it reaches a point where I'm having none of it and I interrupt her.

"Mom, I'm worried. When did you get the shot?"

"We got it three weeks ago. Both of us had sore arms and a little headache. We took some Tylenol and now we're fine."

"Last time we talked, you were going to hold off. You were concerned about the mRNA technology. What changed?"

Mom all but screams at me, "What changed is your dad went into a diabetic coma, got pneumonia, and almost died of that horrible virus! I am not taking a chance on losing your dad, and he doesn't want to lose me. We got the first shot. No more discussion!"

I slowly breathe in and out. It's really hard, but I need to let this go. Like most anything related to my mother, there's nothing I can do.

"Just so you know, we're getting our second one in a couple days. If we have any problems, I'll let you know.

"Mom, I really wish you would reconsider."

"Jennifer, your cousin Tyler works for one of the pharmaceutical companies making the shot in Michigan. He told us that it's perfectly safe."

I know it's not the most popular stance, but like forty to fifty percent of the US population, I have concerns over the vaccine. Especially since my parents are determined to get it.

A week after talking to my mom, I get a call from my sister from California. Lori asks, "Did you hear what happened to Dad?"

"No, I didn't. What's going on?" I ask her.

"Dad's been sick in bed for the last four days since he had his second COVID shot. He's got a fever, chills, and feels horrible." Lori continues in a slightly snarky voice, "Didn't Mom tell you that Dad's been sick?

"No, Lori, she didn't tell me. She doesn't want to tell me he's having problems, especially since I advised him to hold off on it. He has immunity. I read you need to wait a few months after having COVID before getting the shot. No wonder he's so sick."

"Mom and Dad are in their seventies. If you were in your seventies, you would get the vaccine too."

Our conversation is going nowhere. "I'm not going to argue with you. I know you got yours. Clint and his family are waiting, and we're definitely not getting it. We've had way too many issues when it comes to vaccines in the past. Our doctor recommended that we continue with the protocol we're on and phone her immediately if we get sick. Based on our allergies and what's in the shot, Mark and I could die if we took it."

Lori travels a lot. She is anxious to have life return to normal. I understand her viewpoint, but I don't agree with it. We have to agree to disagree, just like we do on religion and politics.

Now it's time to be calm and talk about something innocuous. I guess that leaves one topic. "So, how's the weather in California today?" I ask with a slight laugh. Lori and I change the subject to more benign topics and hang up after a few minutes.

My mind goes back to my parents and the situation with my mom. I wish it were easier. And once again, I find myself thinking, *Why me? Why do I always have to be the adult?*

Heck, this is the same woman who used to flirt with my boyfriends when I was in college. How embarrassing, having a mom who would act all helpless and innocent and sweet to my ex-boyfriends.

I can't even go there. This is a memory I need to forget.

Kylie is old enough that she can see with her own eyes and make her own decisions regarding how she feels about people. I believe my mom is stuck in this time loop at the age of sixteen, and all she can think about is herself and what she is interested in.

My dad was horribly sick with COVID and all my mom could think was, "Poor me, poor me." All she could think about was how this was impacting her. Most people would've immediately taken my dad to the hospital. Not my mom, not Patti. She doesn't like to drive and she didn't want to pay for an ambulance, so she waited until it was at a crisis point. Instead of calling the ambulance, she calls the doctor's office. Seriously, who does that?

My dad almost died of COVID, so there's definitely more going on here. I think if my dad died, Clint and I would really have had our hands full. I can't imagine the guilt my mom would be feeling, especially after she just kept him home.

I guess I don't have an answer. I know at some point we will have the conversation. The conversation where we both cry, or at least I cry and apologize for not being the petite, adorable daughter she longs for. A daughter more like my sister, Lori. The conversation where maybe, just maybe, she will be able to apologize for not being there when I desperately needed her. Maybe it will happen before she's on her deathbed.

Then again, maybe pigs will fly.

Epilogue

Patti

The virus changed us in so many ways I didn't expect. A global pandemic the likes of which we have never seen. I don't think Joe could survive another one, and I certainly wouldn't survive being trapped in the house with him again.

I THINK THIS WILL BE recorded as the year that changed history in multiple ways. Many businesses ended up closing. Our favorite restaurant in Grand Blanc closed, as did several in St. Augustine. It's crazy how many people, my Joe and I included, were used to eating convenience foods and going out. The pandemic forced us to rethink quick trips to the grocery store. And we used to go to church every week. Now we watch church online or we do our own thing. Some people lost their connection to God while others got closer.

I've definitely found that I pray more and feel like God has been closer to me and to my family this year. He's helped us get through my depression and Joe getting the virus, and kept the rest of our family safe. Most importantly, God answered my prayers and saved my Joe from dying when he got the virus.

Kind of tongue in cheek, I learned that while I like my hair shorter, I can survive longer in between haircuts than I thought possible. I've been used to getting my hair done several times per month and trimming it every four weeks or so. The pandemic changed that. The first few months, coloring my hair was impossible. I got used to having red and dark brown stripes, and Kylie told me I had "style." I can't remember what you call it, but my blotchy hair color actually has a name, and some people color their hair that way on purpose.

I'm happy and thankful that Joe and I got our vaccines. I almost lost him, and there's no way I want to go through him getting sick again. First time I've ever cried tears of joy about getting a shot.

This is also a year that a presidential election was hijacked. I don't care what the Democrats say, I will always believe that President Trump is our true president and the election was stolen from him. I don't know anyone who voted for President Biden. Jenni won't tell me, but I think even my staunch Democratic daughter voted for President Trump.

It's also been a year of great kindness and great selfishness. For each and every kind act, there were multiple acts of stupidity and meanness. People fighting and disagreeing without a thought of how their actions impacted or affected others. We've become a polarized society. It's no longer okay to be friends with someone from a different political party, and I find that crazy and wrong. My best friend Susie is as liberal as they come and we still get along. So why can't everybody else?

It's also the time when families came together. A friend of mine moved in with her children to help take care of her grandkids while her daughter and son-in-law worked online from home. Workplaces are realizing there are benefits to people working remotely. Clint's company has gotten rid of their leases on two different buildings and he is now officially a remote employee. One of the benefits, he says, of this year from hell. "Companies are realizing they can trust their employees, in many cases, to work from home and save money."

Speaking of family, I'm learning that if you're not there for your kids when they're young, they will not be there for you when you're old. When did it become more important to live up to the image my mother-in-law had instilled in me to be the perfect Clarke wife over being my kids' mom? And why did it take the pandemic for me to see that the secrets I kept are keeping me from the people I love?

The pandemic is teaching me that I've spent a lifetime surrounding myself with fake people. Wearing a mask or not wearing a mask isn't really a big change, but most of the people I'm friends with are fake up to their eyebrows. They have tiny bodies courtesy of their personal trainer, Botox, liposuction, lifts, tucks, and eating disorders. Most of the women I know keep their size zero or size two bodies like it's their job. And to many, it is. They exist as arm candy. If they get too big, their husbands will leave them. I've lost track of the number of divorces we have in our "inner circle," the number of times the guys turned their wives in for a younger, prettier model. I've fallen into the trap of being somehow terrified the same thing will happen to me.

Due to the pandemic, I realized it's literally been years since I've had a piece of chocolate cake with raspberry filling and chocolate butter cream and coconut frosting. I love chocolate cake and I've been too afraid of what it would do to me to allow myself the occasional indulgence. I've always taken a smidge of cake, and the most I allow myself is savoring a bite or two and then promptly spitting it out in the sink.

I didn't gain weight during the pandemic; instead, I found a whole new me. You could say I lost one hundred and fifteen pounds... okay, truth, one hundred and twenty pounds. Instead, I gained a person who is tired of playing the game and putting a mask on every day of her life. I wish I hadn't been so afraid before. So afraid of making a mistake, of failing. Instead of living life, I checked out from it as I made a list of a million things to do each and every day.

The virus taught me how short and fragile life is. We've lost two friends from our Wednesday night card club in St. Augustine. The virus almost took my Joe. I don't know why it spared me. I just know I'm grateful and I need to get busy. I promised Susie that within six months I would talk to my daughter and explain. I've hurt Jenni enough, and I know it's past time. We're almost at the six-month mark.

This weekend, I will sit down, work on my bullet points, and get Joe to practice with me. It's got to be perfect. I have to make sure my Jenni understands why it was so very hard for me to talk to her about my miscarriage. The baby should've made it, and I've always, *always* felt guilty. Like it was somehow my fault.

The biggest, hardest lesson I've learned is secrets will eat you alive. When you keep your pain inside and you refuse to share it, you push away the people you love the most. It's not that I don't love my daughter. If anything, I love her too much, and I'm horribly afraid of disappointing her.

I'm seventy-four years old. This "young" lady needs to make up for lost years. The problem is Jenni and I have gotten used to a certain way of treating each other, and if I want to have a good relationship with my daughter, I have to focus on changing what comes out of my mouth. I remember all the times that she came to me as a young woman and I pushed her away. When she tried to tell me about her latest crush or about her problems with her swimming coach or her friends. I was always too busy, thinking of the next thing on my list. The times I listened - I sat just long enough to cross off "talk to Jenni" from my list.

My beast of a mother-in-law accused me of being jealous of Jenni. Millie told me that I was too weak and insignificant to be the mother of a daughter with as much promise as my daughter. And I think, on some level, I believed her. I let her swoop in and become more of a mom to her than I was.

Before I can fix the relationship with Jenni, I'm learning I have to fix the fundamental relationship I have with myself. I have to make the little girl in me feel warm and safe and loved. At least that's the psycho-babble my online therapist tells me. When I feel uncomfortable or not good about myself, I lash out. Deep stuff, don't you think?

I've got some work to do, some definite apologies to be said to my Jenni and Kylie. I guess it's true what they say, we are only as healthy as the secrets we keep. It's time for me to get healthy. I don't know if

I'll ever have a real, authentic relationship with my girls and with my grandkids, but I'd like to try.

Jen

COVID made our immediate family closer while bringing long-held secrets into the light. The question remains, will my mom and I get past the years of hurt and betrayal?

I REMEMBER BEING ABSOLUTELY TERRIFIED out of my head for the first forty-eight hours or so after COVID-19 blew up in the news and everything started to shut down. I found myself thinking, *We need a vaccine.* In the next breath, I was afraid a COVID-19 vaccine would be developed and mandated. *We need to protect our son.* Even though Mark has a lifetime medical exemption to vaccines, I worried he would be forced to take a shot and he would die. Our family went through so much to get him to this point, and I couldn't imagine losing him to his autism or having his autoimmune issues come back.

A year later, we know a lot more about COVID-19 than we did twelve months ago. In some ways, I feel like I just kept running faster and faster on the treadmill, and in other ways, I feel like I learned a lot this year. Ben and I slowed down enough to stop being two people constantly moving, never having time to relax. It's like we were holding our breath and now we can fully exhale. We have more margin in our schedule and life. Much to my surprise, when I look back at this past year, our family actually thrived in spite of—or perhaps I should say *because* of—COVID-19.

My girls and I had our first ever trip without Ben and Mark, and our mother-daughter relationship went to the next level. I used to think, *I can't be their friend until they are much older.* But that mentality and thought process changed as a result of our trip. The girls were able to see their mom isn't perfect, and it was possible for each of us to show some of our vulnerabilities.

I see so many examples through this last year, during COVID, when our family came together and helped one another. Probably the most important thing I'm learning is how to be there for the people in my life who need me, or pieces of me, while also setting appropriate boundaries. By stretching myself so thin, I wasn't helping anyone, least of all my family and the people I love.

I remember reading about setting appropriate boundaries. I remember learning—if you tell someone no and the person gets angry or talks badly about you or destroys the relationship because you told them no, then the relationship was not important to begin with. That statement resonated with me, and I've slowly started to cull people from my life. What has been a sad experience, the pandemic and Stay Home order, resulted in more time for my family, the work I love, and the friends who matter.

COVID reinforced that time is not infinite. My dad nearly died. There is a part of me that is furious with my mom for continuing to keep secrets from me and other family members. And I can't help but get frustrated over her childish mannerisms. I'm learning to let go and realize my mom is the way she is. I can't change her. Life is too hard and too short for me to bear a grudge against her. It's taken a lot of prayer and introspection for me to get to this point. Sometimes I listened during my prayer time, hoping I'd hear a direct message. Other times, I yelled and questioned and asked the *Why?* question a lot. I've been reminded the only person I can change, the only behavior I can attempt to control, is my own behavior and how I choose to react to the people, places, and things in my life.

And COVID reminded me how special my husband is. Ben works right alongside me as we prepare dinner and teach our kids. His example reminds me that real men help their wives and their families, not quitting until *everyone* can sit down. They love their families, they grow with them, they teach them, and they pray for them.

My children will likely disagree, but thanks to the pandemic, I've been starting down the path of preparing to let them go. I'm realizing each weekend brings one fewer weekend that we are all together under the same roof. Before we know it, they will be off on their own. It's my hope they will soar and find extreme happiness.

For a brief and shining moment, COVID helped our family to pause. The pandemic encouraged us to face our fears and talk through our anxiety and deal with rough emotions. It helped us to slow down and spend time with the people who matter the most. And it's helped me to begin to process some pretty priceless thoughts related to family, thoughts that are geared toward growth and healing.

A few days ago, I got together with a group of friends, a group of my warrior moms, for dinner. It was so fun, so freeing, and felt almost like "normal life." As I exited the parking lot, I narrowly avoided a head-on collision. In an instant, I realized how quickly our lives can be taken from us. Whether it's COVID, a health crisis, or car accident, we are all one breath away from saying goodbye.

I'm still ruminating on how to have an authentic, real relationship with my mom. I don't have the answer yet, but I'm getting closer. If nothing more, COVID has enabled me to choose *joy* and forced me to let go of my feelings of anger and anxiety.

I want to live every second I possibly can, loving and enjoying and being there for the people I cherish the most.

Kylie

Kylie: Because of the RONA, I couldn't play lacrosse my sophomore year in high school. I continued to practice and improve my lacrosse skills through the RONA, and it will be no accident when I make varsity. Like the great soccer player Pelé said, "Success is no accident. It is hard work, perseverance, learning, studying, sacrifice, and most of all, love of what you are learning to do."

I WANT LIFE TO RETURN to normal. When the RONA first hit, I didn't think it was a big deal. I thought it would be over soon. But as it dragged on, I became pissed. And as more time went on, the walls just seemed to close in. Even though I have my family with me, it still feels like I am alone. Being stuck at home is like the worst punishment I can imagine. The pandemic confirmed to me that it's not good for people like me to be isolated. I cried more than I've ever cried in my life. I'm not a person that usually cries, so it was hard.

When the pandemic started, my parents told us we were experiencing history. And since our online school started out pretty light, my mom made us start keeping a journal. It only lasted about a week. Mark flipped out one day and made a big deal telling our parents every day was the same as the one before. Big mistake! After that, Mom didn't make us keep writing a journal unless we wanted to.

But she then decided to start having us experience "joyful" moments together. Mom's idea of joy and mine are completely different. First, we started doing stupid art projects, going for daily walks, sitting in Mom's office, and talking with her every day to make sure we were mentally okay. Oh—and I forgot to mention, we also had to play board games at least once a week in a newly resurrected family game night.

Game night is actually fun. Especially when we play some of my favorites and I kick everyone's butt. The person that is the most fun to beat is Mom. She loves to talk smack, but there's at least two games she can't beat me at. She tries, but I always beat her.

One of my big revelations—big word, eh? — I've learned how important my family is to me. When the pandemic began, I was sixteen and felt invincible. I wasn't worried about getting the RONA. It took Grandpa Joe almost dying for me to realize how serious it was and how much I love my family. Because of the forced stay at home, my mom and I had a lot of time together. We've talked about important things, and I've been able to see my mom as a person, not just my mom.

And—crazy to admit this—I would want to be friends with her even if she weren't my mom. My mom doesn't sugarcoat things, and just like me, she struggles. I've seen her hurt, angry, and I've seen her cry during this past year. I wish I knew why my Granda was so mean to my mom and so nice to me and everyone else. It doesn't make sense. Mom is her daughter. I can't imagine my mom being nicer to my kids than she is to me. And I'm really glad that Jill and I had the chance to go to Puerto Rico with Mom over break. Despite getting seasick, it was a good trip.

I've found out new things about myself this year too. I've never been a very artsy person, but I've learned I'm pretty decent at photography. I had an assignment to take pictures that represented my thoughts on the pandemic. My sister Jill came with me to our high school track to help take some random pictures. I wasn't thinking much about it when Jill said, "Hey, Kylie, take a pic of me walking."

I just kind of pointed and took a bunch of photos, hoping one would turn out. Later, when I was looking at the day's pictures, I found the perfect one. It was of Jill's right foot crossing the finish line while her left foot was arched and not quite over the line. I got an A for this project and I named it "Crossing the Finish Line." It's really good. I printed off a copy for my mom.

I'm not much into symbolism, but my teacher told me this picture is a perfect representation of the hard work we've had to endure this last year. Life is slowly returning to normal, we're back in school, and hopefully this summer we'll be able to go to some concerts, the beach, and outdoor festivals.

I'll never admit this openly or say it out loud, but being home with my family allowed me to get closer to them and stop thinking of my brother Mark as such a pain. Life slowed down. It wasn't always fun or easy and, in fact, there were some pretty painful moments, but I realize how important connection is and how much I need my family.

Right now, I can't wait to finish out my junior year, slide into senior year, and go off to college. I know, I know… I just said how important family is. They are, but I need freedom so I can become my own person. I feel like there's so much I've lost this last year, and there's a part of me that absolutely can't wait to spread my wings and get out of here. *Really*. I can't wait to get out of here!

But no matter what college I go to or where I end up, I'm always going to be a Blake. And I guess that means I'm going to be okay.

JULIE CADMAN

Discussion Questions

1. The pandemic becomes a fourth main character and the backdrop of the novel. Do you remember where you were and what you were doing when you first heard about COVID-19? What about the first time you went to a store and wore a mask?

2. Patti begins her narrative by stating, "I feel like I'm still Kylie's age. Those years between sixteen and now (seventy-three) went by in a *blink*." What do you think causes Patti to focus on acting young as opposed to "acting her age?"

3. The Clarkes isolate at home when their state issues a "Stay Home, Stay Safe" order, yet are able to visit with their extended family at different times. During the pandemic, were you living alone or with family members? How did you cope with the big changes going on?

4. Jen has a strong concern about medical freedom. "Mark has a compromised immune system, and I was instantly terrified for him. He is allergic to so many substances. His neurologist wrote out a lifetime medical exemption to vaccines a few years ago..." Do you agree with Jen's stance on medical freedom? Why or why not?

5. Kylie is struggling as she waits to get her driver's license. She misses her friends and can't take part in her high school lacrosse season. If you've ever had to wait for something you really wanted, what gave you hope to keep going?

6. Of the three women protagonists, Patti, Jen, and Kylie, which one do you identify with the most? If you were in their shoes, what would you have done differently during their family conflict?

7. Of the three women protagonists, Patti, Jen, and Kylie, which one do you identify with the least? What about her character was hard for you to connect with?

8. When Kylie gets her driver's license, her first outing is to visit her grandparents and take her grandmother to lunch. What does this say about her relationship with Patti? How does the relationship change after the weekend?

9. Have you had a moment in your life where a secret was shared that changed the trajectory of your life or someone you are close to? If you were in Jen's shoes, how would you react to your mom sharing a family "secret" with your daughter and asking her not to tell you?

10. Kylie is put in a difficult situation by her grandmother. Do you think she did the right thing in telling her mother the "secret" that her grandmother asked her to keep? What advice would you give to Kylie in this situation?

11. Why do you think Jen becomes so furious with her mother? What is the underlying reason for her anger? Do you think she is right to be angry or do you think her response is unreasonable?

12. Why do you think Patti is afraid to let Jen see who she really is? How do you think Jen's perception of her mother is different from the beginning of the book versus the end?

13. Do you think it's possible for a relationship to move forward and/or be mended without forgiveness? Why or why not?

13. What advice would you give Patti, Jen, and Kylie to help them overcome the family conflict that comes about from the reveal of the "secret?"

15. Clint and Lori both tell Jen that she should just let the conflict stay unresolved and move on. If you were in Jen's place, what would you do? Would you let it go and move on, would you confront your mother about the issue, or would you do something different?

16. Did you change your perspective on any of the characters as the book progressed?

17. Jen is feeling sandwiched between two generations. What advice would you give Jen as she navigates between taking care of her kids and trying to help her parents?

18. Jen and Patti have a challenging relationship, but each talk about wanting to change. What is preventing them from moving past their differences? What do you think each woman has to do in order to bridge the gap between them?

19. How does the relationship between Patti and Kylie compare to the relationship between Jen and Kylie?

20. Patti experiences severe depression during the pandemic and needs to seek help in order to improve her mental health. Do you think her family did a good or bad job supporting her recovery from her mental health episode? Why or why not?

21. What does it take for Patti to finally realize that COVID is serious and for it to become real to her?

22. What skills do you think Kylie and her family developed during the pandemic? Did you develop any new skills during the pandemic?

23. Kylie is feeling stressed and trapped at home. If you had any teens or young adults living at home during the pandemic, did they react in a similar way? What advice would you give or actions would you suggest to Kylie to get through this period of time?

24. Patti reveals another secret from her past that concerns the first three months of Jen's life. Do you think she should tell Jen this secret and, if so, how do you believe Jen will react?

25. When Joe gets sick, Patti promises God that she will apologize to Jen and Kylie if he will spare Joe. Do you think Patti will fulfill her promise if Joe is spared?

26. Do you think the Clarke ladies will eventually sit down and explain their actions to each other? Why or why not? What do you predict will change in their relationships if they do so?

27. Share a favorite scene or quote from the book. Why is it your favorite?

28. Every family, no matter how perfect, has an elephant in the room—what elephants are in the room for the Clarke family? How do they deal with them?

29. What character in the book would you most like to meet?

30. If you got the chance to ask the author of this book one question, what would it be?

Acknowledgments

WRITING THIS BOOK HAS REMINDED me of those who inspire, encourage, and walk with us on our journey.

My sincere thanks go to my family and friends who have encouraged and cheered me forward. To my grandfather Carl, the first great reader in my life who encouraged and supported my lifelong love of reading. To my parents Booth and Barbara, who kept me supplied with reading materials and celebrated the writing of my first mystery in the third grade.

To my husband Dana, a fellow reader and author, who has listened and re-read *UnMasked* and knows the characters almost as well as I do. Your support and constant belief in me has been life-changing. The character Ben has much to learn from you. I love you so much!

To my amazing children, Jessica, Katie, and Luke—my inspiration for Kylie, Jill, and Mark. Thank you for allowing me to share some of life's exciting moments with you and to ask questions, like, "What word do you think Kylie would use?" And, most of all, thank you for being excited with me throughout this whole process—even the moments when you ate dinner without me because I was deep into character mode. I love you all so much, and I'm so grateful to be your mom.

Thank you to Kary Oberbrunner for your Facebook writing challenge during the pandemic and to Holley Gerth—your "Be a Kick-Butt Writer by Friday" course got my butt in a seat and helped bring Jen, Kylie, and Patti to life.

It was an honor to be selected as one of the five finalists for the When Word's Count Pitch Week. Thank you to Steve Eisner, Barbara Newman, Emma Irving, Amber Griffith, Athen Desautels, Ben Tanzer, Marilyn Atlas, and Colin Hosten, and my co-finalists, Amy, Rebecca, and Shawn.

Thank you to Ann Waker and Peggy Moran, early editors who encouraged and helped shape my ideas for Jen, Kylie, and Patti.

And a *huge*, extra special thank you to Alison McBain, my editor, fellow author, friend, and the gold winner of When Word's Count Pitch Week. You're a gifted author as well as editor—I've enjoyed the process with you! And special shout-out to Jeff Blashill, my wonderful cover designer.

To my dear friends Bunny LaMere, Donna Moyer, and Beth Thayer—so grateful for your friendship. And friends from Puerto Rico, Annie and Derry—I cherish your love and hospitality. Thank you to my niece Mackenzie and nephew Eric Mojica—so excited to talk mysteries and music with you, and I can't wait for our next Murder Mystery Party!

Thank you to my friends (you know who you are) who shared their sandwich generation stories as well as how their families managed during the pandemic. I really appreciate the support and encouragement of my Soul Sisters—Kathy Dougherty, Cyndi Wehrli, Mitzi van der Harst, Gail Kobal, Karen Orlando, Karen Schoonover, Christine Maurer, Jodie Lenney, Jaclyn M., Amy Lapain, Oliva Chan, Sherry Richter, Amy Geyer, Julie C., Kathy G., and my special friend, Carol Lewis—we love and miss you, and we're watching over your precious family. You ladies are incredible. Always encouraging, praying, and there for each other—thank you for your love and support.

To my Warrior Mom Friends—Michele Gordon, Nicole Grabowski, Laura Burr, Maryann Baker, Tammy G., Heidi S., Carla Marymee, Lisa Wernette, Jessica Lizardi, and so many more, who understand the character of Jen better than *anyone*. You are all such remarkable, incredible friends.

To everyone not mentioned specifically here, I want to thank you for all your help and assistance through this adventure.

To God for directing my path and turning devastating experiences into blessings I couldn't imagine. Thank you for entrusting me to pay forward what I've learned, and for putting everything in place at the perfect time, so I could tell Jen, Kylie, and Patti's story. And for the reminder to trust in the Lord, Proverbs 3:5-6.

About the Author

JULIE CADMAN IS A FORMER automotive and healthcare executive, co-founder of the nonprofit Healing Complex Kids, as well as an author of nonfiction and fiction books. Julie was born and raised in Michigan, and lived in Puerto Rico, Texas, and Wisconsin before she returned to her birthplace. For as long as she can remember, she's loved reading, and it's been her dream to write.

Life got in the way of her dream at first. She got her BS in psychology with a minor in business administration from the University of Michigan, went to work for General Motors, and received her MSA in administration from Central Michigan University. After twelve years at GM, which included an international assignment in Puerto Rico, she left to manage the General Motors account for two different tier one suppliers. In 2001, she married her husband, Dana, and they adopted their son and two daughters internationally. Julie began working in healthcare before co-founding a medical recruiting company. She learned about being a mom to children with special needs, autism, and chronic medical conditions.

When the pandemic happened, she decided *not* this time… this time, she was going to find time for her dream. So, she began writing in the creases of her day. At night, between eleven PM and two in the morning, she spent eight months writing two books.

She is the publisher and contributing author to *Pathway to HOPE 2021 Resource Guide*. And she was one of five authors from across the

US and Canada selected to compete in an author's pitch week for *When Words Count*. *UnMasked* won a silver medal award in the contest.

Julie is a consummate multitasker and began writing as her personal form of self-care. She gets her steps in by walking and wearing her headset as she loudly lip syncs to her favorite songs ("Uptown Funk" tops the list). Her family frequently has to remind her they can hear her lip syncing. She and her family live in the Midwest with their goldendoodle Kerby. For more information, you can visit:

Website: www.JulieCadman.com
Facebook: AuthorJulieCadman
Instagram: @Julie.Cadman1

A Gift for You

I've created a companion journal to *UnMasked*. This journal contains fifty-two quotes with writing prompts from the characters to help you foster and reflect upon your relationships. As a special bonus, you can download a free digital sample of the companion journal at: www.JulieCadman.com/journalsample.

I hope you enjoyed reading *UnMasked* as much as I enjoyed writing it. You would do me a huge favor if you took a few minutes to leave a short review on Amazon, Goodreads, and/or BookBub. As a fellow author told me, "One of the greatest compliments you can give a writer is a review."

Thank you,
Julie Cadman